'Well, now . . .' Lionel murmured thoughtfully, turning to regard Catherine with a speculative frown. 'What are we to do with you, I wonder?'

She was taken momentarily aback, and then saw the expression in his eyes. 'I hope, sir,' she said, smiling, 'that you will set me free.'

'You think you deserve that?' He began to move towards her, but slowly, his eyes devouring her. 'After all the trouble you've caused, driving your brother and me nearly demented?'

Catherine took a step towards him, forgetting in her urgency that she was still bound by the wrists to the stern rail. 'But I shall make amends, Lionel . . .'

'Indeed?' he said softly, slipping his hands about her waist. 'Then you had better begin . . .'

Joyce Holms was born and educated in Glasgow but has had eleven homes in the last twenty-three years ranging from a hotel on the island of Arran to an apartment in Andalucia. Writing is her one abiding passion and she has been writing articles and short stories for magazines and broadcasting for almost twenty years. She is a self-confessed 'health nut' and starts the day with a brisk three-mile circuit of the 'Meadows' in Edinburgh where she now lives with her husband and two teenage daughters.

Her first Masquerade Historical Romance, MISS MACINTOSH'S REBEL, was published earlier this year.

THE MAGNIFICENT MISS FRAZER

JOYCE HOLMS

MILLS & BOON LIMITED
15–16 BROOK'S MEWS
LONDON W1A 1DR

First published in Great Britain 1985
by Mills & Boon Limited

© Joyce Holms 1985

Australian copyright 1985
Philippine copyright 1985
This edition 1985

ISBN 0 263 75272 0

Set in 10 on 11½ pt Linotron Times
04–1285–64,300

Photoset by Rowland Phototypesetting Limited
Bury St Edmunds, Suffolk
Made and printed in Great Britain by
Cox & Wyman Limited, Reading

CHAPTER
ONE

'Offer to look after her?' Mrs Frazer repeated, her tiny silver-grey head trembling with agitation. 'Of course I did not offer to look after her! Who in the world would *offer* to look after Catherine? The girl was thrust upon me—positively *thrust*!'

'Oh, Elspeth, surely not?' Mrs MacIntosh tried unsuccessfully to hide a smile behind her teacup. 'And yet I had always imagined Catherine to be your favourite grandchild. You must have told me so a hundred times.'

'Ay, and so she is; but in small doses, Margaret, in small doses! Not for six weeks at a stretch! I don't have to tell you—Catherine is, after all, as much your grandchild as she is mine—that she is not at all a comfortable person to live with. I am utterly worn out already and she has not yet been with me a fortnight.'

Mrs MacIntosh nodded comfortingly and swept some cake crumbs from her lap with a plump hand. 'She always was something of a handful, I know. But what can you do, dear, when her papa insists on indulging her to such a ridiculous degree? I never knew a father so besotted with his offspring as dear Colin.'

Mrs Frazer's spine stiffened imperceptibly, but she essayed a tight smile. 'Do you think so? He is, no doubt of it, an affectionate father, but I would have thought our granddaughter's nature to be the result of heredity rather than of excessive leniency. Her mother was, in her youth, inclined to be . . . headstrong, was she not?'

'Isobel?' This seemed to come as a surprise to Mrs MacIntosh. She screwed her face up as though she were having great difficulty in casting her mind back twenty-five years. 'Was she? Dear me, it all seems so very long ago. Yes . . . I dare say you may be quite right, Elspeth, but I am persuaded that Isobel was much less *energetic*. Catherine is much too exhausting for either of us to cope with, and I must say I think it very shabby in Colin and Isobel to foist her on to you like this. If only you had been forewarned, you might have been forgiven for fobbing them off with some excuse.'

'I seem,' said Mrs Frazer, with an extremely acid smile, 'to have been the only one of Catherine's immediate family who was *not* forewarned. I have since discovered that her Aunt Fiona claimed her entire brood was down with chicken-pox, her uncle Laughlan and his wife fled to London and even you, Margaret, were stricken down by some unspecified ailment which appears to have been of very short duration.'

Margaret MacIntosh giggled unrepentantly and passed her cup to be refilled. 'Really, dear, it would have been so awkward for me to have her just now. Poor James is suffering from gout, and . . .'

'Fiddlesticks!' Mrs Frazer said, quite pleasantly. 'Your husband is suffering from the same complaint as mine, an overdose of Catherine! Johnnie endured her company for two days and then bethought himself of some urgent business at Transk which could not await his attention, and off he went. It's all a hum, of course. As you know, he made over the estate to Colin when we bought this place and I'll swear he hasn't spent above a sennight in the house for years. Ten days now he has been gone while I am left to cope with Catherine single-handed.'

'Only for another four weeks,' said Mrs MacIntosh bracingly, accepting the offer of another slice of cake. 'And I shall be at my sister's house in Irvine for at least another fortnight, so you can send for me if you need me. Forbye, you will have Jamie to turn to. Isobel told me he had promised to stay with you and bear his sister company while she was here.'

'Oh ay, he promised all right, but where is he? No sooner had his parents sailed for France than he up and left his sister and me sitting here like a couple of nuns, and we have seen neither hair nor hide of him since.' His grandmother's cup rattled furiously on its saucer. 'Catherine tells me he is dangling after some Glasgow belle. He met her quite recently when she was staying with her aunt in Inverness, but now she is returned home to Glasgow and Jamie needs must follow her. We have had but one letter from him since he left, and I think this is another, just arrived.'

Stepping to the fireplace, she stood on tiptoe to bring her eyes above the level of the high mantelpiece. A moment's groping among the profusion of ornaments and knick-knacks thereon produced a letter which she offered for Mrs MacIntosh's inspection. 'Your eyes are better than mine, Margaret. Is that his hand? Yes, I thought so. But, as you can see, it is directed to Catherine, so we must wait to see whether or no it will tell us when to expect him.'

Mrs MacIntosh had the grace to look a little shamefaced. 'It's really too bad, Elspeth. No wonder you feel the family have let you down. But I make no bones about it, dear. It is Colin and Isobel who are at fault in the first place for refusing to take Catherine with the three younger ones to France with them as they had intended. A rather severe punishment—don't you think?—for what was, after all, the merest indiscretion.'

Mrs Frazer's hand remained frozen for an instant, in the act of returning the letter to the mantlepiece. '*Indiscretion?*' She drew herself up to her full, unimposing height and fixed Mrs MacIntosh with an incredulous stare. 'My dear Margaret, you never cease to amaze me! I never thought to hear you excuse such shocking behaviour in any young lady—far less in your own daughter's child. To my mind Colin acted with remarkable forbearance. Think of the scandal if it had got out? When I heard . . .'

She became abruptly aware of the alert and interested gaze which was being directed at her, and realised that she had fallen into a trap. Frowning at her own stupidity, she said unwillingly, 'You don't know the details?'

'I don't believe I do, precisely.' Margaret removed a cake crumb from the corner of her mouth. 'Isobel forgot to tell me when she wrote.'

'She didn't forget,' stated Mrs Frazer, not mincing matters. 'She merely did not wish you to know. She did not wish me to know either, for that matter, but I had the whole story out of Colin the day he delivered Catherine.'

Mrs MacIntosh smiled encouragingly, looking like a fat satisfied tabby-cat in her brown dress and écru lace. 'Yes?'

'Oh dear . . . One hesitates to pass on such a damaging story, but I know you wouldn't dream of letting it go any further.'

'Mmmm?'

Taking this as a promise, Mrs Frazer put on a prim expression which gave her the appearance of having had a thread run round her lips and pulled tight. 'It seems that Catherine was discovered fencing with Jamie in the stable-yard at Transk.'

Catherine's maternal grandmother seemed, at first,

not to have heard this statement. Her china blue eyes remained fixed on Mrs Frazer's, and her expression did not change till the latter repeated with emphasis, '*Fencing*, Margaret. With *foils*! And dressed in her brother's shirt and breeches, forbye. It was the minister who came upon them.'

Mrs MacIntosh's cherubic face crumpled as though she were about to burst into tears, a reaction which her informant could have understood better than the high cackle of laughter which presently emerged.

'The minister! My certes! Wouldn't you know it would have to be the minister? That girl will be the death of me yet! Do you think it was all a plot to shock the old man? It would be like Catherine.'

'Far from it,' Mrs Frazer returned, looking indescribably shocked by this response. 'Indeed I have a strong suspicion that it was in no way an isolated occurrence—Colin denies it, but that's nothing to the point. You and I know that Catherine is too much in the company of her brothers. Before Sean married, he and Jamie and Catherine were inseparable, and now that the twins are fifteen they have replaced Sean in their escapades. Caroline is still only a child, but the others all run together in a pack!'

'Well, and what if they do?' said Mrs MacIntosh, embarking on a pastry. 'What could they possibly get up to at Transk that would be so very terrible?'

'For the boys, nothing! I have no objections to their pursuits, but I do object, most strenuously, to Catherine's participation in—*not* only fencing, you know—but in pistol-shooting, cock-fighting—yes!—and even, I fear, *dicing*!' Making a supreme effort to remain calm, she rose and trod to the window, parting the curtain to stare out in the manner of one who dreaded what she might see. 'One cannot altogether be sorry that it has all

come out, since it has forced Colin to put an end to it,
and in a manner which will pacify the minister.'

'Well, yes, I can see that he would want to make sure
that justice was seen to be done.' Mrs MacIntosh sighed.
'But it does seem a little harsh, all the same. The poor
girl was looking forward so much to going to Paris.'

'I dare say she was,' agreed Mrs Frazer, returning to
her seat. 'But if she is overcome with melancholy, she
hides it very well! She charges through life like a bull at a
gate, and in less than a fortnight she has the whole
neighbourhood by the ears. I have every young buck
within twenty miles on my doorstep at all hours of the
day, tramping mud into the hall, drinking my best
Bohea, while Catherine roams the moors with them on
that enormous grey of hers. How she handles it I don't
know, but my groom tells me he has the greatest difficulty in keeping up with her. Why, only yesterday . . .'

The events of the day before, however, were to
remain a mystery to Mrs MacIntosh, for at that moment
a wild shriek cut across Mrs Frazer's words, making
both ladies start violently and turn towards the window
in time to see two mounted figures career across the
lawn and draw up with a spurt of gravel at the front
door.

'Catherine,' uttered Mrs Frazer in failing tones, as her
granddaughter sprang down from her horse without
waiting for the assistance of either her escort or her
laggard groom who was now approaching by a more
orthodox route. She was hatless, and the wind was
whipping free long strands of black hair and curling them
into her eyes and mouth.

'Just look at her!' Mrs Frazer twittered, passing a hand
across her eyes. 'What would her mama think? But I am
powerless to control her, Elspeth. Powerless! Only per-
ceive what havoc she has wrought! My lawn!'

Mrs MacIntosh did not reply, being intent on watching the drama that was unfolding at the front door.

The head gardener, a truculent ancient with a face like pine bark, had emerged from the shrubbery and was bearing down on Catherine with purposeful tread and ominously clenched fist. His words did not carry as far as the drawing-room window, but neither of Catherine's grandmothers was in any doubt as to the nature of his remarks. They were all the more intrigued, therefore, when the two culprits followed him meekly back to the scene of their crime and helped him to replace the divots, while Robert, Mrs Frazer's young groom, maintained a virtuous aloofness.

'Well, I declare!' Mrs MacIntosh exclaimed, letting the curtain fall across this edifying scene. 'Your worries are over, Elspeth. If no one else can tame Catherine, it appears your gardener can!'

Mrs Frazer shook her head with a pitiful travesty of a smile. 'Would that were true! I assure you I would double the man's wages tomorrow. Unfortunately, he holds no more sway over her than I do. The difficulty, you see, lies not in making her sorry for doing wrong but in preventing her from doing wrong in the first place. If one could only foresee her intentions, all would be well, but one cannot say, "Please don't ride over the lawn when you come home", when the idea of doing such a thing would simply never occur to anyone but Catherine. As you just witnessed, she is always most contrite and eager to make amends, but—pray tell me—*what* is she going to do next?'

They fell silent, pondering this question, but presently a door slammed, tinkling the china ornaments on the mantelpiece, and a clarion call rang through the house.

'Grandmama! Where are you, Grandmama?'

As the two elderly ladies exchanged speaking glances,

the door was flung open and the room was suddenly filled with noise and movement and ferment, as it always seemed to be when Catherine entered. She threw her gloves and crop on a table, narrowly missing the teapot which happened to be in the way, and darted to the window, which she proceeded to throw open.

'Oh, it's so dark and suffocating in here, Grandmama! How can you bear to be cooped up like a hen in a basket? Just look at what you are missing!'

She turned to wave a beckoning arm, and gave a squeal of surprise. 'Why, Grandmama MacIntosh! I didn't notice you sitting there in the gloom. How lovely to see you! Come and look at all the excitement the gale is causing. There's a tree down across the river, and . . .'

'*Catherine!*' Mrs Frazer managed to gasp, as she made a vain attempt to stem the blizzard of writing-paper which the draught was sweeping from her desk. '*Please* close that window immediately! Just look at the mess!'

Her granddaughter slammed the window shut with more haste than decorum and helped to restore order without once breaking the flow of her remarks.

'That *hooligan* wind is turning the place quite upside-down, you know. It whisked the hat clean off my head, and we chased it for miles before it fell in the river and sank! You cannot conceive how exhilarating it is to gallop along with a wind like that. We climbed Gifford Law—right to the very peak—and it seemed one need only spread one's arms and leap to come swooping out over the valley like a sparrow-hawk! You ought to . . .'

'Catherine, dear!' Mrs MacIntosh interrupted strongly, since Mrs Frazer was clearly unable to defend herself. 'I do wish you will sit down and be still for a moment. Your Grandmother Frazer and I are no longer young, and I must confess that we find your exuberance a trifle wearing.'

Catherine's mobile face stilled abruptly as she seated herself on the very edge of a chair in the exact position expected of a young lady: her hands clasped loosely in her lap, her back rigidly erect, her green eyes demurely downcast. This won a smile from both ladies, but each of them was sharply aware that the overall impression was one of agonisingly pent-up energy.

Mrs MacIntosh said gently, 'I'm glad you enjoyed your ride, dear. We watched you come in.'

'Oh, were you watching? Then you must have seen me win our race.' Catherine's face was alive again, sparkling with enthusiasm, but she was clearly making an effort to subdue her tone, as she went on, 'It was neck and neck all the way from Campdon to the river, but Sir Charles was forced to give way at the little bridge because it will not take two horses abreast, you know, and as you saw, he was unable to make up the lost ground. Oh . . . the lawn!' She turned to Mrs Frazer with unfeigned remorse. 'Grandmama, I am indeed sorry! Your lovely lawn! But old Mr McBride says it will be as good as new in no time. He was really very understanding about it considering all the trouble he has had with it—the moles and the clover and . . . I forget the other things he mentioned. However, Sir Charles made him a peace-offering—"greasing his palm", he called it! Isn't that quaint?'

'But *not* a suitable expression for a young lady!' gasped Mrs Frazer, flinching visibly. 'It doesn't matter about the lawn, Catherine, but I am compelled to say that I do not approve of you—or Sir Charles either, for that matter—crawling around in the mud to help McBride to replace the turves. If you wished to apologise, that is one thing, but the groom might have put the damage to rights.'

'Ah, but you cannot have noticed, Grandmama.

Robert did not cross the lawn, he came round by the drive. Only consider how unfair it would have been to have made him suffer for my crime. Sir Charles, however, was equally guilty, so I made him make amends.'

Mrs Frazer glanced at Mrs MacIntosh for help, but finding that lady struggling with an insistently curving lip, she said only, 'I take it Sir Charles has gone home?'

'Yes. I asked him to come in and take a dish of tea with us, but he was full of excuses. Do you know, Grandmama, I truly believe he is terrified of you!'

Her rich, full laughter filled the room, sounding almost sacrilegious in the crypt-like gloom. Mrs MacIntosh touched her handkerchief to her mouth, trying to avoid looking at Mrs Frazer's outraged scowl, and purposefully began the long process of struggling to her feet.

'Have them send my carriage round, child. I must be on my way if I'm to be home before dark. No, no, don't come down with me, but ride over and see me one day soon—when you have an *hour* to spare—and give my love to Jamie when you write.' She touched her cheek to Mrs Frazer's and sailed out of the room with a prodigious rustling of petticoats, while Catherine ran to the window to watch her being installed in her carriage.

'My certes! What a smart equipage, Grandmama. A carriage like that would be just the thing for you instead of that great cumbersome old coach you still keep. Do come and take a look at it.'

Mrs Frazer sighed as she contemplated the utter impossibility of ever installing an inkling of correct behaviour into her granddaughter's head. 'Indeed I will do no such thing, Catherine. It would be most improper. Do come and sit down. See . . . there is a letter for you on the mantleshelf. It arrived when you were out, and I believe it may be from Jamie.'

Catherine crossed the room in what appeared to her grandmother to be two leaps, totally unconscious of the fact that the train of her habit had whisked her embroidery basket off a footstool, scattering its contents.

'It is! It is from Jamie! Oh how I miss him! I do hope . . .' Tearing open the missive, she became gradually inarticulate as her eyes ran across the lines. Then her mouth twisted in a wry smile. 'Oh dear! It is all about Judith again, Grandmama. How beautiful she is, what "uncommon refinement of sentiment and purity of manners" she possesses! It's all very strange. Judith Cameron never seemed to me to be anything at all out of the ordinary, and I knew her well, you know. We went to dancing school together, and I spent a week at her home once, before we came out. Surely, if she had had a "face like an angel" and "the sweetest voice imaginable", I would have noticed?'

Mrs Frazer abstaining from comment, there was a short silence while Catherine appeared to lapse into profound thought. Her grandmother watched her uneasily, reminding herself that nothing good had ever emerged from Catherine's periods of reflection in the past. But Catherine, rousing herself, said only,

'I'll tell you what, Grandmama. I'll go up now and finish reading this while I change for dinner, so that we can discuss Jamie's news over our meal.'

Mrs Frazer steeled herself for the inevitable door slam, but when its echoes had died away she permitted herself a small sigh of self-pity. Another four weeks to go! Twice as long—dear God!—as she had already endured! At this rate she would be in her grave before Colin and his wife returned home. Feeling very old and frail, she levered herself out of her chair and paced sedately to her room, comforting herself that in only a few hours it would be bedtime.

Had she realised just how harrowing these hours were to be, she would have remained in her room, but she had no indication of the tempest until she was already seated at the dinner-table.

Catherine had made the most of her time in transforming herself into a very elegant, smoothly coiffed and beautiful young lady. She wore a simple dark blue dress, which had previously won her grandmother's approval, and she carried herself with such an air of soft-spoken gentility that her aged relative would have been seriously alarmed if her wits had not been dulled by exhaustion.

For several minutes the table-talk centred on the food, the price of candles, and whether or not the wind were dying down. Then Mrs Frazer made the mistake of asking if Jamie had said anything interesting in his letter.

'Oh dear . . . I don't perfectly know how to tell you this, Grandmama.' Catherine said, wrinkling her brow and making her grandmother's heart miss a beat. 'Jamie appears to have got himself into a dreadful pickle, and it looks as though I am going to have to post off to Glasgow straight away. If I set off first thing in the morning, I'll have no difficulty in being there well before dark.'

Mrs Frazer's knife clattered to her plate as she tried to reassure herself that her ears were playing her tricks. 'What—What did you say?'

'Oh, it's nothing for you to worry your head over, Grandmama. You know what Jamie's like, forever flying up into the boughs over the most trivial occurrence. But he needs me to straighten things out, so I have no choice but to go to him. Really, for a man of almost twenty-one, he is singularly inept!'

'But . . . But, Catherine dear, who is to take you? You know I cannot undertake such a journey at such short notice . . .'

This objection was brushed aside with an airy wave.

'Of course not, dear, you mustn't think of it. I shall apply to Sir Charles. He will be delighted to take me in his chaise, and of course I shall have my maid with me.'

'On no account!' Mrs Frazer cried out, her mind reeling. 'I don't know what you can be thinking of, child!'

'You don't wish me to take my maid?'

'I don't wish you to *go*! In all the world, girl, what would your mother think of you? Gallivanting about the country with an unmarried man, and no one to lend you countenance but that impudent hussy you are pleased to call a maid. Six months ago she was a cottar lassie on your father's estate, and she has not the remotest idea how to go on. If I were your mother . . .'

'Jessie is an excellent maid, Grandmama. She suits me very well, even if she doesn't mind her tongue as she ought, and . . .'

Mrs Frazer silenced her with a raised hand, and drew several deep and calming breaths. After a moment's reflection, she said tentatively, 'Forgive me, Catherine, but I must say it strikes me as extremely odd that Jamie should apply to you in his hour of need. *Not*—I assure you—that I consider it misguided of him to do so, but it did not escape my notice when he was here that his opinion of your intellect is not flattering. May I . . . ah . . . May I ask if he solicited your assistance in so many words?'

'Oh, his letter made it quite clear that he needs me,' Catherine returned, gesturing vigorously with her knife, to the close peril of the serving-maid who happened to be refilling her wineglass. 'I only wish I might tell you the whole story, Grandmama, for you would see I have no choice but to go, and as quickly as may be arranged. But, of course, I'm not at all sure that Jamie would wish me to speak of his affairs.'

'Well, I am most sorry, Catherine, but I fear I cannot permit you to go to Glasgow alone.' This was uttered with a Trojan firmness which would have ended all argument there and then had it not been delivered in a bird-like treble. 'You must see how irregular it would be. And, besides, where would you stay?'

Catherine leaned across the table to squeeze the thin old hand. 'Darling, you are putting yourself in a taking for nothing. Glasgow is only a few hours away, not in darkest Africa. I shall stay with Jamie at the Saracen's Head, which is the most respectable of inns, and I shall not be gone above a day or two. What harm could I possibly come to in Sir Charles's chaise, with . . .'

'*No!*' Mrs Frazer's minuscule bosom heaved with strong emotion. 'Definitely not! Your parents would not countenance your travelling with Sir Charles, and neither do I. You must write and tell Jamie so. The matter is quite closed. I absolutely refuse to discuss it any further.'

She took a large sip of wine and fanned herself briskly, rather pleased with herself for having squashed the matter so firmly. 'Good God!' she muttered, more to herself than to Catherine who had returned her attention to her cooling meal, 'Sir Charles's chaise, indeed! The idea of even considering such impropriety! All the way to Glasgow, no less! In my day, a lady would no more have ridden in such an equipage than in a wheel-barrow! You may not approve of my "great cumbrous old coach" as you call it, but let me tell you, with a good coachman and at least one groom, a lady travelling alone could be assured of privacy, at least. Whereas . . .'

'Oh, well, I dare say you are quite right, Grand-mama,' Catherine murmured submissively, rising and dabbing her mouth with her napkin. 'I should have enjoyed the chaise better, of course, but if you do not feel entirely comfortable about it, then the coach it will have to be. Forgive me if I leave the table now, but I must just see Jessie and tell her what to pack.'

The door slammed behind her with a thunderous crash, and Mrs Frazer received a momentary impression that she was tinkling in her chair in much the same manner as the ornaments on the mantelpiece.

For some seconds she remained staring at her plate as though it might provide a clue to the sudden turn of events. At one moment she had had everything under control, and at the next—chaos! As an illustration of the difficulties of handling Catherine, it was fairly typical, and Mrs Frazer was much inclined to admit defeat. While she could not view her granddaughter's solitary trip to Glasgow with anything but the strongest disapproval, the thought of a few days' peace and quiet for herself did much to reconcile her to the idea.

Leaning forward, she picked up her wineglass and drained it with unaccustomed bravado, almost enjoying the first guilty conscience that had troubled her in years.

CHAPTER
TWO

CATHERINE COULD imagine no crueller form of torture than to be boxed up in a coach all day. Her grandmother's housekeeper had done everything possible to make her journey comfortable, with extra cushions for her back, a rug for her knees and a hot brick for her feet, but nothing could relieve the hour upon weary hour of tedium.

McRae, the mouldering coachman, refused to exceed the decorous speed at which he thought it proper for a lady to travel, and this, added to the ancient and ornate design of the coach, turned the journey into a solemn procession. Catherine was mortified to be seen riding in such ostentatious state and hid in a corner till she could be fairly certain of encountering no one who knew her.

'A fine figure of fun I shall make, arriving at the Saracen's Head in this monstrosity!' she remarked to Jessie. 'Did you notice how those cottagers we just passed doffed their caps? I'll swear they thought that we were royalty!'

Jessie had not only noticed, but had derived no small amount of entertainment by acknowledging the salutes with a regal bow. 'It's no' that bad. A wee thing old-fashioned, mebbe, but I like it fine.'

'Do you?' returned her mistress, reflecting that it was no great hardship for Jessie to spend the day lolling among the cushions, since she would otherwise have had plenty of work to keep her occupied. 'Well, I do not. I had much rather have gone with Sir Charles in his nice travelling chaise but Grandmama nearly flew up in the air when I suggested asking him. It would have been much more amusing than bouncing along in this plaguey coach, and very likely I could have prevailed upon him to let me take the reins for a stretch. He has done so before, you know, on more than one occasion. He thinks I have good hands.'

'Oh ay,' said Jessie in tones that made Catherine look at her sharply.

'You think he might be prejudiced in my favour?' She gave this a moment's serious thought. 'No, for he does not, in any case, approve of young ladies who wish to do such things, and would prefer me to sit quietly with my hands folded. Besides, Jamie let me drive his greys at Transk, and they are so tender-mouthed I know he would never have trusted them to me if he had thought me at all cow-handed.'

'Hmph! I'll wager your father never knew about that!'

'No. And if he finds out, I'll know who told him,' Catherine returned pointedly, but with no great degree of heat since she was well aware that it would not occur to Jessie to tell tales. Mrs Frazer might look for other qualities in a ladies' maid, but Catherine had her own priorities.

It would have been nice to have had a more diverting companion for the journey, but she could not blame Jessie for, presently, disposing herself comfortably and dozing off. There was nothing to see from either window except a seemingly endless expanse of moor, and it was impossible to read for any length of time since the coach bounced and swayed upon its springs as though it were a ship in a howling gale. This left Catherine with nothing to do but practise yawning and drumming her nails on the window-ledge and in minutes she was ready to scream with boredom.

Finally she rummaged through her pockets and drew out Jamie's letter, smoothing it out on her knee. If she could only hold it steady for a few minutes, she might be able to understand it better at the second reading than she had done at the first. Jamie was an unwilling and therefore an impatient letter-writer at best, and it was quite plain to Catherine that the only reason he had invested, this time, in a second sheet was in order to fill the first one with praise of Judith Cameron.

Skimming over this with the inattention it deserved, she came at last to the only paragraph of significance in the letter. Even without the paper jiggling before her eyes, it was not easy to decipher. Jamie had scribbled:

You will not have forgotten that I had the most bitter quarrel with Lord Marbrae in London last year. I remember writing to you about it at the time, and no doubt you thought it silly of me to lose my temper over so trivial a matter as a pair of horses. The fact is, they were something quite out of the ordinary and I was furious at having let them slip through my fingers. It seemed devilish underhand, somehow, that Lord Marbrae's offer should be accepted before I even had the chance to bid, and I have to admit that I flew into a passion and told him so to his face. I wish to God I had cut my tongue out first! There was the devil to pay because of it, since Marbrae, as I soon discovered, is one of the darlings of London society, and ever since then he and his cronies have made no secret of their dislike for me. Of course, I would be quite happy to apologise—indeed I would gladly grovel to him—but my dear J. will not hear of my speaking to him at present. The matter, meanwhile, is weighing on my mind so heavily that I can get no sleep for thinking on it.

The remainder of the letter was taken up with vague promises of his return to his grandmother's house at Ayr in the near future, but Catherine ignored these and returned to studying the mysterious paragraph for the third time.

She remembered the story of the disagreement, but had not at the time afforded it more than a moment's thought. Jamie's quick temper was a by-word in the family, and his periodic squabbles were too frequent to give rise to comment, except by his mother who was inclined to excuse his irritability on the grounds that he was going through a phase. Catherine did not wholly accept this theory, but it did seem, on reflection, that her elder brother had lately shown a distinct tendency to count to ten before exploding. Either the years were teaching him wisdom, or his tiff with Lord Marbrae had taught him a salutory lesson.

It was clear that he regretted his foolish outburst, but why, after all this time, he should still be losing sleep over it was completely unfathomable. If he expected his sister, as his tone implied, to appreciate the significance of his remarks, he was very far from the mark. She was quite at sea, and impatient to tell him so.

The name of his antagonist had rung no bells when he had mentioned it at the time of the quarrel, but now she discovered that she could put a face to it. She had met Lord Marbrae some years ago, in Edinburgh, either at an Assembly or at the home of some friend of her mother's. He was a rather sweet, roly-poly old man with merry eyes and an old-fashioned bag-wig. He had spoken to her about the standing stones on his estate in

Perthshire, pinched her cheek and called her a spirited little filly.

It was excessively difficult to picture him falling out with Jamie over the purchase of a pair of thoroughbreds, and it was totally impossible to believe Jamie capable of venting his frustration on such an inoffensive old greybeard as Lord Marbrae. Yet, since he had irrefutably done so, why should the wonderful Judith be so adamant that he should not apologise?

The whole business was a confusing hotch-potch of unanswerable questions, each one of which irked Catherine like a stone in her shoe. Several times she crumpled the letter into a ball and thrust it back into her pocket only to retrieve it a moment later to scan it once again in case she had missed some nuance that would make all clear. She hated conundrums of this sort, and was more than ever impatient to reach Glasgow and learn the answer.

However, while they were halted for refreshments at Kingswells, an idea occurred to her which was to postpone her reunion with her brother even more. Judith's home, Monkwood, she suddenly realised, was situated on the outskirts of the city at no great distance from the road upon which they were now travelling. A half-hour spent with Judith would not only solve the mystery but greatly alleviate the excruciating tedium of the journey.

This proposal met with considerable opposition from McRae, who had strict instructions from his employer that her granddaughter was to be delivered straight to the Saracen's Head by the shortest possible route and to be shielded, meanwhile, from all contact with the rest of humanity. He was too deaf to be swayed by argument and too old to succumb to charm, so, in the end, Catherine was forced to resort to Sir Charles's methods,

which, she was relieved to see, worked just as successfully with coachmen as they did with gardeners.

Consequently, about six in the evening, they turned
into a narrow side road and drew up before the tall iron
gates of Monkwood. Catherine, by this time, was beside
herself with boredom and had driven Jessie to despair by
making her play guessing-games to pass the time. Not
only were her muscles protesting at the prolonged confinement, but the meal she had eaten at Kingswells,
having been well churned by the nautical motion of the
coach, was beginning to make threatening noises. She
let the window down while Robert, the young groom,
jumped down off the box to go to the gatehouse, and the
fresh air tasted like wine.

No one appeared at the gatehouse door in answer to
Robert's knock, but she saw him stroll round to the neat
garden at the back and presently he returned in the
company of a pretty, dark-eyed young lady. This transpired to be the daughter of the gatekeeper, and she was
able to inform Catherine that Miss Judith and her
mother had just set forth to a tea-party and were not
expected home till late in the evening.

This information pleased nobody. Catherine was fran-
tic to get out of the coach, Jessie was more than ready for
a break from her mistress's fidgeting, Robert had just
met the girl of his dreams, and McRae now discovered
that the road was too narrow to turn the coach in.

Catherine solved everyone's problem by demanding
that the steps be let down. 'I must and I *shall* have some
fresh air,' she said decidedly, cutting short McRae's
objections with a furious wave of her hand. 'If you
cannot turn your horses here, you must drive on till you
come to a wider part of the road. There is no turning-
point any wider in the drive till you reach the house, and
that is at least a mile and a half from this entrance. I shall

walk quietly in the grounds till you return for me. No, Jessie, I don't need you. Robert and this young lady will take excellent care of me, I don't doubt, and you will only be gone for a few minutes.'

'Are you sure?' Jessie threw after her, and added with engaging concern, 'You'll wish you had me by you if you lose your dinner!'

Ignoring this remark, Catherine found herself in a pleasant beech-lined drive which she remembered well from her last visit. Robert paced sedately behind her, but she had noticed the lingering glances which passed between him and the gatekeeper's daughter, and waved him back with a smile. 'No need to stick to me like a burr, Robert. You can wait here. I'll only be going a few steps up the drive.'

He looked a shade doubtful at this, but as he could see at least half a mile along the drive before it curved, there was plainly no need for him to intrude on her privacy. He turned eagerly back to the blushing young lady, and Catherine could see that she herself was speedily forgotten.

It was bliss just to be alone, to be able to stretch her legs and to breathe in great lungfuls of the sweet, loam-scented air. She was surprised to find how well she remembered Monkwood: the long forest rides, the rose garden, the house among the trees. Over there, she remembered, lay the walled garden, and on this side, screened by the line of beeches, was the ferny glade where she and Judith had picnicked one sunny afternoon.

It had been a very happy holiday, and realising that the smell of wood smoke and pine forest that lay heavy on the breeze was sharply evocative of that time, she had paused to breathe it in when she heard, quite unmistakably, the faintest ring of blade upon blade.

Somewhere, and at no great distance, a sword-fight was in progress.

It took only a second to pinpoint the direction. To her right, a narrow path led downhill through a tangle of bushes, and as she followed it, the sound came more clearly, luring her on. In a few hundred yards the river came into view below her, deep, brown with peat, and swirling round in a wide arc. Within this arc lay a green stretch of sheep-cropped turf. A perfect spot for a duel, a fencing lesson or a friendly contest.

It was not immediately apparent which it was that she found herself watching now. Certainly both men seemed to be fighting with firm determination. She could hear their voices from time to time, but from thirty or forty feet above them, it was impossible to guess at the words. Luckily, the path zig-zagged down among the broom and brambles to within feet of the greensward, and in a few moments Catherine was in a position to view the combatants at close range.

This was like no sword-fight she had ever seen, and, for a delicately-reared young lady, she had seen a great many. Fencing was a favourite pastime of all four of her brothers and she had, many times, had the opportunity of watching them tilting with each other and with their friends. Added to this, her recent series of lessons with Jamie had, while giving her no small opinion of her own skill, also taught her to know a real master when she saw one.

These were both first-class swordsmen, fast, strong and very proficient, and although they fought for pleasure—she could now see the buttons on their foils— every lunge and thrust was executed with total resolution. They fought barefoot, using every inch of space available to them, forcing each other to and fro from one end of the green to the other.

They were also very well matched. The taller of the two, who was probably several inches over six feet, had the advantage of reach, but he was slower on his feet and relied on a rigidly upright stance and a considerable strength of wrist to get himself out of trouble.

His adversary was only two or three inches shorter, but he moved with a speed that made Catherine doubt her eyes and he fought intelligently, using the features of their tilting-ground to his advantage. At one moment the taller man would find himself backing into the river, the next, his sword would be entangled in overhanging branches.

'Curse you, sergeant!' he cried angrily more than once, while his quicksilver opponent danced back out of reach, laughing with gleeful derision.

Catherine, too, found herself laughing silently at the audacity of the 'little sergeant'—as she began to think of him—though, in truth, he was little only in comparison with his lengthy opponent. His back was turned to her from the moment she was able to see him clearly, and it was several minutes before she began to realise that the pleasure she derived from watching him was not entirely due to his skill as a swordsman.

There was something about the way he moved, something very confident, perfectly co-ordinated, that held her spell-bound. She could see the long, deeply indented line of his spine where his sweat-damp shirt clung to his back, and his close-fitting buckskins outlined a waist and hips that were as slim as a girl's. As he thrust and parried, swaying, crouching, springing like a cat, her eyes followed him avidly and a pulse beat fast and strong at the base of her throat. And then he swung to face her, and it seemed that her heart stopped beating altogether.

He was, quite simply, the most beautiful creature she had ever seen.

Beautiful, strangely enough, not handsome. She had known handsome men before, many of them, but not one of them was such an overpowering delight to her eyes as this one. He was as sunbrowned as a ploughman, his features too strongly chiselled to be thought refined, his expression almost grim, yet—yes!—he was beautiful, as a thoroughbred stallion is beautiful, with the same gloss of health and vigour and the same proud lift of head. His shirt was open at the throat to show a slim, strong column of neck, and the sun that had turned his skin to bronze had gilded occasional strands of his tawny hair so that his head seemed haloed in the amber light of the setting sun.

Jessie—McRae—the monstrous coach awaiting her at the gate—all were forgotten in the sheer joy of watching this golden Apollo. Indeed it seemed, later, that all her other faculties had closed down temporarily in order to allow her brain to concentrate on the flow of information delivered by her eyes. Only the abrupt and unexpected ending of the contest brought her back to full awareness.

'Hell's teeth!' The tall man staggered back as his foil went sailing into the trees. 'That was a dirty trick, sergeant! As—As dirty a trick . . . as I've seen in a . . . a twelvemonth! Damme if it wasn't! . . . God, I'm blown!' He sat down on a convenient rock and wheezed painfully, while the sergeant retrieved his sword for him. 'Touched in the wind, I fear, like the parson's mare!'

'Ah well,' grinned the victor, returning to throw himself on the grass at his feet. 'You're not as young as you used to be, you know. Can't expect to keep going the way you did when you were my age.'

'Insolent pup! I'm not thirty-one yet! I'd like to see you in seven years' time!'

Catherine knew that she had tarried much too long, but they were both facing her now across only a few feet of grass, and she was afraid to move in case they noticed her among the broom. It would be embarrassing to be caught eavesdropping, and she did not have time to waste in explanations, but her retinue would already be worried about her and might arrive on the scene at any second. Fortunately, the tall man, at least, was making preparations to leave. He had drawn on his boots and now stood up, reaching for his coat.

'I am sentenced to a party at Lady Blair's house tonight,' he was saying dolefully. 'My mother has gone on ahead, but I had to promise to put in an appearance later in the evening.' He smoothed his hands across his hair. 'Coming?'

The sergeant shook his head and said, throwing Catherine into a panic, 'I think I'll have a dive in the river before I go up.'

His hands were already at his shirt-buttons, but he turned to watch the other man stride away down the river bank, and Catherine, not daring to wait for a better opportunity, gathered her skirts and fled up the path as silently as she could. In a few steps the bushes grew thickly enough to hide her completely, and she felt confident enough to slacken her pace a little.

Evidently, she thought as she climbed, the tall man was Judith's elder brother. What was his name . . . ? Leonard . . . ? No, *Lionel*! He had been away in the army when she had last visited Monkwood, but she had heard Judith speak of him often and with great affection. The other swordsman was clearly a fellow-soldier. They seemed—for an officer and an enlisted man—to be on uncommonly friendly terms, although much the same relationship existed between herself and Jessie. Possibly fencing instructors occupied a special position in the army, regardless of rank . . .

At that second there was a rustling of bushes close

beside her, and the sergeant stepped out directly across her path.

She was more amazed than frightened. He was still in his shirt-sleeves and bare feet and must have taken the direct route straight up the bank, but he gave no sign of any particular exertion. His hair was perhaps a little dishevelled, a few curling strands fallen across his brown forehead, but he did not look like a man who had just scaled a precipitous rock-strewn slope in a few seconds. What he *did* look like, she thought a little breathlessly, was a very dangerous ruffian, and he was smiling at her in a manner which did little to inspire confidence.

The sun had sunk behind the hills, and it was so gloomy under the trees that she could not see his face at all clearly. The way he stood, however, balancing on the balls of his feet, his arms held a little way from his body, told her that he was ready to catch her if she tried to run past him. But when he spoke, his voice was low-pitched and slightly amused.

'Well, now . . . ! Not the kelpie I thought I was pursuing . . . not even a wood nymph . . . but only a young lady who has lost her way. Yet, I must confess, at this moment I cannot find it in my heart to be disappointed.'

Catherine took instant exception to the familiar tone. He might enjoy Lionel's friendship, but she was not in the habit of encouraging implied flattery from strange men, even of her own class, and certainly not in such a precarious situation. She lifted her chin.

'I have not lost my way,' she said crisply, betraying her uneasiness by only the faintest tremor. 'I have been visiting Mr Cameron's sister, and the sound of your contest attracted my attention. And now, if you will kindly step aside, I will be on my way.'

He tipped his head on one side, and although she

could not see his eyes, she was aware of their scrutiny. It was quite clear that he did not believe her, which—she had to admit—was not entirely surprising, since young ladies did not normally wander about their friends' woods in the falling dusk. If he had caught only a glimpse of her as she quitted the river bank he might have taken her for a poacher, but now he was plainly puzzled.

'These woods are full of poachers,' he said, as though reading her thoughts, 'and I'm quite sure Miss Cameron would wish me to escort you to . . . wherever you are going.'

'That will not be necessary.' Catherine returned hurriedly. He might wish to satisfy his curiosity as to where she had come from, but she could well imagine the repercussions if she were to emerge from the woods in the company of this disreputable and barefoot vagabond. 'I have my own servants in attendance, and no doubt you have other duties to attend to.'

His teeth gleamed in a most disquieting grin as he replied disrespectfully, 'Oh, I have, ma'am, I have. But none so agreeable. With your permission, I will accompany you at least as far as the lodge gates.'

He stood aside to allow her to precede him, and as she swept past, she said, 'I wish you will not bother. If I am seen with you it will give rise to conjecture, and I am in no need of your protection.'

He offered no reply to this but turned to accompany her, walking—not deferentially behind her—but at her shoulder, perhaps even a little in front. Yet, if his manner were less than obsequious, his attentiveness left nothing to be desired. He seemed to exude an aura of protectiveness that she found strangely potent, and as he kicked a fallen log out of her path or held a bramble spray aside from her skirts it was hard not to feel quite ridiculously precious. To one who had grown up among not particularly doting brothers, this was a novel experience and one which was to return to her thoughts with surprising frequency.

As they walked, she was aware that he was trying to get a better look at her face, but she kept her chin ducked so that the brim of her cap thwarted his curiosity. He no longer alarmed her, but she was sharply conscious of the fact that he was a man and she was a woman and that darkness was gathering fast. Luckily, it was only a short climb to the drive, and in a moment she saw the blue shadows of the thicket give way to the afterglow that still filtered through the beeches on to the carriageway.

'You may leave me here,' she said, halting abruptly. As he began to demur, she lifted a hand, and snapped, 'I have no wish to be delivered back to my servants by you. Please do as I say immediately, or I shall be forced to complain of you to Mr Cameron!'

'As my lady wishes,' he said quietly, after a moment's hesitation, and melted back into the greenery, from where, to her astonishment, a faint whisper reached her which seemed to say, 'Au revoir!'

Before she had time to assimilate this impertinence fully, a movement caught her eye and she realised that Jessie was hurrying up the drive towards her, her skirts hitched to her knees for speed. Whether she had seen the sergeant or not Catherine could not be sure, but clearly he had seen Jessie and had, at least, had the decency to make himself scarce.

'Well . . . I don't mind telling you . . .' Jessie was beginning in a truculent tone, but Catherine, conscious of the eavesdropper in the bushes behind her, was not going to be read a lesson.

'I dare say you don't, Jessie,' she said crisply. 'But I mind listening. Come along. I have been longer than I had intended, and it will be dark by the time we reach the Saracen's Head.'

'You're still looking a wee bittie peely-wally,' said Jessie, in what her mistress regarded as unnecessarily ringing tones. 'Did you puke up your . . .'

'No, I did *not*!' Catherine interrupted, blushing hotly and dragging Jessie inexorably down the drive. 'I feel perfectly all right now. All I needed was a breath of fresh air.'

As she pressed ahead, she was goaded by a suspicion that he was keeping pace with her on the far side of the beeches. There was neither sight nor sound of him, but knowing that he was suspicious of her, she felt he would be bound to follow to see what he could find out so that he could make a full report to Mr Cameron in the morning. If he was indeed there, she thought, simmering with chagrin, he would be astounded by the sight of the coach, which was drawn up athwart the gates like something that had recently been a pumpkin.

He was also, in all probability, privy to the heated scene outside the gatehouse where everyone was blaming everyone else for the delay. Jessie had already fallen foul of McRae, who was more interested in keeping his horses moving in the cool breeze than in helping to look for Catherine. McRae had blamed Robert, and the groom had taken exception to being described, in front of the gatekeeper's daughter, as a great havering chanty-heid who shouldn't be allowed out without his mother.

The result was an undignified wrangling which Catherine put a stop to by climbing into the coach and rapping on the window in a peremptory manner. 'If you wish to clapperclaw each other you may do so when we reach the Saracen's Head. Get in here, Jessie, and let us for pity's sake be on our way.'

Jessie was of the opinion that Robert would be the

better for a good skelp round the lug, but Catherine caught her by the sleeve and dragged her almost bodily aboard. She was on tenterhooks till they pulled away, wondering what more they could do to embarrass her. She could tell from his clenched face that McRae was furious with her and could scarcely wait to deliver himself of a blistering rebuke, but fortunately he was in a hurry to see his horses stabled and contented himself with muttering beneath his breath.

It was, of course, ludicrous that she should care what the sergeant's opinion of her might be, but she told herself that she was more concerned about what he might pass on to Judith's brother. She would certainly be calling upon her friend in the next few days, and she did not particularly wish Lionel to have formed an unflattering opinion of her. Bad enough to be suspected of trespassing without being labelled as the mistress of a very eccentric and acrimonious band of servants!

As she had predicted, it was already dark by the time they reached Glasgow, but the Saracen's Head was just warming up for the evening's business. Alighting at the front door in a confusion of town carriages and sedan chairs, Catherine was swept into the lobby in a throng of elegantly dressed gentlemen and ladies. Most of these, it transpired, were not guests at the inn but were *en route* for an Assembly which was being held in the ballroom on the first floor. The sight of such festivity cheered Catherine enormously, making her feel that the long, boring journey had been well worth the effort.

Her first objective was to contact Jamie, but here she struck an obstacle as he had gone out for the evening and it seemed unlikely that he would return before bedtime. However, the room next to his was, fortuitously, vacant, so she was able to console herself with the prospect of giving him a pleasant surprise in the morning.

It was a delightful room (one of the best in the house, she was assured), and the windows gave her an excellent view of the comings and goings at the front entrance as well as a commanding prospect of the main thorough-fare. There was plenty of space for a truckle bed for Jessie, and when the fire had been lit in the large, ornate fireplace, Catherine was inclined to pronounce it one of the most comfortable and well-appointed rooms she had ever lodged in.

'Oh ay,' said the maid, passing a warming-pan over the sheets. 'But just you wait. You'll mebbe no' be so sonsie when you get the reckoning.'

This consideration had not occurred to Catherine. On the few occasions in the past when she had stayed at an inn her father had been with her and had, naturally, settled the bill, so she had not the remotest idea how much a room like this was likely to cost her. Such mundane matters, in any case, rarely held her attention for any length of time. She habitually overspent her allowance, and her doting father, just as habitually, gave her a gentle scolding and paid her debts. Something similar, she supposed vaguely, would happen in the matter of her reckoning at the inn: either her allowance would cover it, or Jamie would settle it with his own.

After a light supper in front of the fire, she climbed into bed and lay listening to the faint sounds of music from the Assembly, the more distinct clatter from the taproom directly below her, and the rattle of wheels on the cobbles outside her window. After the silence of her grandmother's tomb-like residence, no lullaby ever sounded sweeter. Now that she had escaped from her incarceration, she would take care not to be recaptured in a hurry. There was nothing to amuse her in Ayr. The odd card-party, perhaps, or the dull company of a few rustic squires, but no assemblies, no theatres, and assuredly no beaux of the calibre of the little sergeant.

She pulled herself up sharply, opening her eyes and halting that train of thought before it got out of hand. The sergeant might epitomise everything that was desirable in a man, but he was not for the daughter of Frazer of Transk. She herself might be willing to live with him in a cottage, but it would break her parents' hearts. Better to put him out of her mind right away than to risk the inevitable anguish later.

Turning over, she focused her mind on the treats in store for her on the morrow, and planning a reconnaissance of the city, a shopping expedition and a visit to Judith, she fell happily asleep.

CHAPTER
THREE

THE NOISE started again at first light: carts of vegetables and wicker baskets on their way to market, noisy washerwomen bound for the wash-house on the green, a travelling chaise being brought round from the stable yard for a departing guest. Dogs barked, pattened feet clattered on the cobbles, and gradually, inch by slow inch, Catherine surfaced from a deep and contented sleep.

She woke conscious only of an obscure sense of well-being, but as the mist of dreams coalesced into an awareness of her surroundings, she was all at once as wide-eyed as a marigold. Scrambling out of bed, she ran to the window and threw back the curtains.

It had rained in the night, and heavily to judge by the running gutters, but the sky was now clearing and a pallid sun showed fitfully between the clouds. The street was now busy with tradespeople and merchants. A hunchbacked bellman appeared, ringing his bell to attract the attention of passers-by and announcing in raucous tones that fresh herring were to be had at the Broomielaw, three for a penny.

Catherine whirled away from the window and pounced on the truckle bed where Jessie was still restoring her strength for another exhausting day. 'Jessie! Wake up, you slugabed! Quick, quick, and you will see the bellman. He is the funniest little man imaginable—

with a big hooked nose and a hump on his shoulder like Mr Punch. Hurry!'

Jessie woke with a choked snore and staggered to the window, but the bellman had gone before she had properly come to her senses.

'Well, never mind,' her mistress comforted her, skittering across to the fireplace to poke hopefully at the embers of last night's fire. 'I dare say he will be back tomorrow. Have them send me up some hot water and some breakfast, and as soon as I am dressed Jamie can take me out to see the sights. You shall take him a note right away so as not to waste any time.'

'I hope he had a good night's sleep,' muttered Jessie cryptically, but the inference was lost on Catherine, who was now throwing everything out of her boxes in the search for paper and goose-feather.

'I wish I had thought to leave him a note last night, for there is no saying but what he may have gone out early this morning. He will be prodigious surprised to find I am in the room next to his, will he not? I wish I might see his face when he reads this!'

'Ay, me too,' said Jessie drily.

'Well, now.' She smoothed her writing-paper thoughtfully. 'I shall have some fun with him, I think. How would this be: "Sir, The lady in the room next to yours would be excessively obliged if you would do her the honour of calling upon her at your earliest convenience. As the matter is of some urgency, she begs that you will not delay." There, now. Don't let him see you slipping it under his door, but knock loudly in case it escapes his notice.'

'He'll surely not visit a strange lady in her room at this hour.'

'I'll wager you this that he does.' Catherine brandished a lace-edged handkerchief that happened to be lying on the dressing-table. 'Jamie's curiosity will out-weigh his sense of propriety any day of the week. You'll see.'

In less than twenty minutes she had won her bet. She had just donned her petticoat and was seated before her mirror preparatory to having her hair dressed when there was a discreet tapping on the door, and in answer to her carefully disguised 'Enter!', Jamie stepped over the threshold.

He halted just inside the door, his eyes widening and a deep flush mounting his cheeks. The sight which met his eyes was hardly one to inspire confidence. The lady at the dressing-table was turned towards him, but her face was obscured by the hand-mirror which she was holding before it. One glance, however, was sufficient to tell him that she was dressed—to put it mildly—informally, and as his eyes slid in amazement from low décolletage to neatly-turned ankle, his hand was already groping be-hind him for the doorknob.

At that moment a husky murmur bade him approach and, hesitating, he saw one hilarious green eye regarding him round the edge of the hand-mirror.

'Kate!' he ground out viciously, and strode forward with malevolent intent. 'You ought to be thrashed, you brat! What a plague you are!'

'Mercy!' Catherine gurgled, between whoops of laughter, defending herself with the hand-mirror. 'Mercy, you great gowk! You should thank me for teaching you a lesson which may one day save you from the clutches of a wicked woman.'

'One of these days I'll teach *you* a lesson, minx!' snarled her brother, fighting back a grin. 'What are you doing here? When did you arrive—and who is chaperon-ing you? Not Grannie Frazer, surely?'

'You shall hear all presently,' Catherine returned

evasively. 'But first sit down and let me finish dressing, for I want you to take me out to see the sights this morning and we shall have plenty of time to talk.'

'You couldn't have waited till a less ungodly hour, I don't suppose?' He drew forward a chair and bestrode it obediently, folding his arms across the back and propping his chin on them. 'I was at Duffy's last night. It's a gaming-house just along the road, you know. Dropped quite a bundle at hazard, tried to get it back at the faro table, failed, and didn't get back here till the small hours.'

Catherine looked at him out of the corner of her eye as Jessie went to work on her hair, but before she could say anything, he gave a short laugh and shook his head.

'No, you needn't raise your eyebrows at me. I'm not falling into evil ways. It's one way to pass the time when I'm unable to be with Judith, that's all. Which reminds me, Kate. I can spare you one hour this morning, no more. I am engaged to go riding with her, and I can tell you now that I have no intention of breaking that appointment.'

'Oh, of course not. I wouldn't dream of asking you to do such a thing,' Catherine assured him, scolding him with a look. 'I shall be delighted to come with you. I am looking forward to seeing Judith again. Indeed, I called at her house yesterday on my way here, but she was out.'

Jamie did not seem unduly excited by this prospect, but fell to toying with the various bottles and jars on the dressing-table in a rather depressed manner. 'You called at Monkwood?' he said, after a moment's thoughtful silence. 'You're devilish impatient to see Judith suddenly! Just what are you up to, puss?'

Catherine put on a look of outraged innocence. 'What

should I be up to, for heaven's sake? I was bored and travel-sick, that's all. I needed a respite, and Judith's house was convenient.'

'Another half-hour's ride and you'd have been at the Saracen's Head.' Jamie regarded her with narrowed eyes, and gave his head a slow shake. 'Don't tell me any of your bouncers, Kate. You are bent on some knavery or other and you needn't bother to deny it. Certes! If I can't tell by now when you are up to your tricks it's not from want of practice. Come, now; out with it! What are you doing here?'

'Oh, it's that awful house of Grandmama's.' Catherine shrugged, removing a bottle of perfume from his fingers before he spilled any more of it. 'It's so dark and silent, and all the servants creep around like lost souls. Poor Grandmama was ready to be carried off with an apoplexy every time I so much as ran downstairs, so I felt we both needed a little break . . .'

'She's not with you? Then who is?'

'Oh, just McRae and Robert . . . and Jessie, of course.' She saw his brows come down threateningly, and continued speaking very fast. 'Grandmama insisted that I travel in that rolling nightmare she calls a coach, with McRae cosseting his horses all the way and Robert perched up behind in case we were set upon by highwaymen! It was like a royal progress. The coach is to return to Ayr today, but I had to promise to keep Robert by me and not dare to sally forth without I am accompanied by either you or him.'

His face had darkened with displeasure, but it was a mark of his new self-control that he kept a tight rein on his temper. 'The devil fly away with you, Kate! If this reaches Father's ears—and it will, you may depend on it—it will be my head that will roll. He told me I was to stay with Grandmama and keep you out of mischief until he got back from France, and now, the minute I turn my back . . .'

'Hardly "the minute" dear,' Catherine placated him, giving his cheek a pat. 'You do exaggerate, you know. Besides, if Grandmama gave her permission, I don't see how Papa can blame you.'

'She did *give* her permission, I hope?' Jamie's hands tightened suddenly on the chair-back. 'You're not gammoning me, are you? Only I can't imagine how you prevailed upon her to let you come—and with no one but your abigail.'

'Oh, as to *that*,' Catherine returned sunnily, 'it was the easiest thing in the world. Your letter arrived the day before yesterday, so I simply told her—well, it was perfectly true, in a way—I told her you were in a little trouble and needed me to help you sort things . . .'

Jamie's furious countenance stopped her in mid-sentence, but he was, at first, too inarticulate with annoyance to take advantage of this opening. 'Oh wonderful!' he got out at last. 'You really don't mind dropping me in the soup, do you? Father is going to be furious with me for this! And what do you mean by "perfectly true"? I'm not in the least scrap of trouble— at least, I wasn't till you arrived—and if I were, I'm not such a gudgeon as to want you sticking your nose in!'

'Well, but you are *so* in trouble,' Catherine countered briskly. 'You said in your letter that you could get no sleep for worrying about your quarrel with Lord Marbrae. That's trouble, isn't it? And I'm sure I can easily persuade him to let bygones be bygones because I met him in Edinburgh, you know, and we got along famously . . .'

'*No!* Confound it!' Jamie leaped violently to his feet, catching the chair before it hit the floor. 'I did not say I needed you to help me and I do *not* need you to help

me—in fact, I can think of nothing I need less at this
minute! Forbye'—he pointed a finger between her eyes
as though he were aiming a pistol—'if you insist on
helping me against my will, I shall very likely end up
strangling you with my bare hands. I will not have you
meddling in my dealings with Judith. Now, if that is
not perfectly clear, just tell me so and I'll go over it
again.'

'Oh, it is, it is. Absolutely,' Catherine smiled, without
making any specific promises. 'Except that I don't see
what Lord Marbrae has got to do with Judith, or why you
should be so upset about his dislike of you.'

He sat down again, the better to see her face. 'I
thought you just said you knew him?'

'I did. At least I met him once, years ago. I thought
him a very sweet old gentleman.'

'Oh, I see. That must have been Judith's uncle.' He
began absent-mindedly opening jars and sniffing at the
contents. 'He died, you know, two years ago. I thought
Judith might have told you. Her brother Lionel in-
herited the title, and since her father is dead, Lionel,
Lord Marbrae, is head of the family. In short, he is the
man I shall have to ask for Judith's hand in marriage.
And he hates me like poison.'

His tone was carefully matter-of-fact, but there was no
hiding the pain in his eyes and Catherine was stricken
with commiseration. And yet, at the same time, she
realised that this was just the sort of heartbreak that she
was studiously avoiding by refusing the little sergeant a
place in her thoughts. She might not be succeeding,
entirely, but at least she recognised the desirability of
nipping such an ill-starred romance in the bud.

'You must have known from the beginning that Lord
Marbrae would refuse his consent,' she said, out of a
strong sense of superiority. 'You have only yourself

to blame for allowing yourself to become so deeply involved.'

'I didn't know Lord Marbrae was Judith's brother until she returned to Glasgow a fortnight ago.' He had now found a rather expensive jar of lip-salve which he was experimentally massaging into his thumbnail and buffing it off with her hare's-foot. 'Both Judith and her aunt referred to him only as "Lionel", and why should I connect "Lionel Cameron" with "Lord Marbrae"? I nearly fainted when I discovered they were the same person.'

Catherine removed the lip-salve to a place of safety and eyed him thoughtfully. 'I think you are probably making a mountain out of a molehill, you know, Jamie. If you have continued to see Judith since she returned from Inverness, Lord Marbrae must know about it. If you have not run into him at Monkwood, his mother will have told him that you are paying advances to Judith, and he would have put a stop to it if he had disapproved as violently as you seem to fear. Isn't that so?'

This elicited no reply at all, and he seemed strangely unwilling to meet her eyes. Instead he fell to cracking his knuckles—a habit that made his sister's spine creep—which forced her, after a moment, to replace the lip-salve within his reach.

Finally she became suspicious of his silence. 'Jamie,' she said curiously. 'Lord Marbrae does know that you are . . . friendly . . . with his sister?'

He got up and strode to the fireplace, where he set about poking the logs with the toe of his boot till half of them fell out on the hearth and made the room blue with smoke.

'We thought . . . That is, Judith thought . . .' he muttered over his shoulder. 'We decided that it would be wiser if I did not visit Monkwood till we could devise some way of making my suit appear less unwelcome to Lionel. Neither he nor his mother are aware that Judith is seeing me. I cannot like it, of course.' He swung round, glaring at Catherine as though it were her fault. 'But Judith is so afraid to put the matter to the issue that she is reduced to tears every time I suggest bringing the matter into the open.'

Catherine hid a smile. Judith's most enviable talent, as a child, had been an ability to make tears come into her eyes at will. Evidently she was still using the trick to good advantage. 'So, meantime, you must be content to meet her when she is out riding? How romantic!'

'It is not at all romantic!' Jamie was very sensitive of his honour and clearly hated being persuaded into acting in an underhand manner. The wonderful Judith must have quite an influence over him. 'We meet only once or twice a week, and only in the presence of her groom. Or, if she is in town with her mother, she occasionally calls at the milliner's with her maid and we are able to exchange a few words. It's all very hugger-mugger and I utterly deplore it, but I'm hopeful that it will not be for long. There is a masked ball at Eastwood House next week to which Judith and Lionel are going, and I have also been sent an invitation. It's a pity you will be back in Ayr by that time, otherwise I might have taken you with me.'

Catherine had her own opinion about that, but knew better than to voice it. She examined her finished hair-style in the mirror and nodded her approval. 'I must say, I agree with Judith wholeheartedly.' She got up and gave him a quick hug. 'Try not to be so blue-devilled about it. She's quite right, you know. There is bound to be some way of winning over Lord Marbrae if we could only think of it.'

'I don't mind your thinking about it,' he said grimly, setting a threatening fist against the point of her chin.

'Just don't *do* anything. All right?'

'Oh pooh! You are worse than Grandmama!' She made a face at him and drew him towards the door. 'I am almost ready now. Do you go and choose me a decent mount at the livery stable—not some spavined old hack that I shall be ashamed of in front of Judith—and I shall be down presently.'

Pushing him out, she turned to see Jessie watching her with an expression of strong foreboding.

'Well, now,' she said, giving her maid a decided nod. 'That was most interesting. You are thinking the same as I am, no doubt? That it's time I took a hand in this matter. Jamie has not the slightest notion how to handle the situation, but once I have heard Judith's side of the . . . What's the matter, Jessie? Do you have the toothache?'

Jessie opened her eyes, muttered something under her breath and said, finally, 'Just a twinge, miss. Which habit is it to be?'

'My good cream one with the brown waistcoat and the brown jockey cap . . . or shall I wear the cocked hat?'

This important decision settled, she stepped presently into the stable-yard and found Jamie waiting for her. He had found her a neat little sorrel mare which was extremely skittish and inclined to jib at the least excuse, but which settled down nicely once they got going.

The promised hour having now largely evaporated, Jamie would permit only the most cursory appraisal of the surrounding streets before setting off for his rendezvous with Judith, but it was clear to Catherine from the little she did see that this was a much more modern and prosperous city than Edinburgh. The streets were wider and cleaner, and many of the buildings were colonnaded at street-level to form a covered pavement backed by tradesmen's booths.

Glasgow's prosperity was built on the tobacco trade, and this was evident everywhere from the scarlet-cloaked merchants—commonly known as the Tobacco Lords—whom they watched pacing up and down in the Trongate to the fleet of gabbards unloading at the Broomielaw. Catherine, however, was much more interested in seeing the shops, the theatre and the latest fashions as worn by the Glasgow ladies.

She was very careful not to initiate any direct discussion on the subject of the length of her stay, but Jamie made it quite clear that he regarded her visit as little more than an overnight stop, and she was left with the impression that, were it not for his assignation with Judith, they would both, at that moment, be upon the road to Ayr.

This did not worry her unduly. She had not the slightest doubt of her ability to thwart any plans he might make to return her to captivity, but the necessity of affording some thought to the problem made her unnaturally withdrawn as they crossed the Clyde and rode southwards for Monkwood. Once past Gorbals, a picturesque little village with neat thatched cottages, they gave their horses their heads and enjoyed a fine gallop across the moor till Jamie drew rein in the lee of a low copse of alders.

'Here we wait,' he said. And there they waited for several minutes, which, as Catherine pointed out with indisputable if unappreciated logic, might have been better spent in the fascinating environs of the Trongate. However, the sun had come out and it was not too tiresome to sit admiring the view and speculating idly on how their parents, the twins and little Caroline were enjoying their visit to Paris. Jamie did his best to appear relaxed, but he was so clearly on tenterhooks that Catherine breathed a sigh of relief when they finally heard the sound of approaching hoofbeats and Judith emerged from the trees, followed by an elderly groom.

Catherine was absolutely staggered by the change in her. If she had ever remotely resembled the picture that Catherine's memory retained of her—shy, insipid, freckle-faced and pallid—all similarity had disappeared. Her hair had surely never been such an eye-catching shade of guinea gold? And that face, with its pert little nose and pointed chin—could it really belong to poor little Judy Cameron who couldn't even execute a *pas de bas* without tripping over her own feet?

Two enormous long-lashed brown eyes opened wide as they swept from Jamie to his companion, and a soft cry of surprise issued from a mouth as pink and sweetly curved as a rose petal.

'Catherine? Is it really you? What a delightful surprise! Oh, but of *course*! I see now that it must have been you who came to call yesterday when we were out, only when Lionel asked me which of my friends were in the habit of paying calls in a coach and four I was *quite* at a loss, especially as I could think of no one who could be described as tall and lissom and exceedingly beautiful and with a mind of her own! But, my word! Lionel was eaten *alive* with curiosity, and made me promise to introduce him to you if you should call again, although why . . .'

'I don't think that would be a good idea,' interposed Jamie, earning his sister's gratitude. In one respect, she thought dazedly, Judith had improved not at all. She had always been a chatterbox—and even her letters, over the years, had been marvels of verbosity—but at least she had been wont to draw breath occasionally.

'You would have to introduce her as Catherine Frazer of Transk, and Lionel would immediately connect her with me and—I don't know—I just don't think it would be advisable to remind him of our . . . our difference of opinion at this moment. Besides, she'll be going home tomorrow, so I doubt there will be time for her to visit you at Monkwood.'

Judith, who had followed this speech with her brow furrowed with concentration and her eyes glued to Jamie's lips rather in the manner of a deaf mute, now turned to Catherine and cried out, 'Going home tomorrow? But you *can't*, Catherine, not without spending *some* time with me when it has been more than two years since I last saw you and I have so much to tell you, and every time I am in Inverness you are in Edinburgh, and when I am in Edinburgh you are at Transk, and you never say anything—*really*—in your letters, so it would be altogether too unfair of you to go without telling me all your news. Don't you agree, Jamie?'

She paused enquiringly, but since Jamie was momentarily at a loss for words, Catherine said at once, 'I had hoped to stay for at least a week, Judith, but Jamie does not at all approve of the idea and is afraid that some dreadful fate will overtake me if he does not return me to my grandmother's house forthwith. See if you can prevail upon him to change his mind?'

Judith swung round on Jamie with a look compounded of reproach, entreaty and absolute trust, and Catherine was treated to a graphic demonstration of the effect, on a stubborn man, of a pair of soulful brown eyes and two softly pouting lips. Jamie melted visibly, just like a chocolate soldier which Catherine had once, as a child, put in front of the fire to warm.

'I've no objections to her staying a day or two,' he said mistily, but the gaze did not waver till he swallowed hard, and added, 'or as long as she wants to, actually, unless our grandmother objects. I dare say no great harm will come of it as long as my father doesn't find out.'

'Who is to tell him?' Catherine shrugged. 'Not Grandmama, surely, for he would only be miffed at her for allowing me to come in the first place. Robert and McRae are not likely to be in contact with him, and Jessie, thank heaven, does not consider herself to be my keeper.'

'Then that is settled.' Judith clapped her hands together with delight, earning herself an infatuated smile from Jamie. 'We shall see a great deal of each other while you are here, Catherine, although it will be awkward if I am not to introduce you to Lionel—but still, I'm sure Jamie is quite right upon that head for he always knows just what should be done, but anyway Lionel is out most afternoons either on business or with his friends and, in fact, he went off to see his shipwright just before I set out to meet you and he won't be back till dinner-time, so why should you not come back and take tea with me now, Catherine?'

'Why not, indeed?' she replied before Jamie could think of any objection. 'An excellent idea. You don't mind riding back alone, do you, Jamie? I'll be staying only a couple of hours at the most, so you can send Robert to fetch me at about three.'

Jamie glanced uncertainly at Judith. 'What about your mother? If she meets Catherine, she may mention her to Lionel.'

'Well, then, we will not go up to the house. There is a pleasant summerhouse above the rose garden where we often have tea, so there should be no occasion for Catherine and my mother to meet if you do not think it wise.'

He could retaliate with no further objections, so she gave him her hand to kiss, and they spent several seconds looking into each other's eyes with such similar expressions of tender passion that it was all Catherine could do not to snigger. Out of decency, but also to preserve her gravity, she walked her horse a few paces away and turned back only when she heard him say, 'Till tomorrow then, dearest.'

As she approached, he caught her eye in a look that spoke volumes. 'Very well then, Kate. I will see you this evening. In the meantime, please try to behave yourself and don't get into any scrapes, will you?'

Catherine opened her eyes at him, looking indescribably maligned. 'Why, Jamie,' she said in a hurt voice. 'As if I would.'

CHAPTER
FOUR

IT WAS NOT impossible to hold a conversation with Judith, but merely very, very difficult. There was an art to it which Catherine had once mastered, but which returned to her only gradually as they trotted over the moors to Monkwood.

Several times during the ride she was reminded of her first driving-lesson at the age of nine. Jamie had—most reprehensibly—allowed her to take the reins of the dog-cart with a very skittish little black mare between the shafts, and Catherine, in spite of Jamie's shouted instructions, had experienced the greatest difficulty in imposing her will on the fickle creature. The ensuing tussle was still sharply etched in her memory and it amused her to reflect that Judith demanded the same concentration, the same light touch to change her direction, and an even more determined effort to get her to stop.

However, properly handled, Judith could impart more information in a five-minute monologue than her friend could have hoped to elicit in a half-hour's question and answer. By the time they reached the familiar gatehouse, Catherine was in possession of the true facts regarding the quarrel between Jamie and Lionel as well as much gratuitous information regarding Judith's recent journey from Inverness, her mother's penchant for sick headaches, and the new yacht which was being built for her brother.

'I *thought* there was more to the quarrel than Jamie was willing to admit,' said Catherine, refusing to be seduced by these digressions. 'Certainly, he told me he had insulted Lord Marbrae, but he didn't say it was in public. No one could have blamed your brother if he had challenged Jamie to a duel.'

Remembering the quite awe-inspiring sight of Lord Marbrae at practice with the sergeant, she could only shudder at her brother's stupidity, and actually gasped with horror when Judith replied,

'But Jamie *did* offer him satisfaction, you know, but Lionel was very rude about it and said—most contemptuously, Jamie says—that he didn't fight with schoolboys, which I thought quite beastly of Lionel and not at all like him since Jamie was very nearly twenty and Lionel was not all *that* much older than he . . .'

'He was quite old enough to call him a schoolboy . . .' Catherine put in, her sympathies entirely with Lionel, but Judith was not to be deflected.

'. . . but I dare say Lionel is challenged to a great many duels, *not* because he is in the habit of offending people but because he is quite famous as a swordsman, and perhaps other swordsmen might wish to see if they could beat him, so, you see . . .'

'Well, he was beaten yesterday evening,' Catherine interjected. 'It was by a trick, admittedly, but I must say I thought his adversary had the upper hand all along.'

Judith stopped as though she had hit a brick wall. She stared at Catherine for several astounded seconds and made a few false starts before she succeeded in murmuring dazedly, 'Enoch? How very strange! Lionel told me that you had been watching Enoch and him fencing down by the river, but he did not mention that Enoch had beaten him, which is the strangest thing, because there is such rivalry between them and I have often heard Lionel say . . .'

Catherine's mind wandered away into a consideration of the sergeant's name. Enoch . . . She had to admit that it had never been one of her favourite names, conjuring up, as it did, a picture of someone rather weak and ineffectual. The only Enoch she had ever known had been a youth of that kidney, a circumstance which no doubt coloured her subsequent reaction to the name, but now that she came to consider it anew, it *did* have a certain ring to it. Applied to the golden swordsman of the night before, it sounded quite rakish—even dashing! Enoch . . . Yes . . . She rather liked it.

As they progressed, chatting, along the drive towards Monkwood House, she was aware that part of her mind was alert to the possibility of his sudden appearance. Try as she might, she could not ignore the way her pulse quickened at the prospect of seeing him again, or the disappointment when they reached the summerhouse without encountering him. It was in the hope of leading Judith on to speak of Enoch that she said, as they dismounted, 'Your brother was in the army when last I visited you . . .'

'Ah, yes, but he had to resign his commission in the Scots Greys a long time ago—oh, two years, at least— first Papa died and then my uncle died, and with both estates to manage, how could we go on with Lionel in the army? Of course, he was very upset as he loved the army life, but there was nothing . . . There goes Ewan, my mother's errand laddie. He can take our horses to the stables. *Ewan!*' She delivered the reins into the hands of the small boy who came running up in answer to her summons, and leaving Catherine sitting in the sun, went herself in search of refreshments.

The silence when she had gone was like the calm after a storm. A blackbird sang in the trees at the foot of the sloping lawn, and somewhere near at hand water gurgled and splashed on the stones of a busy little burn, but the sounds were lost in the tranquil silence that, for Catherine, would always characterise Monkwood House. She had fallen in love with the house and its grounds on her last visit, and it was pleasing to find that the remembered atmosphere of peace and felicity still remained.

It was strange, she thought, letting the sun beat redly through her closed eyelids, that she should feel so at home in a place that was the very antithesis of Transk. She loved her father's home, the resolute old stone house with its turrets and crow-stepped gables, the blood-red moors and the ring of mountains that rose on every side. Yet only here, at Monkwood, had she experienced this perfect peace, this feeling of truly belonging.

All too soon Judith was back, her tongue beginning to clack as soon as she was within earshot. At her heels, bearing a tray of tea-things, was a tall negro footman whom, Judith divulged, Lionel had brought back from a recent visit to his plantations in Jamaica.

'. . . and I was so looking forward to Lionel coming home, since I wanted him to meet Jamie, and I *knew* they would like each other prodigiously, for Lionel loves sailing and horse-racing and fox-hunting just as much as Jamie does, and they are so alike in a hundred other ways and—oh, Catherine!—I could have *wept* when Jamie told me that they had quarrelled, and I have tried so hard to decide what to do, indeed I have thought of several *excellent* stratagems which would have made Lionel think more kindly of Jamie, but Jamie thought they wouldn't serve, and I know he is much more clever than I and always knows what is best to be done, only . . .'

'What were they?' Catherine wedged in. 'These stratagems you thought of?'

Judith thought deeply for a moment or two, and finally held up four fingers. Pointing to the first of these, she said earnestly, 'The best one, *I* think, was to engage a highwayman—it need not be a real one, of course—but someone who would pretend to accost Lionel late at night in a lonely spot, and then Jamie could ride up as though *quite* by chance, and single-handedly . . .'

'Um . . . yes . . . I think I can guess the rest,' Catherine muttered, resisting an impulse to hold her head. 'Don't bother to tell me the others. I have a feeling something more sophisticated will be necessary to sway your brother.'

'Oh, Catherine!' cried Judith immediately, catching hold of her friend's hand and squeezing it happily. 'You were always so good at solving problems like this and managed to get us out of *so* many scrapes when we were younger! Don't you remember the time you climbed up on the wash-house roof to steal a bottle of the whisky old Angus used to hide there? You threw one down to me, and when I spread my skirts to catch it, it went straight through and smashed at my feet!'

Catherine blenched. 'Ye gods! You could have been killed, Judith! What a dreadful child I was to have involved you in my hoydenish pranks!'

'Oh no! You were always such exciting company and if we did get into a muddle now and then you always saved us from retribution. I shall never forget how terrified I was to face my mother with a great three-cornered tear down the front of my good muslin dress, but you made me pick her a big bouquet of lilac—remember?—and how could she rail at me for an accident which she assumed had occurred when I was doing something to please her?'

'There is no escaping the fact,' said Catherine, uncomfortably aware that this incident was only one of many, 'that I was an extremely mischievous and deceitful little girl, and I am very much afraid that I frequently led you into situations which would have been quite foreign to your own nature. I am thoroughly ashamed to think of it now, but you may be sure that I will make recompense by doing everything in my power to reconcile Lionel and my brother.'

'Then the matter is as good as settled!' Judith cried triumphantly. 'I just *know* that you have been sent in answer to all my prayers for guidance, and I am quite confident that whatever you decide to do will turn out just as we would wish it to!'

Her limpid brown eyes fixed themselves on her friend's face in an expression of complete trust, and her lips parted as though she were in instant expectation of Catherine's producing an immediate solution to the problem.

'Um . . . well . . .' Catherine obliged, for the sake of saying something. 'Don't you know anyone who knows them both and who would be willing to act as mediator? Someone whose opinion might carry weight with Lionel?'

Judith set both elbows on the table and cupped her chin on her hands, staring blankly out into the sunshine. Catherine could almost hear the wheels of her brain grinding rustily round. 'I'm afraid not,' she said apologetically after a minute or two of deep reflection. 'Jamie does not know a great many people in Glasgow, since, like you, he is used to spending the winter in Edinburgh, and anyway Lionel is rather dogmatic and rarely allows himself to be swayed by anyone else's opinion, even his best friend, whose estate marches with ours and who has been like a brother to him since they were in petticoats . . . !

'Have you tried crying?' Catherine interrupted, suddenly recalling this talent of Judith's which had got them both out of many a tight corner in their regrettable past. 'You used to be able to make tears come to your eyes at will. Can you do so still?'

'Yes . . . but . . . At least I *think* I can, for you know it has been an age since I have tried to do so, but, Catherine, I am not at all sure that it would work with Lionel, indeed I know he would only call me a silly wet-goose and tell me to stop piping my eye.'

'Indeed!' said Catherine with a strong reprobation that ignored the fact that her own personal experience of brothers would not have encouraged her to hope for a different reaction. 'Very well. We shall abandon that plan. I'm sure there are any number of gambits we can try. Think, Judith! How can we make Jamie indispensable to Lionel? What does Jamie have that Lionel would give his right arm for?'

'I don't know,' Judith groaned, a deep frown marring her damask brow. 'I don't think he has anything . . . Oh! If only he bred fighting-cocks! I overheard Lionel talking about a black-crested red which he would dearly love to see beaten, but it weighs over five pounds . . .'

'*Judith!*' Catherine said through clenched teeth. 'Do try to be a little more practical! I doubt me if your brother would be persuaded to exchange you for a fighting-cock, not even if it weighed five *stone*!'

Judith appeared, at first, to be disposed to be hurt by this rebuke but then subsided in a fit of giggling. 'Five stone! Only conceive, Catherine! A fighting-cock weighing five *stone*!'

But Catherine had just experienced a blinding flash of inspiration and was not to be distracted. 'Just a minute, Judith. I think I have it! You must begin associating with someone *totally* unsuitable . . . an impoverished fortune-hunter, say, or a half-pay officer . . . and you must make Lionel believe that you are madly in love with the fellow and mean to marry him, no matter what he says or does. Just think how worried he would be if he thought there were a danger of your eloping with some dreadful man! Why, he would be so beside himself that he would fairly *leap* at the chance of seeing you safely married off to Jamie!'

Judith drew a deep breath and held it for several seconds while this new idea penetrated her understanding, then threw her arms around her friend's neck and hugged her gratefully. 'Oh, Catherine! You are so clever! I knew you would think of something and I am convinced that Lionel would dislike it excessively if I were to contract an alliance with someone who was not respectable . . . only . . . only . . . I don't think I am acquainted with anyone who is not of the first respectability, because Mama is always with me and I have no opportunity of meeting anyone who does not meet with her approval.'

'Oh come!' Catherine said crisply, raising her eyes skywards in search of patience. 'Surely you could meet someone unsuitable if you put your mind to it? The world is full of unsuitable people! You met Jamie, didn't you?'

'Yes, but Jamie is not unsuitable, and he was introduced to my Aunt Maude by Lady MacIntosh, which made him *quite* unexceptionable . . .'

'Surely . . .' inserted Catherine thoughtfully. 'Surely your Aunt Maude would have written to your mother to tell her that Jamie was visiting you regularly? And, if your mother knows that he is paying court to you, why has she kept Lionel in the dark?'

'Oh, did not Jamie explain all that? It all came about because of Aunt Maude's deafness, you see. When Lady MacIntosh introduced him as "Mr Frazer", Aunt Maude thought she said "Mr Mather", and by the time we realised that she had picked up his name wrongly we knew that Lionel and Jamie were at loggerheads, so it seemed wiser not to say anything to the contrary. Only, Mama now thinks I have a beau in Inverness called "Mr Mather", and because Aunt Maude was so taken with him and told her so, she is forever asking me if I have heard from him again and it quite puts me to the blush, but I have resolved to say nothing of the mistake, so . . .'

'But you are often in town with your mother,' Catherine said, bringing her firmly back on course. 'Jamie tells me that you are able to meet each other occasionally at the milliner's. Surely you could find an opportunity to strike up an acquaintance with some merchant's son or the like? What about the Assemblies? You must be allowed a little freedom there, at least.'

'Well, yes . . . but it is Lionel who takes me to the Assemblies now because the music brings on Mama's migraine, and although Lionel does not stand over me his eye is on me all the time, and if he thought I were stepping beyond the bounds of propriety he would swoop on me like a hawk. Besides, there are no unsuitable people at the Assemblies. Mr Niven tried to bring in a very *vulgar* woman once and he was turned away at the door. To be sure, there is Andrew Ford who talks to himself a great deal, but he is quite elderly and Lionel would never believe me if I were to tell him that I had formed an attachment for him. And Mr Parry . . . Oh, Catherine! You *must* see Mr Parry before you go home, otherwise you will not be able to say you have seen all the sights of Glasgow! Everyone calls him "Pretty Parry" and Lionel says he is a "Macaroni", and it is all the rage in London where one may see a dozen such in the space of a ten-minute stroll down the Strand—such a monstrous wig and enough paint and powder to cover the Town Hall!'

'Yes, I have seen Macaronis before,' Catherine smiled. 'Do you think Lionel would object to your running off with Pretty Parry?'

'Oh, yes, indeed he would dislike it above anything, for he thinks Mr Parry the greatest dunderhead and called him an "abomination" when I remarked upon him on the way home last week. But . . . But, Catherine . . . I am not at all sure that I could *attach* Mr Parry, at least, not without spending a good deal of time on the attempt, and . . . and we don't *have* much time . . . Jamie is so impatient to speak to Lionel, and every day that passes brings him closer to the breaking-point. He hates all the subterfuge we are forced to employ, but if we could only make him wait for a few days . . . there must be a way to soften Lionel's heart . . . I would do anything . . .'

Her voice tailed away wistfully and they both fell silent, brooding despondently, oblivious of the sunlit garden that surrounded them.

Catherine was unwilling to relinquish the idea of the unacceptable suitor. She was well aware that one or two of her own friendships had, in the past, caused her father many sleepless nights, and although the thought of marriage had never once crossed her mind she knew that both her parents were keen to see her comfortably—and safely—settled. Such a lever would be a powerful tool to use on Lionel, she knew it in her bones. He had only one sister to dispose of, and the Cameron fortune was more than enough to make her a matrimonial catch of the first water. Lord Marbrae would never suffer to see her throw herself away on a cockscomb or a penniless wastrel. But where could one find a suitable candidate within the next few days?

The difficulty was that it would have to be someone with whom her brother knew her to be already acquainted. Someone with whom she had had time to fall in love. Perhaps someone she had met during her stay in Inverness. 'Mr Mather' . . . ?

Catherine's chin came up, and she stared, arrested by a sudden idea, into the distance. Gradually an idea began to take shape. An idea so bold and yet so certain of success that she was hard put to it not to throw back her head and crow with triumph to the skies.

'Judith . . .' she said in a whisper, restraining herself with great difficulty and speaking very slowly so that she would not be misunderstood. 'Listen . . . All we need is someone who will *pretend* to be enamoured of you and willing to run off with you if Lionel refuses you permission to marry him. Now, Lionel and your mother must believe you to have known him for some time, so we shall call this fictional suitor "Mr Mather". I know your Aunt Maude gave a good report of Mr Mather, but it will take some time for Lionel to get a letter to her to confirm this, and we must hope your aunt will not reply too promptly.'

Judith was plainly at a loss already, but her trustful, long-lashed stare never wavered. 'But will it not appear strange to Lionel that Mr Mather does not come to call on me?'

Catherine shook her head. 'Lionel *will* see Mr Mather, but only from a distance. We will dress him as a Macaroni. The wig and the powder and paint will make an adequate disguise, and he will also be instantly recognisable as your new beau even though he never gets close enough to your brother to be in danger of receiving a direct set-down or—we must be realistic—physical violence.'

Judith thought this over, and a faint gleam of hope began to kindle behind her eyes. 'And who will you ask to play the part of "Mr Mather"?'

'Why, no one, you daft gowk!' Catherine laughed, '*I* will be "Mr Mather". Even Jamie wouldn't recognise me.'

Catherine had never actually heard a death-rattle, but she assumed it must sound very much like the noise which issued, piteously, from Judith's throat.

'Now, Judith,' she said trenchantly. 'You are not about to cry, are you? There's not the slightest need, I promise you, for there's no question of our being found out. As I said, Mr Mather and Lionel will never come face to face. In fact, it may only be necessary for Mr Mather to make one appearance—well, perhaps two—and we will choose situations where he can easily escape from your brother, should he appear to wish to force a confrontation.'

Judith was leaning back weakly in her chair. She said nothing, but her lips appeared to Catherine to be moving in silent prayer.

'I think the Assembly Rooms would provide an excellent venue for his first appearance,' she went on, disappointed but not entirely surprised by her friend's lack of enthusiasm. Judith had always been slow to appreciate the brilliance of complicated schemes, but she usually went along with them unprotestingly and followed instructions to the letter. 'There will be plenty of people there and it's very easy to lose oneself in a crowd. Besides, if Lionel *should* corner me, he will be forced by good manners to behave in a restrained manner. After that, it will be up to you, Judith, to persuade him that you have been seeing Mr Mather in secret since you were in Inverness, and that you love him to distraction and intend to marry him. Lionel will, of course, forbid you to see him again, whereupon you will scream and rend your raiment and swear to elope if he does not relent.'

'I'm not perfectly certain that I shall be able to rend my raiment,' Judith whispered, a small worried frown etching a line between her brows. 'Perhaps my green polonaise . . . it has muslin at the front . . .'

'I was speaking figuratively,' said Catherine with commendable restraint. 'Don't worry about rending anything. Just try to imagine it's Jamie he is forbidding you to see again, and act accordingly. If you are successful in convincing him of the depth of your passion, we need display Mr Mather to him only once more—just to let him see that you are willing to defy him. That can easily be accomplished at a fair distance, for if he were to see you out riding, say, with a companion, he would not require to be close to you to be able to see that you were in the company of a Macaroni—*ergo*, Mr Mather. And, I assure you, Judith, it would be a strong man who would turn down the heir to Frazer of Transk if he came offering for you after that!'

'Yes . . . Yes, I'm sure you are right!' Judith clasped her hands at her bosom, and a little colour returned to her face. 'I cannot be altogether happy at the prospect of causing dear Lionel so much worry, for—to tell you the truth, Catherine—he is, in general, the most amiable of brothers and I know he only wants what is best for me, but yes! . . . I *will* do it! If it is the only way to make him look favourably on Jamie, then I have no choice—I'll fight him like a tiger!'

'Well said!' cried Catherine, overcome by this uncharacteristic display of ferocity. 'We shall plan to present Mr Mather at the next Assembly, then, shall we?

That gives us just under a week, which is not long, but I imagine we will contrive to be ready in time. I must own that I am vastly entertained by the prospect of being a Macaroni, if only for a few hours, but it will take a great deal of planning and preparation to do the thing properly. Never mind, it's all in a good cause.' She stood up and smoothed down the skirt of her habit. 'But now I must start for home. Robert will have been waiting for me at the stables, and I must take care not to be late home lest Jamie should lose patience with me and decide to return me to Ayr.'

Judith walked down to the stable-yard with her and saw her on her way, and if she was noticably less talkative than was her wont, there was a determined lift to her chin and a grimly obstinate set to her mouth that caused Catherine to smile wonderingly as she rode away. Strange how love could change people, making a wild-cat out of sweet, gentle little Judith and turning the hot-tempered Jamie into a—comparatively—tolerant fellow.

Even the normally taciturn Robert was showing signs of uncommon light-heartedness, breaking into an occasional note or two of song and looking about him with appreciation as though seeing the beauties of the countryside for the first time. No doubt he had made the most of his time while awaiting Catherine at the stables, and there was every sign that his relationship with the gatekeeper's daughter was progressing in a satisfactory manner.

Love, she reflected, seemed to be in the air just now, and at that second—just as her thoughts returned unbidden to the sergeant—they turned a bend in the road and there he was, standing on the grass verge in conversation with a farmer who was trimming the hedge.

For a split second she absolutely refused to accept the

evidence of her eyes. This simply could not be the same man she had watched fighting barefoot on the river bank!

There was no mistaking him, this time, for anything but a gentleman. From the immaculate cut of his military style frock-coat, from the shine on his French top-boots, and from the pristine whiteness of his linen it was easy to deduce that her previous estimation of his station had been embarrassingly at fault. The magnificent jet-black gelding whose bridle he held whinnied as he turned to face her, and two giant deerhounds leapt up from where they had been lying at his feet, growling suspiciously.

Taking instant fright, Catherine's little mare threw up her head and began to dance and buck like a cork on a whirlpool, while she herself, quite dazed with shock, fought to bring her under control. But before she could do so, before even Robert could spur forward to her aid, the cause of all the commotion took two strides across the road, caught the mare by the bridle and brought her, trembling, to a standstill.

Catherine was much inclined to be infuriated by this high-handed interference. She disliked being made to look as though she was unable to handle her mount, and was about to say so, when she met the look he was directing at her and the words withered on her tongue.

'I fear the Fates are determined to damn me in your eyes, Miss Frazer,' he said, and she discovered for the first time that he could frown and grin at the same time, and with quite devastating effect. 'I am but this minute returned from calling at the Saracen's Head to apologise for last night's misunderstanding, and now I am come within an ace of unhorsing you! Not an auspicious start to our acquaintance, but I shall pledge myself to become more engaging with time!'

As far as Catherine was concerned he was quite

engaging enough as it was, in fact it was all she could do to maintain a composed exterior when inwardly she was in total disarray. At close quarters and in full daylight— as she had never seen him before—she could mount no defence against him. Had he, in truth, turned out to be the obscure fencing-instructor she had supposed him to be, it would have made no difference. No consideration of duty to her station, regard for her parents or thought of personal advantage could have made her strong enough to resist him.

He seemed to glow in the sunlight as though lit from within. The faint sheen of his dark gold skin was rekindled in the whites of his eyes and on his strong, even teeth, and as he stroked the mare's neck the reflections from her coat ran like fire along the clean line of his jaw. And yet his eyes, beneath the down-drawn brows, were dark, and forbidding and the muscles about his mouth seemed to resist his grin. For all his expertise, Catherine thought inconsequentially, even Lord Marbrae would think twice before crossing swords with this man in real earnest.

Finding that her own face had arranged itself into an expression of dewy-eyed euphoria, she straightened it hurriedly, and said with an admirable assumption of cool civility, 'I'm surprised you know my name. Judith told me that, until this afternoon, she had been just as puzzled as anyone to my identity.'

'Ay.' He nodded, wryly. 'You provided food for much speculation, none of it profitable, so I was forced to track you down as far as the Saracen's Head, which I had chanced to overhear you mention to your maid. There, of course, I drew a blank, but at least had the satisfaction of learning your name. Had I known that you were, at that moment, visiting Judith, I would have made haste to intrude upon your tea-party.'

She shook her head wonderingly. 'There was not the slightest need to go to such trouble to apologise. Nor, indeed, was any apology necessary, since, I see now, it was I who caused much of the confusion. You must have thought it odd that any friend of Judith's would be unaware that her brother was no longer "Mr Cameron" but had been "Lord Marbrae" for years.'

'That was, I must confess, one of the things that whetted my curiosity, but it was most reprehensible of me to allow you to remain under a misapprehension. In fact, I was about to set matters straight,' his grin widened imperceptibly, 'when you threatened to complain about me to Mr Cameron.'

She was too late to choke back a gurgle of laughter. 'Dear me! What a tangle of false impressions we concocted between us! You suspecting me of being a trespasser—or worse—and I quite confident that you were some sort of fencing-master.'

It was immediately apparent that he did not consider this a compliment. 'A *fencing-master*?' He fell back a step, and clapped a fist to his chest as though wounded to the heart, while his eyes seemed to search vainly for a friend to support him in this crisis of the psyche. 'A fencing-master? Certes! I knew you had taken me for a servant—perhaps even a menial—but a fencing-master!'

'But an extremely *good* one!' offered Catherine, in mock contrition. 'And only because, while I was watching your fencing-match, I heard your friend address you as "sergeant".'

'Ah! Then I forgive you. A perfectly natural mistake.' Prompted by a butt on the shoulder by the neglected mare, he returned to scratching her forelock, and said apologetically, 'It's a nickname, of course, dating from the days when he and I fought many a bloody campaign together, with our hobby-horses and wooden swords.

He, being the elder and much the bigger, was, naturally, the officer, while I never managed to rise from the ranks.'

A vague memory stirred of Judith mentioning a life-long friend of Lionel's whose estates marched with Monkwood. What a pity she had not thought to ascertain his second name. She could hardly address him as 'Enoch', and he obviously assumed that she had learned his identity from Judith. 'It seems to me,' she said smilingly, 'that the blame for this imbroglio is fairly evenly distributed between us, so we need not argue about who is to apologise to whom.'

Becoming aware that Robert had been clearing his throat pointedly for some moments, she held out her hand to Enoch in farewell. He took it, but without raising it to his lips he said plaintively, 'I'm not sure that I like leaving things like that. If I am to be deprived of the opportunity of making you a formal apology, I shall have no excuse for calling on you.'

This remark had the effect of making her fingers clench spasmodically in his, but she managed to laugh lightly as she said, 'I'm not sure that it would be proper for me to receive gentlemen callers at the Saracen's Head, since I am, at present, chaperoned only by my maid. However, I will be often at Monkwood during my stay. Perhaps we will meet there.'

He made no effort to hide his disappointment, but good manners precluded argument. He thus had no option but to bow, and say, with a rather brooding look, 'Be assured, ma'am, I shall make every effort to see that we do.'

And with *both* of them making every effort, Catherine mused as she resumed her journey home, it would be strange if she and Enoch could not contrive to meet frequently at Judith's house. There could be no impropriety in doing so, as long as Judith were present, and there would be less danger of Enoch meeting Jamie and, perhaps, mentioning him to Lord Marbrae.

Behind her, Robert began to whistle a high-spirited strathspey, and Catherine felt that her heart was beating time.

CHAPTER
FIVE

DURING THE next few days, however, a return visit to
Monkwood proved totally impossible to arrange.
Judith's letters—delivered all unwittingly by Jamie—
warned that it would be too difficult to avoid running
into Lionel. He had become involved in breaking in a
promising yearling from the Monkwood stables, and, as
a result, could not be relied upon to be absent from
home with the same regularity as of late.

Although he was now aware of Catherine's identity,
he had made no mention of his previous encounter with
Jamie, and Judith was not sure if he realised that they
were brother and sister. Better to follow Jamie's advice,
she argued, and avoid reminding him of the quarrel as
long as possible. Besides which, the less he saw of the
face which was soon to appear in the guise of 'Mr
Mather', the better chance they would have of hood-
winking him.

In any case, Catherine was already finding herself with
very little time for visiting. Within twenty-four hours of
inventing Mr Mather, she had discovered several serious
defects in her plan. Foremost among these was the fact
that very few of Glasgow's tailors had even heard of a
Macaroni, far less dressed one, and none of them was at
all anxious to do business with a woman.

Undeterred, Catherine armed herself with a sketch of
her requirements and a fictitious brother with a broken

leg, and sallied forth to demand the services of Alexander Jamieson in the Gallowgate. This gentleman was—if his advertisement in the *Glasgow Journal* were to be believed—much patronised by gentlemen of fashion and well known to be a master of his trade. Unfortunately, he was not of a particularly gullible nature, and only the offer of a substantial deposit finally persuaded him to undertake the task of outfitting milady's questionable brother.

It then transpired that accurate measurements were necessary, since no self-respecting Macaroni would show himself in public in a coat into which he did not require to be eased with all the strength and cunning of at least two helpers. This degree of perfection demanded expert cutting and fitting, so Catherine was forced to explain soulfully that her brother was in such pain that he could allow no one but herself to measure him and that, of course, any miscalculation which might arise from this arrangement would be her own responsibility.

Finally, having chosen the most sumptuous materials that Mr Jamieson could offer, she emerged triumphantly into the street and prepared herself to do battle with the wig-maker and the cobbler. Both of these worthy tradesmen were quite amenable to her wishes, but here again she was impelled to offer a down payment as a spur, and it began to dawn on her that the project was likely to prove a considerable strain on her finances.

Each of Mr Mather's two suits of clothing (for he could not be expected to wear the same outfit when riding out with Judith as he had worn at the Assembly) had to reflect his foppery and conceit, and both his shoes and his wig were so unlike the staid Glasgow mode that they had to be specially made. But whatever the cost, she told herself, it was too late to turn back now, and one either did the thing properly or not at all.

But, to do the thing properly, one had to invest in all the little extras that were so necessary a part of a Macaroni's ensemble: the fobs and seals, the tall beribboned cane, even—against her better judgment—an umbrella that had just come into the shoemaker's possession in part payment of a debt and which could be relied upon to mark Mr Mather as an affected popinjay of the first water.

It was an expensive business, to be sure, but it did not occur to Catherine to worry unduly about where the money was to come from when the accounts began rolling in. By then Jamie and Judith would be safely betrothed, and even Jamie could not be so ungrateful as to refuse to help foot the bill. In fact, the thought of his impending gratitude made Catherine feel, as she confided in Jessie, quite overcome with emotion.

In the meantime, it was no easy matter to keep him in the dark. He puttered in and out of Catherine's room at all hours of the day, clearly uneasy at her failure to make demands on his time, and she was forced to hide Mr Mather's finery, as it arrived, in a box under the bed. A slight cold in the head had to be hurriedly invented to account for her lack of interest in the fleshpots of Glasgow, but he had known her too long to be lulled into a false sense of security; she knew that he smelled a rat somewhere.

However, he was unable to surprise her at any activity more suspicious than writing furiously at her table, and when he asked what she was writing, he was told innocently that it was a letter to Grandmama and did he have any message he wished to be included?. In fact, although she had received two exceedingly agitated letters from her grandparent, both demanding her instant return, she had not the slightest intention of replying to either of them, and all of Jamie's messages of filial affection fell on stony ground.

The half-legible scrawl with which she covered page after page spelled out every detail of the stratagem which she could possibly plan in advance. She was more determined than ever—considering the danger of the matter coming to Enoch's ears—that nothing should go wrong, and she spent long hours in laborious planning and organisation. Judith was sent a detailed script to memorise, lest at the critical moment she should be short of words to describe her passion for her fashionable beau and her determination to be his bride. Even Mr Mather's words and actions could not be left to the inspiration of the moment, but were carefully considered and practised rigorously before the glass till they became almost second nature.

Jessie watched these preparations with a jaundiced eye, maintaining the uncritical silence which was her chiefest gift, but when the hour came for her mistress to walk forth in public dressed in an outrageous satin coat and skin-tight breeches, her face was a study of dismay.

'Try a wee thing more o' that black stuff on your eyebrows,' she insisted anxiously, re-tying the band of the enormous wig for the third time, lest it fall off and expose the coiled tresses beneath. 'It makes them look bushier.'

Catherine regarded herself in the small warped mirror, holding up her coat-tails and turning to peer over her shoulder. 'There's something wrong with these breeches. They don't look the same as Jamie's.'

'It's your arse,' said Jessie kindly. 'It's just not the right shape, nor ever will be, but with your coat-tails down, no one will notice.'

They both subjected 'Mr Mather' to one long final scrutiny.

'Is there enough padding in the shoulders, think you?'

'Ay, they're fine. Keep sniffing that nosegay; it hides your face a bit.'

'You don't think I could be recognised? Perhaps some more carmine . . .'

'No, leave it! I wouldn't recognise you myself. Just pray to God your wig stays in place.'

Catherine lifted the tiny three-cornered hat and perched it atop her monstrous wig with a hand that felt almost too weak to bear its weight. Her knees were trembling so violently that the tall cane, with its garland of tassels and ribbons, was not merely an accessory but a necessary means of support. And yet, while one part of her mind cringed fearfully at what she was about to do, another part was in a white-hot state of excitement. She had never been given to introspection, and so she appreciated only hazily the fact that danger affected her in much the same way as a bumper of brandy might have done: speeding her pulse, lifting her spirits and making her feel, generally, that life was sweeping her along at a dizzy and exhilarating speed.

She took a chair to the Town Hall and could have wished the journey longer, because when she alighted in the Trongate she was still experiencing difficulty in forcing air into her lungs, and, in consequence, doubted her ability to speak intelligibly. Fortunately, the august personage at the door understood the language of the coin she slipped into his hand, and although he did not demean himself by checking its value, she found herself bowed ceremoniously through the portal.

The sudden transition from pitch darkness to the brilliantly lit interior made her halt, dazzled, a few paces into the reception hall, so that she was not immediately aware of the stares which her entrance attracted. When she did so, she was further unnerved by the discovery that another Macaroni was staring at her from the far side of the room, and although she did not dare to return the stare too directly, she was fairly sure that this must be the renowned Pretty Parry.

His attire, although bizarre, was so magnificent and worn with such an air of confidence that it seemed, for him, the only suitable mode. His head, in its bulky wig, was thrown up in an attitude of proud disdain, and his slim, straight figure displayed a superb burgundy coat and striped breeches to elegant advantage. In one hand he carried a tall, amber-clouded walking-stick with gold tassels and in the other was a posy of wild flowers, which he was holding to his nose in an attitude of faint boredom.

All this flashed into her mind in the split second before she realised that what she was looking at was not Mr Parry but a reflection, in a full-length mirror, of Mr Mather. The effect of the full ensemble, which had not been visible in the small mirror provided by the Saracen's Head, was so striking that Catherine was filled with a heady sensation of invincibility, and it was with rock-steady confidence that she turned, with a languid movement of the head, and began to climb the stairs to the ballroom.

Heads turned at her approach, conversations faltered and died, but she gave no sign that she was not totally absorbed in a slightly disparaging study of her surroundings, and the faint, amused curl to her lips was entirely genuine. The ballroom was particularly crowded, and it took several minutes to locate Judith. She had hidden herself in the centre of a group of chattering young ladies and only one glance was needed at her small, rigid face to see that she was consumed with terror. She caught sight of Catherine while she was still some paces away, and her enormous brown eyes seemed to bulge from their sockets.

'Ah! Miss Cameron!' Mr Mather, the focus of every pair of eyes in the room, executed a complicated bow which was embellished with so many flourishes that it took several seconds to complete. '*Chère mademoiselle!* I had scarcely allowed myself to hope that you would be here tonight, but I dared not stay away for fear of missing you.'

Judith's colour faded from fish-belly white to a poisonous eau-de-nil. She made two or three abortive attempts to speak, but it appeared that her teeth were stuck together with carpenter's glue. Clearly, she would have to be removed from this close circle of attentive ears if she were not to give the game away immediately.

'Dare I ask you to stand up with me, ma'am? Pray do not refuse, else I am desolated!' Catherine deposited her nosegay and walking-stick and took firm hold of Judith's icy fingers, leading her out to where a country dance was forming. They began to move to the music but Judith's face remained a mask of purest panic and her steps had the jerky stiffness of a marionette. It was, Catherine thought, like dancing with a corpse.

'Don't you think I look extremely well?' she demanded, trying to instil in her friend a little of the buoyant delight that filled her own breast. 'You'd never have recognised me in a hundred years, would you?'

Judith's lips parted, but no words came.

'Oh, mercy on us, Judith!' Catherine whispered furiously. 'You will have to do a great deal better than this, otherwise we are betrayed. Smile at me . . . flutter your eyelashes . . . don't you know how to flirt?'

'I'm . . . so frightened . . .' If a dead flounder could talk, Catherine reflected, it would sound like that: limp and watery and totally without hope.

'Oh pooh! What is there to be frightened of, you shatter-pate? It is I who am running the risk of being recognised, not you. And if I am not afraid, there is not the least reason for you to be so faint-hearted. Try to bear in mind how happy you will be when you are married to Jamie.'

Judith dragged in a deep breath. A little colour came back into her cheeks and she managed a small smile. 'You . . . you do look splendid, Catherine. I'm sure no one could possibly recognise you with all that rouge and powder . . . and such a wig! You look prodigous well-to-do.'

'I am a great deal *less* well-to-do than I was last time we spoke,' Catherine returned in an undertone. 'All this finery doesn't come cheaply, you know. Indeed I am already in debt to the tune of . . .' She hesitated, realising that the exact figure might damage Judith's already beset nervous system beyond hope of recovery. 'But that's nothing to the point, anyway. I'm sure Jamie will think it money well spent, if it succeeds in . . .'

She broke off so abruptly that Judith started and began to look alarmed. 'What . . . What . . . ?'

'Smile!' ordered Catherine urgently, stretching her own carmined lips in a lascivious grin. 'Your brother is watching us. No! Do *not* turn around, Judith! Oh, was there ever such a ninnyhammer? You must simper and flirt and hide behind your fan. That's better. He's still looking. Oh, mercy! His friend Enoch is speaking to him now, and they are looking this way and laughing. Quick! Hit me across the knuckles with your fan as though I had said something roguish—*ouch!* For goodness' *sake*, Judith! Ah, they have dismissed me as of no account and have gone into the room beyond the arch. What is it—a card-room? But he is sitting where he can keep an eye on you, so try to laugh a little.'

By the time the dance ended, Judith was trembling with nervous tension.

'There, now!' Catherine said, hearteningly. 'That wasn't so bad, was it? The worst is over. We shall stand up for one more dance presently, another later in the evening, and then I shall melt away in the crowd before your brother has the opportunity to speak to me.'

They seated themselves on the fringes of the group that Judith had been part of earlier, and Catherine set herself to the task of coaching Judith in the part that she would have to play solo. 'Now, if Lionel should tell you to hint Mr Mather away, you must be firm as a rock, Judith. Try to imagine it's Jamie you are fighting for, and you won't go far wrong. You need not threaten to run off with Mr Mather—not in so many words—but make sure he knows the thought is in your mind.'

'It *is* in my mind.' Judith's small pointed chin jutted mutinously with the same surprising burst of resolution that had manifested itself once before. 'I would run away with Jamie tomorrow rather than be forbidden to see him.'

'Yes, dear, but you would never get Jamie to agree to a runaway marriage.' Catherine possessed herself of her friend's fan and began to ply it for her like a courtier. 'He is much too sensitive of his honour. Men are strange that way. However, I am persuaded that such extreme measures will be quite unnecessary if you frighten Lionel enough. He will certainly tell you tonight that your friendship with Mr Mather must cease forthwith, whereupon you will tell him that you would rather die. Then, tomorrow, we put the final part of our plan into operation: we show Lionel that you are prepared to defy him and go on meeting Mr Mather in secret. Now, where can we be sure that Lionel will see us together? It must be somewhere that has a clear line of retreat, for I must be well away before he has a chance of catching up with us.'

Judith's eyes slid furtively around the circle of intrigued faces behind her, and she moved her head closer to Catherine's to whisper, 'He goes out with the hunt tomorrow morning about nine. If we are on the ridge up at the wood where I meet Jamie, he could hardly miss seeing us from the road. There is a path through the wood which comes out just before the bridge at Gorbals. If you were to ride away in that direction, Lionel would never be able to catch you.'

'Excellent. He will be worried sick.'

'He might be very miffed . . .' Judith's ephemeral courage began to show signs of slipping away again. 'I would have to face him when he returned home, and he would be sure to read me such a lesson . . .'

'Judith! If you are to cower every time a man shouts at you, you had better not marry Jamie, for he can shout louder and longer than anyone else I know,' Catherine informed her frankly. 'Indeed, I rarely see him but he finds the necessity to shout about *something*.'

'Yes, but if *I* were your brother, I dare say I would shout at you also, Catherine,' said Judith with a smile that was totally innocent of criticism. 'I'm sure he means it for your own good.'

'Moonshine!' She became aware that the conversation round about them had virtually ceased, and that the other girls were straining to hear the whispers that were passing between Judith and her new beau. There were two stone-faced matrons sitting with the group, whose frigid stares stated clearly that the *tête à tête* had gone far enough. 'Come,' she murmured, drawing Judith to her feet. 'We will dance this cotillion and then I will take myself off for a while. Our third dance can wait till it is almost time to go home, then it will not look too suspicious if I suddenly disappear afterwards.'

'Oh dear! Do I really have to dance with you three

times?' Judith moaned as they took the floor. 'Things may be different in Edinburgh, but here it is considered very *fast* to dance with the same man more than twice. I would not allow even Jamie to monopolise me like that.'

'Yes, but we must impress Lionel with your lack of restraint where Mr Mather is concerned. Remember—You love him to distraction.'

The proximity of the other couples in their set precluded any further conversation, but she continued to ogle Judith for her own amusement and for the edification of her brother, who was still seated just inside the card-room. It seemed likely that he had missed neither their cosy chat nor the fact that they were dancing again, but he was clearly more interested in his cards than in Judith's activities. His arm was hooked over the back of his chair and his long legs stretched out before him, crossed at the ankles, and only an occasional glance flicked back over his shoulder towards the dancers.

Even Enoch, across the table from him, looked more watchful, and as she and Judith moved down the set, she could see out of the corner of her eye that his head turned to follow them. This scrutiny was a little unsettling, but, she decided, it was of no moment, since even if he disliked seeing his friend's sister so amicable with such a jackanapes, it was none of his business and he would be unlikely to interfere.

At the same time, one did not wish to take chances, so, having returned Judith to the safety of the group of curious damsels, she lost no time in burying herself in the farthest corner of the room and keeping well out of sight. Now she had nothing to do but to wait till it was time to dance her third dance with Judith. It would have been amusing to try out her charms on some other unsuspecting miss, but since Mr Mather was supposed to be devoted to Miss Cameron, it behoved him now to languish like a lost soul.

Accordingly, Catherine procured a tall, misted glass of lemonade and disposed herself in an attitude of deepest gloom against a secluded pillar. She was still an object of interest to most people in the room, and although politeness held their astonishment in check, she could tell that few of them were likely to associate themselves with her to the extent of coming over to chat. If she could have seen Enoch from her hiding-place, she would have been quite happy to pass the time in looking at him; watching the play of expressions across his strong brown face and the sure movements of his hands as he sorted his cards. But he was hidden from her, and consequently the minutes dragged by like hours.

At first the small measure of entertainment she was able to derive from diverting her audience was enough to keep boredom at bay. But she soon grew tired of posturing and preening and was trying to smother a yawn when she heard a discreet cough at her elbow and turned to see a small, rather ugly gentleman straightening from a bow.

'Forgive the intrusion, sir. Captain Peter Smart. Your servant.'

Catherine bowed ostentatiously, taking her time about it, realising she had not decided on a christian name. Christian . . . ? Why not? 'Christian Mather. At your service, sir.'

The deeper, rougher voice she had practised so assiduously sounded a little thin, but Captain Smart appeared not to notice anything at all strange. He had the sort of face one might expect to see reflected on the back of a soup-spoon, Catherine thought. His chin and forehead both sloped away sharply from a large, bony nose, and his eyes seemed to tilt upwards like those of a mischievous elf.

'You do not dance, sir?' he said with a sprightly smile and a sideways dip of his head. 'We in Glasgow are great admirers of Mr Campbell's music, but I dare say I should not be far out if I guessed that *you*, sir, are used to dancing at Almack's.'

Catherine essayed a world-weary smile. 'I would not for the world demean the music, Captain. Pray acquit me! I do not dance, because the one lady I would care to partner is denied me.'

'Oh fie! You must not allow yourself to repine!' His merry laugh made his eyes disappear in a wreath of wrinkles. 'Life has many consolations to offer, you know. Come! Allow me to show you the card-room. There are worse ways of passing an hour than in taking a trick at the cards.'

'In truth, Captain, I am not a gambling man,' Catherine said hesitantly, turning over in her pocket the few coins she had left to her. In fact, there was nothing she would have enjoyed better than a round or two of hazard or, better still, faro. She had, over the years, gambled away a fair proportion of her pocket-money with her brothers and was reasonably sure of her skill in a number of games, but she did not feel confident enough of her disguise to risk too close an encounter with a group of strange men. Captain Smart seemed simple enough, but he might have friends in the card-room who were not so easily gulled.

But Captain Smart could see her regret. 'Not even a few hands just between the two of us? Chinese whist, perhaps, with a guinea on the rubber, just for the fun of it?'

Glancing sideways in indecision, Catherine saw Lionel dancing by with a tall blonde woman, and immediately yielded to temptation. With Lionel out of the way, what could be the harm in a little card-play?

'Perhaps just a hand or two . . .'

It came as something of a shock to find Enoch still sitting at the table beyond the archway. Somehow, she had assumed that he would have returned to the ball-room with Lionel, but he had been joined by a group of young cavalry officers and showed no signs of moving. The only free table was next to his, but, feeling his eyes on her as she came in, she was careful to place herself back to back with him so that he could not get a clear look at her face.

Captain Smart shuffled the cards, his square hands moving with unexpected dexterity, and offered them to her to cut. 'What say you, Mr Mather? Shall we have a guinea on the rubber? Or two?'

Catherine had exactly five guineas to her name—minus, of course, the balance of the tradesmen's bills for the clothes on her back, but she tried not to think about that. At one guinea per rubber she could afford to lose five times, but it would not do to appear too penny-pinching. She made a careless movement with one limp hand. 'As you will, Captain.'

'Two guineas, then!' cried Captain Smart, like an old lady playing backgammon. 'And I hope, sir, that you will not bankrupt me entirely!'

He was one of those who like to chat as they play. So was Catherine, normally, but with her last five guineas at stake she would have been happier to give all her concentration to her play. What with trying to appear nonchalant, providing vague answers to the Captain's questions about herself, and deciding which card to play, she had enough to occupy her thoughts without being further distracted by Enoch's voice behind her.

She had scarcely noticed, at their previous meetings, just how attractive a voice it was, but now it seemed to wash over her, gentling her as he had gentled her mare, running down her spine like warm oil. At one point he laughed softly at some remark of his companion's, and she was so bemused that Captain Smart had to cough gently to regain her attention.

'Oh, a thousand pardons, Captain. I was wool-gathering,' she said, playing a card at random. 'What were you saying?'

Captain Smart took the trick. 'I was merely enquiring whether it were your intention to remain long in Glasgow.'

'A week or two, no more,' Catherine said, and feeling that she ought to make up for her lack of attention, added inventively, 'I am faced with the unpleasant necessity of visiting my estates in Yorkshire.'

Glancing up from her hand, she surprised a somewhat calculating look on the Captain's face, but it was replaced by a quick smile as he said, 'Then I hope that you will allow me to show you a little hospitality before you go. A dinner, perhaps?'

'You are too kind, Captain,' she smiled, only half listening to him. 'I would, of course, be delighted.'

Naturally she had no intention of having dinner with him, but it was easier to accept than to think of an excuse. If he made the invitation more specific she would have to procrastinate, but at this moment she needed to watch her play. Fortunately, Captain Smart was a better conversationalist than a card-player, but she took no chances, and presently, to her secret delight, she found herself two guineas the richer. The Captain's face was a study of disappointment as he gathered up the cards.

'For shame, Mr Mather! You have been deceiving me! No gambling man, forsooth! But I shall mind my game next time, never fear. Shall we have another guinea on it?'

'By all means.' Catherine had the bit between her

teeth now, and with seven guineas in her pocket she could afford to be a little reckless. Even if she lost the next two rubbers, she would be left with a guinea and could then call a halt without losing face. Besides, although the stakes were mere chicken-feed compared to what was changing hands at the tables around them, they were much larger than any she had played for before and she found the excitement quite intoxicating.

She was no longer distracted by the Captain's chatter or by Enoch's mellifluous voice. She could keep up a conversation with a small part of her mind while the rest of her attention watched the fall of the cards, calculating the options and dissecting her opponent's play. He was a careless player, much given to rash decisions, and he allowed himself to be constantly distracted by what was going on at the other tables. As the game proceeded, she became certain that she was much the better player, and it was no surprise to her when she again succeeded in winning the rubber and relieving the small gentleman of a further three guineas.

'Dash it all, sir!' he muttered with good-humoured dismay. 'But you have the most confounded good luck! Yet I shall have the better of you this time, I feel it in my bones!'

'In that case . . . Shall we say five guineas on the rubber?' Catherine could hardly believe that it was her own tongue that had formed the words, but her mouth was dry with excitement and she had to force herself to remain lying back indolently in her chair.

Captain Smart gave a chortle of amusement. 'If you were not a gambling man before tonight, my boy, you are certainly become one. Five guineas it is, and devil take the loser!'

The next hour passed, for Catherine, in a blur. Judith was forgotten, her own precarious situation faded into the background as the guineas in her pocket multiplied like rabbits until there were twenty-five of them boasting mutely of her skill and daring. She was immensely elated, and, as she told Captain Smart, could hardly bear to drag herself away.

'Well, then, we must do the same again, and soon,' cried the good Captain with the utmost geniality. 'You shall dine with me tomorrow night at the Black Bull and accompany me later to Duffy's. You are familiar with the gaming-house in the Gallowgate?'

Catherine's dejection at having to refuse was patently genuine. 'Alas, I ride to Edinburgh tomorrow, sir, and may remain a few days . . .'

'Then we shall say Friday? You'll be back by then, surely? Come, I won't be refused!' For all the joviality of his speech there was a certain stoniness in his eyes that gave Catherine pause. Perhaps it was a serious breach of etiquette to refuse an opponent the opportunity to recoup his losses. This was the sort of nicety which was not on the curriculum at her brothers' gambling-school, but she was quick to see that it would be very easy to make the sort of slip that might bring her under suspicion. Better to accept now and to send a note, on the evening, to say she had been taken ill or called away. It was unpleasant to be forced to hoax Captain Smart, after all his kindness, but at least she could save him the cost of the dinner.

'I am, unfortunately, engaged for dinner next Friday, but perhaps we could meet at Duffy's later in the evening?'

He seemed quite satisfied with this arrangement and followed her out of the card-room with a fatherly hand on her shoulder. Catherine would as lief have rid herself of his company, since her throat was beginning to hurt with the strain of talking in the deep voice, but he stood beside her watching the dancers and beating time with his fingers on the breast of his waistcoat.

Judith was dancing with a tall, rather handsome man, who looked to be in his late thirties and with whom she appeared to be on intimate terms. She was laughing and dimpling at him in a very natural fashion and had clearly regained much of her confidence.

'Are you acquainted with Dr Anderson?' asked the Captain, following her curious stare.

Catherine started guiltily, and, to cover up, pretended to be jealous, frowning a little and compressing her lips. 'Never saw the fellow before in my life. But I know the lady.' The more people who were aware of Mr Mather's adoration of the fair Judith, the better.

'Ah . . . I see. But, my dear fellow, you have nothing to fear from the good doctor. Dear me, no. A respectable married man, I assure you. But . . . perhaps I should mention . . .' He stopped, looking uncertain, and then dropped his voice confidentially. 'There is, I believe, another suitor.'

Catherine swung on him with a look of dismay that could not have been bettered by the real Mr Mather. 'What . . . Who?'

Captain Smart glanced about him to make sure he was not overheard. 'Gossip, Mr Mather, is anathema to me—always has been, always will be—But just this once—for I've taken a liking to you, my boy, I don't deny it, and I don't like to see you hurt . . .'

Something in Catherine's piercing gaze recalled him to the point. 'A lad called James Frazer. One of the Frazers of Transk, I believe.'

'How do you come to know this?' Catherine asked carefully. Certes! If it was common knowledge, the fat was in the fire, for it would not take long to reach Lionel's ears.

The Captain laid a finger against his considerable nose. 'Saw them with my own eyes, m' boy. Not a week since. At Mr Fowlis's exhibition of oil paintings. Oh, her mother was there, but I could see she knew nothing of what was going on . . . the glances . . . the hands touching . . . but hush! Least said . . . ! Wouldn't have mentioned it, but that I'd have you aware of the opposition. But, och, you need have nothing to fear from that quarter. There is an elder brother, I believe. Lord Marbrae will be looking for better than a second son for his only sister.'

'I fear you are mistaken, sir,' Catherine returned rather stiffly, flushing a little with irritation at hearing her brother so belittled. 'I happen to know that James Frazer will come into quite a bit of property when he comes of age in a few weeks' time. Even Lord Marbrae could have no objections to him on that score. However, it would suit my purposes if this story did not go any further. I'm sure I can rely on your discretion, Captain.'

'Oh certainly . . . certainly . . . not a word! Wouldn't have dreamed of mentioning it . . . as I said!' The Captain was plainly covered with embarrassment and could have bitten out his tongue. He waited only a few minutes longer before taking himself off with many assurances that he would be waiting at Duffy's on the following Friday.

Catherine wasted no more time in seeking out Judith and giving her a brief résumé of her successes.

'Twenty guineas clear profit! I was never so diverted in my life! And he had not the slightest suspicion that I was a female, I'll swear to it. Perhaps'—she added wickedly, for the fun of seeing her friend blench—'Perhaps I will have dinner with him at the Black Bull and win enough to buy you a handsome wedding gift! Hush! Of course I won't. I'm only hoaxing you. Shall we dance now and get it over with? For I confess I have had enough excitement for one night and I am ready for my bed.'

'Must we?' Judith whined, casting about to be sure that Lionel was at a safe distance and not in a position to snatch her back to her chair. 'It is sure to be talked about . . .'

'Hoo!' returned Catherine rudely, leading her out. 'Your credit will stand a tiny indiscretion like that. In two or three weeks from now you will be engaged to Jamie, and no one will even remember Mr Mather.'

This delightful prospect so cheered Judith that she brightened instantly, and anyone marking their progress across the ballroom would have thought them to be wholly enchanted with each other's company. At least one pair of eyes marked them very closely.

Catherine could see Lionel leaning nonchalantly against a pillar at the side of the hall, but although his slight frown followed them round the room, his attitude was not one of impending aggression. This was a little bit disappointing to Catherine, since her whole plan hinged on Lionel's taking an instant aversion to Mr Mather and regarding Judith's preference for him with the greatest possible distaste. If he were going to refuse to act as hoped, then all her planning and expenditure had been for nothing.

She communicated these depressing thoughts to Judith as the music ended and the dancers began to leave the floor, but Judith could not spot Lionel through the throng.

'As long as he stays there till you have gone,' she said with feeling, 'I don't care *how* placid he looks. I was afraid we would find him waiting for us when we got back to my seat.'

It was obvious that the danger of a confrontation worried her more than the failure of their plan. She was painfully impatient to be rid of Catherine, and hurried off the floor with many a backward glance towards the pillar that her friend had indicated. 'I can't see him. Has he gone?'

Catherine shook her head, wondering if there was anything wrong with her friend's eyes. 'No, he's still there. Can't you see . . .'

'Oh, my God!' said Judith suddenly, staring straight ahead with an expression that seemed to indicate that she was looking into the mouth of hell. 'It's *Lionel*!'

Catherine spun round disbelievingly, certain that he could not have moved so fast, but could see no one but Enoch standing at the edge of the floor.

'Where?' Then she realised that they were both staring at the same person, and—in a flash—that she had made a terrible mistake. It was the tall, lanky man who was Enoch. This golden Apollo was Judith's brother, Lionel!

The magnitude of the shock, she was convinced, would have proved fatal to anyone of a less robust constitution. As it was, the force of it struck her like a blow beneath the ribs and seemed to lift her feet clean off the floor. For a second everything went black, yet when vision returned, her legs were still carrying her forward, straight to where Lionel waited for them, a nasty smile playing about his lips.

'Oh, my God!' she said, unconsciously echoing her partner, who seemed to be withering and shrinking before her eyes like a burst balloon.

There was absolutely nothing they could do but try to brazen it out. If Mr Mather were to turn and run at this stage he would lose all credibility, and, besides, Lionel could catch up with him in a few strides. Catherine's spine stiffened. Very well, then. She had accepted all along that a face-to-face encounter with Judith's brother might not be avoidable, and she had prepared for that contingency. If, now, it was more than ever important that she should not be unmasked—well, then, she would just have to try that much harder!

Tightening her grip on Judith's elbow, she gave it a tiny shake and muttered, 'If you let me down, my girl, you'll feel the weight of my walking-stick!'

This unequivocal threat steadied Judith faster than any sympathetic encouragement could have done. She had just time to gasp angrily when Lionel loomed over them, as inescapable as the wrath of God.

'Oh, L-Lionel!' Judith croaked, her smile ruined by a nervous tic. 'Th-this is Mr Mather, of whom you have heard me speak . . . Mum-Mr Mather . . . This is my brother, Lord Marbrae.'

Catherine put everything she had learned into her bow. As she told Jessie later, it was a bow the like of which had never been seen in Scotland before and which would doubtless be spoken of with awe for weeks to come. Its effect on Lionel was all she could have wished.

He took no pains to disguise his distaste as he replied, with a curt nod, 'Glad to have the honour of making your acquaintance at last, Mr Mather. I am told that you have been one of my sister's most frequent callers during my absence in the colonies.'

The melodic, melted-chocolate voice was now as soothing as the sound of a saw cutting through metal, and his eyes were better avoided.

'Not during your *entire* absence, my dear sir!' she said gaily, and discovered to her delight that her 'Mr Mather' voice—though painful to sustain—was now convincingly husky. She simpered disgracefully at Judith, who was still looking terminally ill. 'Unfortunately I became acquainted with your charming sister only a few weeks ago, when she was in Inverness. I could scarce believe my luck—to find such a rose among the heather!'

She was aware that the drone of conversation about them had ceased, and that the people in the immediate vicinity had moved imperceptibly nearer. This was something of a comfort, since she could be confident that Lionel would not cause a scene in public.

'I see.' He spoke quietly and with perfect composure, but somehow he managed to make every polite word sound like an insult. 'And are we to have the pleasure of your company, here in Glasgow, for long?'

'That depends,' said Catherine vaguely, burying her nose in her posy and sniffing rapturously. 'To be honest, my dear sir, I had expected to find this city somewhat lacking in enticements, after London, but I am pleasantly surprised.' Another side-glance to the blushing Judith indicated the chief attraction. 'Social life is, of course, virtually non-existent and, as you doubtless are aware, it is quite impossible to buy an article of clothing that would not be laughed to scorn in any civilised community. Why, only last week I sent my man out to buy me some stockings. "Only the best", I told him. "Don't bring me those ghastly bags that pass for hose among the gentry here!" But, great heavens!' She paused to sniff her nosegay, revelling in the attentive hush which awaited her next remark. 'The only hosiery available in Glasgow would have shamed a cowman. That, as I told you, my dear Jud—er . . . Miss Cameron—was the urgent business which called me to Edinburgh. Though, I have to admit, I was equally unlucky there, which is why I come before you tonight dressed like the veriest yokel . . .'

Lionel's face was a study. He appeared quite unaware of the interest their conversation was arousing, but was staring at the ridiculous, mincing creature before him as though it were something that could permanently damage his eyes. 'You went all the way to Edinburgh to buy hose?'

'Why, yes! I assure you, nothing of lesser importance could have tempted me to desert your sister's side at this present. Still, I cannot altogether regret the necessity, since my visit led to the discovery of a wonderful apothecary's shop in the Luckenbooths. I was able to procure some Naples Dew—than which nothing is more invigorating to the complexion, as I am sure you are aware, my lord.'

For a second she thought she had gone too far. A distinctly dangerous light flared momentarily behind his eyes and his hands folded themselves into fists. But almost immediately he had himself in check and was saying in a low-pitched snarl, 'No, Mr Mather, I am not aware. You will forgive me, I hope, if I curtail this most interesting discussion for the present. I have much to say to you, and would appreciate being permitted to call upon you in the near future. Would tomorrow be convenient?'

'I would be most honoured,' Catherine exclaimed, with a wide gesture of despondency, 'but I am called away on business tomorrow—perhaps for a few days. May I venture to suggest that I call upon you at Monkwood upon my return, since I, too, have a matter to discuss which I am most anxious to see settled.'

A burning glance in Judith's direction made it quite clear what this matter was likely to be, and to her utter joy, she saw that he was suddenly stricken with alarm. For some moments he remained quite still, his eyes widening, staring at her in disbelief, then he stepped back with a faint bow and frowned, as he said, 'The sooner the better, I think, Mr Mather, don't you? And now, if you will excuse us, I think my sister is tired and should be thinking about going home. Are you ready, Judith? Mr Mather, your most obedient.'

Catherine offered him another magnificent bow and watched his departure with a strong sensation of triumph. In all her rosy imaginings she could not have dreamed of such complete success, for without a doubt he had been quite staggered when she had hinted that a proposal was in the offing. It might have passed unre-marked by a casual observer, but Catherine had been watching him closely and had seen the quick jerk of his head and the momentary slackening of the muscles about his mouth. There would be questions asked in Monkwood House, this night, and it was to be hoped that Judith would play her part adequately. Lionel was no fool. If he were ever to discover the truth . . .

Catherine pushed the corrosive thought to the back of her mind and walked downstairs to summon a chair.

Altogether, she thought, jingling the guineas in her pocket, it had turned out a more entertaining evening than she had enjoyed for quite a while.

CHAPTER
SIX

THAT NIGHT was arguably the worst that Catherine had ever experienced. She arrived home utterly exhausted and fell into bed in the confident expectation of instant oblivion, but although her body demanded rest, her racing brain would not relinquish its hold on reality.

Too much had happened in the last few hours. Her mind felt overstuffed with half-digested impressions, and throughout the hours of darkness she tossed and turned, reliving every conversation, reading new inferences into every remembered response.

From being wildly exultant at the favourable results of her impersonation, she became filled with the most horrid doubts. Why had Captain Smart smiled in *just* such a way when he said goodbye? That surprised look of Lionel's . . . could it have been caused by the sudden realisation that he was speaking to Catherine Frazer?

She sat bolt upright, screaming silently in the darkness, while every nerve in her body seemed to leap in anguished repudiation of the idea. Oh certes! If he had recognised her beneath the clownish powder and paint, what an idiotic, posturing fool she must have appeared to him! Finding that Jessie was snoring like a beached whale, she threw her candlestick at her, but missed.

When she was fully awake, she knew that these were only nightmares, but as soon as she began to slip back into an uneasy doze the torture began again, sometimes in short painful twinges, sometimes in prolonged bouts of mental suffering.

Lionel figured prominently in these dreams, stalking vengefully after her through dark, labyrinthine passages, dressed in his shirt and breeches and carrying a horsewhip. Sometimes his face loomed over her, so close that she could see the shadows that his lashes cast across his eyes and watch the slow unfolding of his smile light up his face like a golden dawn. But when she spoke his name, reaching out to touch him, the beautiful mask crumbled away to show, beneath, the grotesquely painted face of Mr Mather, laughing obscenely.

With a cry, she was awake again, her heart thudding, her eyes searching the shadows for some reassuring landmark. Finally she gave herself up to insomnia, and propping up her pillows, sat up against them and promptly fell into a deep and dreamless sleep from which Jessie had trouble rousing her in time for her meeting with Judith.

She sat yawning on the end of the bed and allowed herself to be insinuated into Mr Mather's riding-clothes by slow degrees. Her whole body felt indescribably fragile, and there was a large lump of panic lodged under her ribs. This was ten times more frightening than setting forth for the Assembly had been the evening before. Now she knew that it was not that gangling giant, Enoch, who was to be her audience, but Lionel, to whom (it was no longer possible to ignore the fact) she had already lost her heart.

This circumstance made an enormous difference to her enjoyment of the adventure. In the beginning, she had accepted the fact that there would be a certain amount of unpleasantness if she were found out. There would be talk. Her parents would be furious. Perhaps a certain type of very exemplary young man would conclude that she was too harum-scarum to make a dutiful wife. All this had seemed an acceptable risk. She was used to talk, and however angry her parents might be, she knew they adored her and always would. And as for making a dutiful wife, nothing could have been further from her ambitions. In short, there was just enough hazard to lend a spice of excitement to the game.

But with the advent of Lionel, all that had changed. Certainly it was thrilling to play for high stakes, as she had discovered in Captain Smart's company the evening before, but Lionel's good opinion of her was too much to risk. Not for her own sport, not for Jamie's future happiness, not for anything in the world would she gamble away her chance of winning his love.

This once, she decided, she would take one tiny step off the path of righteousness, but only if she could be absolutely sure that there was no danger of Lionel approaching within half a mile of her. Afterwards she would burn every trace of Mr Mather's existence and live thenceforth a life of such virtue and moral rectitude that she would be held up as a model to little girls for generations to come. She would not be breaking any promises to Judith by this defection, since she had hoped from the beginning that Mr Mather would not need to make more than two appearances. Now that his existence was established, Judith, if properly coached, could continue to use him as a threat, but he would never— positively never—appear in the flesh again.

She was determined that nothing could possibly go wrong with Mr Mather's farewell performance. His powder and paint were applied just as cunningly as on the night before, and on her way to the meeting-place, she took pains to reconnoitre the escape route that Judith had suggested, to make sure that the way was clear.

Judith was already there waiting for her when she

emerged from the wood. She was dressed in a most enviable blue broadcloth riding-habit, and her face was so wan and drawn that it seemed to Catherine to be a reflection of her own.

'You're late,' she said tensely, tearing her eyes away from the stretch of road that skirted the foot of the hill. 'I have been on tenterhooks in case Lionel should pass before you got here. He's due any minute.'

'Well, then, you had better tell me what happened last night after you left the Assembly,' Catherine returned, taking up a position where she could not fail to be noticed by anyone passing along the road. 'Did Lionel forbid you to see Mr Mather again?'

'I . . . Yes, I think he did . . . At least, I'm not perfectly sure . . .'

'What are you talking about, Judith? You must know whether he forbade you to go on seeing Mr Mather or not.'

'Well, I was crying, you see, and . . . and he said so many things . . .'

'You had better start at the beginning,' Catherine told her with a crispness that was due partly to Judith's vacillations and partly to the state of her own nerves. 'What did he say when you got into the coach?'

Judith thought carefully, still watching the road. 'I think . . . yes . . . He asked me where I had made the acquaintance of Mr Mather, and I knew, Catherine, I just *knew* that he was going to be very angry with me because he goes quite white round the mouth, you know, when he is about to explode, but I said what you told me to say—that Mr Mather had been introduced to me by a close friend of Aunt Maude, whose name I had forgotten, and, oh dear, I hope he does not write to Aunt Maude to confirm this, because, if he does . . .'

'Yes, yes, I know. What else did he say?'

'Well . . . then he said what did I know of his family and where was he from, and I said oh London, and I thought he was quite well connected, but I don't think I managed that part very well because of my voice being all trembly and when he said, "You don't expect me to believe that you have formed an attachment for him, do you?" I started to cry, and he told me . . . he told me . . .'

'To stop piping your eye?'

'No . . . No, he was quite nice about it, but . . . but *firm*, you know, and said, "Look, Judith, I don't know what you are up to, but it is to stop, do you hear me? I don't want to clap eyes on that fellow ever again." So I did what you said: I thought to myself, this is Jamie we are talking about! And I shouted at him—really shouted, Catherine—that I loved Mr Mather and was going to marry him, and nothing he could say or do would stop me!'

'Oh bravo, Judith!' Catherine clapped her hands together as well as she was able while keeping a grip on her reins. 'I wish Jamie might have seen you, love! He would have been so proud of you. So what did Lionel do then? Was he worried, think you?'

Some of the triumphant flush ebbed from Judith's cheeks. 'I'm not sure . . . not the way we had hoped, I don't think . . . He put his arm around me and wiped my eyes and said, "Very well, then. We will talk about this tomorrow when you are not so tired", and then he said something about knowing since he came home from Jamaica that something was worrying me and it never did any good to bottle things up, and you know, Catherine, I felt so miserable at having to lie to him and make him worried, for really he is not an ogre, but . . . Oh, if only Jamie had not acted so unforgivably to him . . .'

'Yes, yes,' Catherine said soothingly. 'I feel rather guilty about it, too; but remember, it may not take more than a few days to change his mind about Jamie. We must just make very sure that he is made to think an elopement is imminent. When he sees us together this morning he will know that you are not falling in with his wishes, so when you have your interview with him later today try to hint gently that you would not hesitate to run away with Mr Mather if driven to it.'

'Yes . . .' Judith nibbled thoughtfully at her lip. 'And how should I do that, Catherine?'

'Well, you must simply think what you would do if you were really thinking about eloping, and then do it,' returned Catherine a little impatiently. It was really quite fatiguing to have to do all the thinking for both of them. 'You could perhaps pack a bag and leave it where Lionel would be sure to find it. Or, I dare say, if you planned to elope, you might wish to have a little extra money by you, so you could ask Lionel for an advance on your allowance. But remember to be vague if he asks you what you want it for.'

Judith drew a deep sigh and toyed moodily with the thong of her riding-crop. 'I am not precisely *afraid* of Lionel, for he is not a *brute*, you know; but when he is determined to have his own way there is positively no gainsaying him, and I am just a little bit worried about what he might do if he really believed that I might elope—stop taking me to Assemblies, for instance, or prevent me from riding out every morning, which is my only chance of meeting Jamie—and Lady Crawford's masked ball is only a few days away, and I would be *so* disappointed if he said . . .'

'When is this ball?' Catherine inserted with sudden interest. Jamie had mentioned it before, she now remembered, but at the time there had seemed little likelihood of Jamie allowing her to remain in Glasgow for more than a few days. 'I think I should very much like to attend. Will Lionel squire you?'

'Yes, if he does not forbid me to go. But how lovely if you could secure an invitation, Catherine. I should like it above anything. But, of course, Jamie is invited and I'm sure Lady Crawford would be only too delighted to let him bring you with him. It's on Thursday and I do think it is very sweet of Lionel to take me for he has to leave for Greenock the next morning and will not be back till Monday . . .'

Catherine let her rattle on, but her mind was elsewhere. How to prevail upon Jamie to procure an invitation for her? That he would refuse point blank when approached on the matter went without saying, since he was a strong believer in the maxim that where Catherine went, Trouble followed at her heels like a dog. He would doubtless be planning to make the most of the opportunity to be with Judith and would not take too kindly to being saddled with his sister. But then, with Lionel at the ball, *she* would not wish to be saddled with Jamie.

'Judith,' she said into a microscopic gap in her friend's monologue. 'I'd rather you didn't mention to Jamie that I'm intending to go to the ball. Not just yet, anyway. I'll have to pick the right moment to approach him about it.'

Judith was plainly at a loss to understand this reticence, but before she could formulate a question, Lionel appeared round a bend in the road below them. He was mounted on a strong-looking bay hunter with a fine head, and for a moment Catherine was held motionless with the sheer luxury of looking at him. Then he caught sight of the two figures on the crest, and she saw him check his pace in quick reaction.

Catherine's hands tightened on the reins. 'Here we go,' she said curtly. 'You ride straight for Monkwood,

Judith. I will send Robert with a note for you tomorrow; do you try to have one ready to give him so that I may know how things are proceeding.'

Without wasting another second, she drove her heels against her horse's flanks with such force that it reached the security of the wood with two bounds. In another second she was thundering down the mossy path with brambles snatching at her breeches and the diminishing sound of Judith's flight well behind her. Soon there was silence but for the din of her own progress, but she did not slacken pace till she was quite certain that she was not pursued. Even then, she was so cautious that she halted for several seconds to strain her ears for sounds of a chase, and was only truly reassured when she saw, close ahead, the path win clear of the trees and slope gently down towards the village of Gorbals.

Pressing forward those last few yards, she felt as though her emergence into the sunshine was somehow symbolic of the relief she would feel in throwing off the dark cloud of guilt that had oppressed her since the night before. Tonight, as soon as it was dark, she would have Jessie take everything belonging to Mr Mather down to the fire at the livery stable and reduce it to ashes. Only then would she begin to feel safe.

This prospect filled her with such peace that she was smiling dreamily as she rode out of the wood and found Lionel waiting for her at the bridge. Her brain recoiled with shock, refusing to believe that it was indeed he and not some nightmare left over from the night before. He was leaning against the parapet, watching his horse crop the grass, and he looked up as she appeared, not angrily, but as one who would say, 'What took you so long?'

A hot surge of anger took Catherine by surprise, flooding her cheeks with colour. That Judith! Surely she must have known—as her brother had evidently known—that there was a side-path by which he could cut her off!

She did not rein in—she was too stupefied to make a decision of such magnitude—but her horse walked right up to him and stopped a pace away, apparently obeying some unspoken transmission of his will, and she sat there, quite helpless, blinking at him witlessly.

'Well, now, if it isn't Mr Mather,' he said finally, and oh! but the honey was back in his voice. Only she knew now that the whipcrack was coming, and she shivered in anticipation. 'Well met, sir. You and I have a matter to settle.'

His face was completely void of expression and his lash-shadowed eyes unreadable, but at least she could tell from his tone of voice that he had no suspicion that he was addressing a woman, and this steadied her a little. All was not lost, she told herself gamely, as long as she did not go to pieces now.

Dragging in a great gulp of air, she said, rather faintly but with a most elegant gesture, 'My Lord Marbrae! A happy chance, indeed! But I regret I am unable to tarry at this present, as I am bound for Greenock—the business I spoke of last night—and I am already behind time.'

'What is it now?' A corner of his upper lip curled nastily in either a smile or a snarl, she could not be sure. 'Another pair of stockings? A cravat, perhaps?'

'I shall hope to call upon you soon, sir.' She gathered up her reins, ignoring his sarcasm. 'I am most eager to speak to you on a matter of some importance.'

His smile widened without gaining anything in sweetness. 'Am I to understand that you wish leave to pay your addresses to my sister?'

Catherine bowed in assent, but hinted with a raised

brow that this was hardly the place to discuss such a delicate matter. Lionel, however, gave a rude bark of laughter.

'You amaze me, Mr Mather. That you could imagine for one moment that I might give my consent! But, no matter. Since your time is short, I will not detain you by listing the reasons for my refusal. Let me just make it clear to you that your suit is unwelcome, and that my sister will not be at home to you should you call on her. Nor, I might add, will she be allowed to ride out unchaperoned, as she did this morning.'

'I am devastated, sir,' Catherine returned, with a break in her voice which was due entirely to the strain of speaking gruffly, but which sounded convincingly heart-broken. 'Your sister and I have formed a close—and I think, lasting—attachment to each other, and I cannot but think you hasty in rejecting my offer out of hand. Pray consider your sister's reaction to this, Lord Marbrae.'

'I am aware of my sister's reaction,' he said curtly, 'as she must, all along, have been aware of mine. Judith knows me too well to entertain any hope that I would give her in marriage to a man whose mentality and way of life I heartily despise. Where there is no hope, there can be no disappointment.'

Catherine swallowed painfully, trying to steel her courage to the point where she could hint at an elopement. It had sounded easy enough when she had told Judith to do it, but now, with those level eyes looking straight into her mind, she choked on the words. Even Jamie at his abusive worst had never unnerved her like this coldly implacable adversary, and she had to admit to herself that her blood ran cold at the thought of provoking him further. Yet the whole plan hinged on the necessity of making him worry, and if *she* could not bring herself to go through with it, there was little likelihood of Judith being able to summon up the mettle.

Avoiding his eyes by looking blindly away into the distance, she said desperately, 'Yet your decision is a harsh one, my lord. To separate your sister, for the rest of her life, from the object of her affection! Her whole happiness is at stake—and my own! Pray reconsider, sir, lest our thwarted passion should force us to . . .'

He straightened suddenly from his relaxed position, and stepped away from the parapet with a fluid movement which at another time would have gladdened her heart, but which now, she felt, shortened her life-span by several years.

'Force you to . . . what?' he enquired softly, but not in a million years could she have brought herself to go on. He gave her plenty of opportunity, regarding her with cynical patience, but when it became clear that no response was forthcoming, he turned and reached for his horse's trailing reins. Springing up into the saddle, he rode forward till they were almost knee to knee.

'Mr Mather,' he said with slow emphasis. 'I will now give you a piece of advice which you would do well to follow. Do not let me clap eyes on you ever again. Keep well away from Monkwood, and make no move to contact my sister. Believe me, you are playing a dangerous game, and if you do not desist I shall be forced to apply pressure. Is that clear?'

Catherine was speechless, but her sick expression seemed to satisfy him as to the effectiveness of his ultimatum, because he said no more, and, with a brusque nod, rode away at a brisk trot along the river bank.

If she had not already scheduled Mr Mather's cremation for that very night, she thought, he would have been doomed anyway after Lionel's warning, for she could never again have summoned up the courage to don the Macaroni clothes. No wonder Judith was so adamant that Jamie should not approach her brother too hastily. Any suitor sent packing by Lionel would be a brave man to defy him, and it now seemed likely that Jamie, having crossed him once before, was understandably cautious about repeating the experience.

She was seriously depressed as she crossed the bridge and headed back to the Saracen's Head. Her original plan had not taken into account the fact that Lionel would prove to be such a strong and obdurate opponent. Had Judith been a little more discerning, she might have foreseen that her brother would not be easy to bully, but now there was nothing that could be done except pray that Judith's love for Jamie would give her enough strength to stand up to him.

Her first act on returning to her room at the inn was to give Jessie Mr Mather's entire wardrobe—his wig, his umbrella, even his walking-stick—with instructions for their disposal. 'Make sure that not one button escapes, Jessie. And stay until everything is quite consumed. I don't want someone happening by and retrieving something that might later be traced to me.'

'You're awful nervous suddenly,' Jessie remarked, hiding everything temporarily beneath the bed. 'You haven't been found out, have you?'

'Not yet, but I don't intend to take any more chances. I'm not taking the risk of . . . anyone . . . discovering that *I* was Mr Mather.'

'Meaning Lord Marbrae, I suppose?'

Catherine stared at her, her cheeks burning with a sudden blush. 'What makes you say that?'

'Well, just that your face gets like a well-skelped bum every time his name's mentioned, and I couldn't shut an eye last night for you muttering "Lionel . . . Lionel" all the time.'

'*Jessie!*' Catherine slammed her hairbrush down on the table with exasperation. 'Will you mind your tongue, girl? Try to remember that you are supposed to be a lady's maid, not a tavern wench. I don't know what my friends would say if they heard you!'

'They never said anything up till now,' she returned sullenly. 'I don't know why, all of a sudden . . .'

Perhaps fortunately, she was interrupted at that point by the arrival of Jamie, ostensibly to inquire after his sister's health.

'I'm well,' Catherine told him in amazement. 'Why shouldn't I be?'

'Well, when I popped in last night, Jessie told me you had taken to your bed with a sick headache.'

'Oh, *that*!' said Catherine hastily, remembering the excuse she had told Jessie to make in just such a contingency. 'That was nothing. It was gone when I woke up this morning.'

He seemed scarcely to be listening to her reply, but dithered over to the fireplace in a rather abstracted manner, which made her say, 'Are you staying for a while? Shall I send Jessie for some tea?'

'What? Oh, tea . . . Yes, if you like.'

A flutter of uneasiness ran down Catherine's spine. There was something bothering him. God grant it was nothing to do with Mr Mather: she had suffered enough guilty conscience for one day.

He kept her in suspense, chatting about nothing, until after Jessie had brought the tea and gone away again. Then, as Catherine handed him his cup, he said in a tone of half-hearted interest, 'By the way, how's your allowance lasting out this quarter?'

Catherine's hand gave a leap so that the tea slopped in

the saucer, and she had to forbid her eyes to slide to the box under the bed, as she said brightly, 'Why do you ask? Are you about to offer me a subsidy?'

He took a large gulp of tea and winced as it scalded his tongue. 'Matter of fact, Kate, I was about to ask if *you* could subsidise *me*.'

She looked at him in astonishment. 'But, Jamie! What have you done with all your own allowance? You told me Papa had slipped you a little extra in case of emergencies before he left for Paris . . . How much did you gamble away at Duffy's gaming-tables?'

'What does it matter?' he snapped, glaring at her with hot eyes. 'I don't ask you what you do with your money! It's none of your business what I do with mine!'

'Oh, that's fine, then!' Catherine returned with spirit. 'Don't ask me what I've done with my money when I tell you I've none left to lend!'

'*None?*' There was no mistaking the shocked disappointment in his face. 'It can't all be gone already!'

She looked at him through her lashes. 'How much do you need?'

'How much have you got?'

'Tell me the truth, Jamie. How much? Ten pounds? Fifty?'

He dropped his eyes to the fire. 'More than that. A lot more. About a hundred.'

'Certes! It's not like you to drop so much at the tables, Jamie. You would have done better to have stayed at Ayr awhile with Grandmama and me.'

'It's nothing in comparison to what most gamblers win and lose in an evening,' he said stubbornly. 'You don't feel you could scrape it together for me? It *is* rather important, Kate.'

Catherine gave a short laugh and leaned over to up-end the jar where she kept her loose change. 'There is my total capital—twenty-five guineas. And out of that, I must pay my reckoning here at the inn, my livery charges and . . . and some tradesmen's bills which will be due before I get my next allowance.' Her heart sank at the thought of admitting her bankruptcy to the tailor, cobbler, wig-maker and sundry lesser creditors, but Jamie seemed to be even more downhearted at her disclosures than she was herself.

He got up and began to pace up and down, cracking his knuckles with a sound like distant gunfire till Catherine could stand it no longer.

'Jamie,' she said, catching at his sleeve as he strode past. 'You're not telling me everything. You're in real trouble, aren't you? Who is it that's dunning you for this money? Won't he wait?'

She pulled him back down into his chair, and was mildly shocked when he suddenly dropped his head into his hands and said in a muffled voice,

'Some reptile has discovered that I've been seeing Judith behind her brother's back and knows what will happen if Marbrae gets wind of it. A letter was slipped under my door early this morning by someone who sets the price of his silence at two hundred and fifty pounds.'

'Two hundred and fifty! . . . But you said . . .'

'In a normal quarter I could have managed to pay it without borrowing, but these last few weeks, what with buying little things for Judith, and . . . yes, Duffy's . . . and one thing and another, I seem to have got through it faster than usual. I've got about a hundred left . . . maybe a hundred and ten when I've gone through all my pockets. Then I could pawn my pistols and one or two other things. Say a hundred and fifty. Even throwing in your twenty-five pounds, that leaves seventy-five to find.'

'Seventy-five pounds isn't a lot,' Catherine said encouragingly, cudgelling her brains for an idea.

'It is, when you've already scraped the bottom of the barrel!'

'Well, send him the hundred and seventy-five pounds and a note to say that the rest will follow at your earliest.'

Jamie gave a snort of derision. 'Extortioners don't give credit!' he said shortly, and pulled a crumpled sheet of notepaper from his pocket. Reading from it, he said, 'I am instructed to put two hundred pounds behind a loose brick which I will find in the wall of the apothecary's shop in the Saltmarket—the third brick below the brass plaque—not later than six p.m. on Saturday. And if it is one penny short, I can say goodbye to Judith.'

Groaning aloud, he jumped to his feet again and resumed his pacing. 'You see the mess I'm in because I didn't follow the dictates of my own conscience and apprise Marbrae of my intentions right at the beginning! How can I approach him now, with this hanging over me? How can I offer for Judith with this . . . this *leech* bleeding me—yes! and *continuing* to bleed me, whether Marbrae permits our betrothal or not—for he must know that I would have to keep paying to prevent Marbrae from finding out what a scoundrel I have been!'

'Jamie, dear, I think you are taking too black a view of things.' Catherine said strongly. 'Certainly, it was not wise of you to meet Judith clandestinely, for—I must tell you—there may be several people in Glasgow who are aware of your friendship. Indeed I have heard gossip myself—but from a very kind person who is certainly not your extortioner—and I am certain that if Lionel were not so recently returned from abroad he would already have learned the truth. But, in any case,' she added quickly as Jamie groaned again, 'I *know* that when he

comes to know you properly he will realise that you are
the most honourable of men, and that it was only out of
love for his sister that you allowed yourself to be persuaded to act as you did.'

Jamie folded his arms on the mantelpiece and rested
his forehead against them, staring down into the flames.
'If only Father were here. I'm sure he could speak to
Marbrae.'

'The important thing,' Catherine said, rummaging
through her jewel-box, 'is to play for time. We cannot
allow this leech to apprise Lionel of the matter, so we
must find a way to pay him. Perhaps Judith might have
some ready cash?'

'*No!*' cried Jamie in a strangled voice, rearing up in
horror. 'Judith is to know nothing of this, Kate! I will not
have her worried, do you hear? Besides, I will not be
seeing her again till all this is straightened out. I sent her
a note this morning to tell her that I felt I must discon-
tinue our meetings till I had regularised everything with
Marbrae.'

Catherine looked at him with strong fellow-feeling.
She knew how much it cost her to deny herself the sight
of Lionel for a few days; how much harder it must be for
Jamie, who knew his love reciprocated. 'Well, then, we
must just see what we can scrape together. I think you
may be surprised. Here are my pearl earrings, for instance. I'm sure I've no idea what they may be worth,
but surely you could get ten pounds for them, at least?
And there's my gold locket, and these shoe-buckles—
which were probably expensive, for Papa bought them
for me in London. See how it mounts up? There must be
at least twenty-five-pounds-worth there.'

But, having exhausted the possibilities of her jewel-
box, it was difficult to know where next to turn. Neither
of them had any close friends in Glasgow, other than

Judith. The only acquaintance in the neighbourhood whom Catherine could bring to mind was Captain Smart, and it would be out of the question to apply to *him* for a loan on the basis of such an brief association. He would be quite shocked if she were to try to borrow from him, she thought; yet, oddly enough, he would probably lose twice as much to her at cards without giving the matter a further thought.

It was only later that she realised how strenuously her mind avoided acknowledging the obvious solution. Every time her thoughts edged round to Duffy's gaming-saloon she shied nervously away, while the miserable silence lengthened and Jamie cracked his knuckles in desperation.

Finally she straightened her shoulders and tried to swallow the lump in her throat. It was unthinkable that she should allow Jamie to suffer the consequences of his foolish behaviour, especially when it was behaviour that she herself had urged on him. If Judith had not mentioned that Lionel was planning to be away over the weekend, her courage would certainly have failed her, but the thought gave her a surge of bravado.

'Jamie, I've thought of something,' she said, and the look of tremulous hope he turned on her extinguished her qualms instantly. 'I can't tell you what it is, just at the moment, and it will take a day or two, but I am quite sure I'll have the money before six on Saturday. So you can put your mind at rest.'

The glare he sent her was anything but grateful. 'I don't like the sound of that at all,' he said bitterly. 'Now, Kate, you listen to me . . .'

Catherine took instant umbrage. 'You thankless wretch!' she gasped, leaping up. 'You ingrate, Jamie Frazer! I do everything I can for you! I worry about you! I give you my jewellery! I sacrifice myself for you! But *you*—you don't like the sound of it! Well I don't like the sound of *you*—you . . .'

Before her hand could close on a projectile he threw his arms about her in a bear-hug—a method of defence which he had devised over the years and which had frequently proved effective. With her arms pinned to her sides she was unable to throw things, and with her ribs compressed she was too short of breath to shout.

'All right! All right!' he said urgently in her ear. 'You are the best of sisters, but you *do* go off half-cocked at times.'

'I do *not*!'

'All right, you don't,' he agreed equably, dodging her kick. 'But I don't want you getting into trouble on my account. I *am* supposed to be keeping you out of trouble at present, remember? By rights, you should be in Ayr.'

'There's no question of my getting into trouble!' snapped Catherine angrily. 'Let me go! You don't deserve that I should put myself out for you one bit!'

'If there were no question of your getting into trouble, you would not be so secretive about where the money is coming from,' Jamie stated with an insight born of long familiarity. He let her go, but retained a firm grip of her shoulders so that he could look her in the eye. 'I think you had better forget all about it, don't you?'

She frowned at him, biting her lip with vexation. Really, did he think her a child or a simpleton that she needed him to hold her hand all the time? If she could only tell him how much she had accomplished already on his behalf—the situations she had come through unscathed—she would make him feel very small! If she were to tell him about her appointment with Captain Smart, however, he would very likely lock her in her room—but that did not mean that there was the slightest risk in keeping it. She had already established her identity with Captain Sharp, and unless he had been taking lessons in the meantime, there would be no difficulty in relieving him of another fifty pounds. The morality of doing so was another matter. Captain Sharp had been the only one among the Glasgow gentry who had shown the least sign of Christian charity to a lonely stranger in their midst, and it seemed all the more dastardly deliberately to take advantage of his weakness. Nevertheless, it had to be. Possibly she could return the money to him at a later date—anonymously, of course.

Drawing a deep breath, she said soberly, 'You're quite right, of course. I *do* go off half-cocked sometimes—or rather, I *have* done in the past. I dare say I caused a lot of worry and irritation too, and I know I often got other people into trouble, but—people grow up, you know, Jamie. I don't intend to be a scapegrace all my life. You can rest assured that I have no intention of doing anything that will get me—or anyone else—into trouble. You'll have your money by Saturday, but remember, it will have to be repaid off your next allowance.'

This last phrase seemed to reassure Jamie more than anything else she had said. 'Very well,' he said finally. 'I don't know why I believe you, but I do. I think you *are* growing up at last. And you're not a bad soul, Kate, even if you do drive me mad at times. Tell you what . . . Seeing that I won't be meeting Judith tomorrow, how would you like it if I hired one of those neat little rigs they have down in the stables and took you for a drive?'

Catherine accepted with alacrity, not only because opportunities like this did not arise too often, but because she hoped the excursion would divert her mind from too close a contemplation of the imprudence to which she had, once again, committed herself.

CHAPTER
SEVEN

CATHERINE HAD already seen the southern environs of the city, so Jamie decided to show her the western approaches and headed downstream along the wooded banks of the Clyde.

The day was crisp and sunny, and as they bowled along in their hired chaise, Catherine was disposed to be more optimistic than she had been the day before. It was mostly lack of sleep, she decided, that had brought on her fit of the megrims. Today, with the blue sky sparkling and the light breeze fluttering the ribbons of her new straw hat, her confidence had returned in full.

Away from the oppressiveness of Lionel's forceful personality, it was easy to tell herself that she had been childish to allow him to dominate her so shamefully. If she had not been so tired and nervy at the time she would have made a more determined showing, and no doubt Judith, who knew him better, could be safely left to apply the final turn of the screw and bring him to his knees.

Soon all her plans would have succeeded: Lionel would be desperate to see Judith married off to the first reasonable suitor, Jamie would have the money with which to silence his extortioner, and she herself would have cozened Jamie into taking her to the masked ball, where she would be sure to see Lionel again.

To be sure, there was still the trifling matter of her

assignation with Captain Smart to be disposed of, but she was determined not to spoil her day out by worrying about that. There would, after all, be no need for her to arrive at Duffy's much before ten o'clock in the evening, and if she were not back at the Saracen's Head with her ill-gotten gains before midnight, she would be very surprised. There was a little *scrap* of risk to the undertaking, certainly, but so insignificant a particle that it was hardly worth thinking about.

Meanwhile the scenery was delightful, and the little villages they passed through were as neat as book illustrations. Away in the distance she could see the beginning of the Highlands, unfamiliar outlines of ridges and peaks that she knew only from a different angle. The river traffic, too, filled her with interest, for there were cargoes arriving from ports all over the Continent and the American colonies: Antigua, Grenada, Kingston in Jamaica, Leghorn in Italy, Bergen in Norway . . . the list was endless.

The closer they came to Port Glasgow, the busier the river became. The very air was redolent with the scents of cordage and pitch and salt-soaked canvas, and the streets were astir with all manner of foreign seafarers and faces of every shade of brown.

Catherine was vastly entertained, and Jamie, rather pleased with himself at having chosen this route, was moved to buy her a pretty carved and decorated shell from a brown-faced sailor. It cost only a few pennies, but it was, strictly speaking, an extravagance, considering their temporarily straitened circumstances. However, it pleased them both inordinately, and Jamie was moved to give further evidence of his good nature by enlivening the drive home with stirring tales of the great ships that sailed from the lower Clyde.

'One day they will be able to sail right into the heart of

the city,' he told her, plainly glad of an attentive audience. 'There are plans to keep deepening the river so that one day there may be as much as fourteen feet depth at low water at the Broomielaw. Meanwhile, here at Dumbuck, one may walk across at low tide, and all the cargoes for the city have to be unloaded on to flat-bottomed craft for the last few miles.'

'Judith's brother is a keen sailor,' Catherine remarked, not because it had anything to do with the present subject of conversation but because she was compelled, by some inner need, to mention Lionel's name on any flimsy pretext that presented itself. She wanted to say, 'Talk to me about Lionel. It doesn't matter what you say, just let's talk about him', but, balked of this direct approach by Jamie's unenlightened state, she found herself directing the conversation into Lionel-related subjects every few minutes. 'I think I heard someone mention that he is having a new yacht built.'

'Really?' said Jamie in such a dry tone that she looked at him and discovered for the first time that the sound of Lionel's name filled him with less rapture than it did her.

'Oh, Jamie! Don't look so chop-fallen,' she said with a smile. 'Lionel will come round, I'm sure of it. Just give him another week and he will be eating out of your hand—see if he isn't. I told you that we'll have enough to buy off that horrible person who is threatening to report your actions to Lionel, and I know—today I just feel so *confident*—that everything is going to be all right.'

'I wish I felt the same.' Jamie drew a heavy sigh, and seemed to resist an impulse to crack his knuckles. 'If I could just see Judith—that's the worst part, not knowing what's happening to her . . . wondering if her brother is trying to interest her in someone else . . .'

'Oh, don't be so silly! Why should he wish to do that? Besides, you saw her only yesterday.'

'Yes, but when will I see her again? On no account will I have any contact with her till I've spoken to Marbrae. I told her so in my letter, and I meant it. I should have put an end to our meetings as soon as I discovered who her brother was. If I had done so, I would not be subjected to these threats now.'

The more agitated he became, the faster he drove, so that Catherine deemed it prudent to lay a hand on his arm, and say soothingly, 'Yes, to be sure, dear, but we all make mistakes. I think you are doing the right thing in stopping your illicit meetings—for the moment, anyway. It won't be for long, and, besides, you will be able to see Judith at the masked ball on Friday, won't you?'

Jamie slackened pace to think about this. 'I don't know. Perhaps it would be better if I were not to go.'

'Oh, Jamie, you can't mean it!' Catherine said, in considerable agitation. 'There's not the slightest need to forgo the ball just to prove your integrity to Lionel. No one stands on ceremony at that sort of function. If Lionel were worried about whom Judith would meet there, he would not have accepted the invitation. The fact that Lady Crawford issued the invitations must be taken to be safeguard enough. In any case, if you are wearing a mask and hood, who is to recognise you?'

'It's not a matter of whether Marbrae recognises me or not, Kate. It's a matter of principle.'

'Oh pooh!' Catherine snapped her fingers. 'I don't give a fig for principle! What is the principle in letting poor Judith mope around all the evening because you are not there? And forbye . . . to be honest, Jamie . . . I *had* rather hoped you might take me with you . . .'

'What? You wouldn't like it, Kate,' Jamie said quickly, out of force of habit.

'Well, perhaps not, but I would like to be able to tell Grandmama that I saw a *little* of Glasgow society while I was here.' She gave him a sweet, sad smile, like an orphan cast penniless upon the world, and said gently, 'I have tried not to be a trial to you, dear, for I know you have problems aplenty without me badgering you to squire me around. But I would dearly love just one occasion to remember when I go back to Ayr next week.'

Jamie looked at her with narrowed eyes, not entirely taken in. 'I would have taken you to the theatre the night before last if you hadn't taken to your bed with a headache. And I'm taking you out today, am I not? Well, then.'

Catherine folded her lips and kept quiet, but in a pointed way, so that he said after a minute, 'Still, I don't suppose you'll have much fun walled up with Grandmama for the next couple of weeks. Maybe I could take you for an hour or two . . . I wouldn't exchange more than a few words with Judith, of course. And we would have to leave before the unmasking at midnight . . .'

Leaving him to talk himself into believing that he was going to the ball for his sister's sake alone, Catherine allowed her thoughts to drift in pleasurable anticipation of the treat in store for her. Just to be in the same room as Lionel would be thrilling enough, but it would be a strange thing if she could not contrive to have words with him and even—if the fates were kind—dance with him.

The thought of being so close to him, his strong brown fingers curling round her own, brought such a glow to her cheeks that Jamie, setting her down at the Saracen's Head, commented that she looked as though the drive had done her good.

From that moment until the following Friday evening, almost every waking moment was filled with thoughts of the ball. She could have wept with chagrin to think of the new blue ball-gown she had left behind in Ayr, but she comforted herself with the purchase (on credit) of a charming green silk domino with a matching mask through which her eyes blazed like emeralds, ardent and full of dreams.

She spent hours scrutinising her face in the glass, polishing her teeth with McAusland's Mixture (which tasted like equal parts of salt and charcoal), attacking a previously unnoticed sprinkling of freckles with lemon juice, and wishing that there really were such a magically efficacious product as Naples Dew. Her hair had to be washed and rinsed with vinegar, her nails had to be polished till they shone like pale pink shells, and a whole jar of lip-salve disappeared in constant application.

Whether any of this had any noticable effect or not, she could not be certain, but she was considerably heartened when Jamie, handing her into the town carriage he had bespoken for the occasion, told her innocently that if she would but take a few pains with her appearance she might be a deuced good-looking woman, even if she *was* his sister, dammit!

It was a pity that so much of her handiwork had to be hidden by the mask and domino, but sufficient remained visible to turn heads as they entered the ballroom. She was aware of the stares that were turned in her direction, for many of them were much more overt than they would have been without a mask to lend them anonymity, but they interested her only inasmuch as they might indicate that Lionel, too, would find her worth staring at.

The ballroom was not large, and Lady Crawford had perhaps underestimated the number of people who would accept her invitation, so that the result was something of a crush. Already the company had overflowed the ballroom into the adjoining dining-room, and the temperature had risen to such a degree that the french windows at the far end of the room had been thrown open to allow the cool night air to enter.

Jamie eyed the eddying throng with irritation. 'I'll never find Judith in this swarm,' he said bitterly, forgetting that his presence at the function was due solely to his concern for his poor neglected sister. 'Do you sit here with these girls while I go and have a look in the dining-room. I'll be back in a minute.'

'Yes, very well, Jamie. Don't be long, will you?' Catherine murmured demurely, glad to be rid of him. If he thought she would still be here when he got back, he was much mistaken. Lionel was somewhere in this room, and she had no intention of sitting here behind a potted palm and waiting until *he* found *her*.

But before Jamie was even out of sight, her hand was claimed for a strathspey by the first in a series of young men who allowed her no respite for over an hour. In spite of the lack of elbow-room, she enjoyed the dancing, but her mind was not on her partners but engaged in a continuing search for Lionel. Among so many hooded and masked figures she had not expected to identify him without difficulty, but when she finally did espy him it was clear to her that she could not have mistaken either his bronzed skin or the easy grace of his carriage.

He was speaking to a tall, auburn-haired woman, to whom Catherine took such an instant dislike that she quite ignored the deep-hooded gentleman who was, at that moment, soliciting her own hand for a country dance.

'Thank you, I do not wish to dance,' she muttered when she remembered his presence, sending him a fleeting smile without once removing her eyes from Lionel. 'I am still out of breath from that last reel. Perhaps a little later?'

He made some reply, to which she did not attend, and

stepped back with a bow; but as he turned to go, he hesitated and said, 'But pray allay my curiosity, ma'am. I know we have met before, but . . . for the life of me . . .'

Catherine flicked him a quick glance and shook her head. His mask was too large and his hood too voluminous to show her any familiar features. 'I'm sorry, I don't think . . .' she was beginning, when, watching Lionel, she realised that he was about to take the floor with the red-haired lady. The final set was almost complete, but if she were quick, there was just time for Catherine and her partner to join it too.

'On second thoughts,' she said briskly, gripping her surprised partner by the sleeve. 'I am much recovered suddenly. I think I shall dance, after all.'

She fairly trotted him on to the floor and succeeded, by dint of determined jockeying, in inserting her partner and herself into the same set as Lionel. Only then did she have leisure to make the discovery that she was dancing with Captain Smart. This came as a distinctly unpleasant surprise, particularly as he was still studying her with frustrated curiosity.

'I dare say you are laughing at me, ma'am, for failing to recognise you, for I am persuaded we are well acquainted,' he was saying with his familiar, self-effacing smile. 'But I'm blowed if I can think where we met.'

Catherine could feel the smile freezing on her lips. She tried to make her hood slide forward without actually touching it, but without any outstanding success, and had to be satisfied with turning her face away. She was aware of Lionel's eyes on her, and tried to compose herself, but the Captain would not let it alone. He kept staring at her and shaking his head, and muttering, 'No . . . No, it isn't the voice . . . or is it? The smile, perhaps? Confound it, what an old lack-wit I am!'

Finally, Catherine could bear it no longer, and said with a cool laugh, 'Believe me, sir, you and I are not acquainted. But perhaps you have met my brother, who is held to be much like me in appearance.'

For a second she thought his face stilled abruptly, and could have bitten her tongue out, but then he was smiling and shaking his head and cudgelling his brains again. 'Ah no, dear lady, I'll swear it was yourself I met. If I could but remember the where and when of it . . .'

It was a relief to turn her back on him, following the pattern of the dance, and to move down the set, spinning with each of the other gentlemen in turn. Suddenly Lionel was before her, his face still and expressionless, a hand outstretched for hers. She took two paces to meet him, and inexplicably found her foot slipping away and the polished floor swooping up to meet her.

He caught her before she hit the boards, holding her easily by the elbows and righting her with the minimum of fuss.

'My God!' he said, frowning. 'That was devilish clumsy of me, ma'am. I hope you are not hurt? Do you wish to sit down?'

'No . . . I am not hurt,' Catherine ground out, her whole body taut with embarrassment, and then realised, belatedly, that here was an opportunity to escape Captain Smart, who was on the far side of the set. 'Er . . . That is, I—I am a little shaken, perhaps.'

'Of course. Allow me.' He tucked her hand into his arm, and without as much as a glance towards either the Captain or his own partner, led her through the maze of dancers to the nearest vacant seat.

Even this mundane action, it seemed to Catherine, he performed with a panache that she was beginning to recognise as characteristic. Close beside him in the swirl of dancers, she felt again that aura of protectiveness that she had noticed at their first encounter in the woods of Monkwood House. As he supported her with one arm and curved the other in front of her to fend off the more uninhibited of the revellers, the glances he cast at her still startled face were full of concern. When he had her settled on a sofa close to the open windows, he stood before her in an attitude of abject contrition.

'I don't know how to apologise.' he said seriously, 'I can't think how I came to be so awkward.'

Catherine shook her head and dimpled at him, rearranging her hood which was in danger of slipping off. 'You were not at all to blame, sir. I think I tripped over my own feet.'

'No . . .' He drew back his chin as though he were afraid she might swing a punch at it. 'I have to confess that it was my foot you tripped over. Thank God I was able to catch you.'

'Since there was no harm done, I shall forgive you,' she said judiciously, trying to resist beaming at him like an infatuated schoolgirl. 'Indeed, I am indebted to you for giving me an excuse to sit down for a while. I have scarce stopped dancing since I arrived, and I am sorely in need of a respite.'

'In that case, may I be permitted to join you for a few minutes?' His attitude showed that he was prepared for a rebuff, but nothing was further from her mind. She did, however, have the forethought to pretend to a moment's hesitation before drawing her skirts aside to allow him to sit beside her.

He sat sideways, with his arm along the back of the sofa, and his eyes, behind his mask, studied her obliquely.

'Your partner . . .' She avoided his look by turning to watch the dancers who were now leaving the floor. 'I fear you will not be in her good graces, thanks to me. I will not be offended if you wish to go and make your excuses to her.'

'Dear me, yes,' he said, without excessive remorse and with barely a glance in the direction of the dancers. 'I feel sure she will never speak to me again! But what would you?—it was an errand of mercy. I could scarcely have left you to fight your own way to a seat.'

She feigned a close interest in the handle of her fan. 'She will surely say my safe conduct might have been left to my own partner.'

'Yes, but it *was* my foot, after all,' he murmured, grinning. 'And, besides, if I had relinquished you to your partner, I would not now be *tête à tête* with the most beautiful lady in the room.'

Catherine raised her eyebrows at him. 'You must have a very discerning eye, sir, if you can make so confident a choice among a group of masked women!'

'Not so!' A corner of his grin lifted whimsically. 'Having once, if I am not mistaken, seen beneath *your* mask, I have no need to see beneath the others.'

Catherine's heart gave a surprised leap, and she felt the colour creep into her cheeks.

Leaning towards her, he touched the back of her hand with one lean brown finger, and said reproachfully, 'You led me to hope that we might meet again at Monkwood, Miss Frazer. I would be disappointed to think that you meant only to fob me off.'

Since she was to be given no encouragement to pretend that she did not recognise him, she could only smile frankly, and say, 'Not at all. I had every intention of calling on Judith during the past week, but other engagements intervened . . .'

At that moment, Jamie appeared at the edge of her vision, striding purposefully among the chairs at the edge of the dance-floor. His head was turning from side to side as though he were searching for someone, and it was plain to see, even at a distance, that he was boiling with fury. Realising that the object of his search was most likely herself, and that in a moment he would turn and see her with Lionel, Catherine rose swiftly, saying, 'I must go now . . . I'm sorry . . .'

Lionel broke off what he had been saying—something, she thought, about hoping to be allowed to call on her—and jumped up to lay a detaining hand on her sleeve.

'I'm sorry,' he said quickly. 'I'm too importunate. Please don't run away, Miss Frazer. I promise I won't coax you any more.'

Catherine was at a loss as to what to reply to this, since she had been unaware that he was coaxing her, but she knew that Jamie and Lionel were within seconds of coming face to face unless she took immediate action to prevent it.

'Later . . .' she said, vaguely, willing Jamie not to look in her direction until she had put some distance between herself and Lionel. In a few hurried steps she reached the edge of the group of chairs and stepped on to the dance-floor, crossing it at an angle to bring herself into Jamie's line of vision.

'*Catherine!*' he mouthed, waving and beckoning her towards the door with a venomous jerk of his head that boded a stormy scene ahead.

'I waited and waited for you to come back for me,' Catherine lied placatingly as she caught up with him, but he cut her short by taking her arm and propelling her towards the exit.

'Where on earth have you been?' he said heatedly. 'I've been looking for you for hours. Come on. We're going home.'

'Not I,' said Catherine pleasantly, thinking it only fair

to disabuse him of that notion without delay. 'I agreed to leave before midnight, but not as early as *this*. Not unless you can give me a very good reason why I should. And, by the by, I shall take leave to tell you, Jamie, that your demeanour is unlikely to guarantee you an invitation to Lady Crawford's next function. Is it necessary to look quite so malevolent?'

'I *feel* malevolent,' he said, breathing heavily. 'I've just had the most dreadful row with Judith, and I've told her I don't want anything more to do with her.'

Catherine faltered in mid-stride and had to clutch at his arm for support. 'What? *Why?*' she cried, dragging him to a halt. 'You can't mean this, Jamie?'

A closer look at his dejected face told her that he did indeed mean it, and was suffering agonies in consequence. She cast about dazedly and spotted a window seat in a quiet corner. 'Come over here and tell me what happened. I'm sure it's all a misunderstanding.'

Jamie allowed himself to be drawn across the room like a docile ox to the slaughter, but refused to sit down. 'She has been deceiving me,' he groaned, shaking his head in disbelief. 'God knows how long it has been going on—*weeks*, if what the tattle-mongers are saying is true—and I've suspected nothing!'

'This is rubbish!' Catherine stated flatly, glaring at him. 'I don't know what you can be thinking of to be listening to such malicious gossip. I simply don't believe it.'

'Nor did I!' Jamie retorted, setting to work on his knuckles as though he meant to wrench his fingers out of joint. 'I told Andy McKellar that, when he came to me with the story. "Load of moonshine!" I told him. "Not Judith. Not a word of truth in it, depend upon it." But then he told me he'd seen them with his own eyes.'

'Then he's a liar!' Catherine stated unequivocally,

beginning to be very angry indeed. 'I don't know this
Andy Whatever-his-name-is, but I can tell you that
Judith has not been deceiving you, and never will! She
loves you to distraction, Jamie. If you do not know that
by this time, then you must be a great deal sillier than
you appear to be.'

'It's true, though. There *is* another man.'

'Balderdash!'

'She was with him at the Assembly last week.'

'Fiddlesticks! . . . er . . . What?' Catherine came to
an abrupt halt, while her mind caught up with a rush.

'She doesn't deny it!' Jamie muttered, too enveloped
in his own misery to notice Catherine's thoughtful stillness. 'And what makes my blood boil is that the fellow is
some simpering fop—a Macaroni, no less! A damned
effeminate dandiprat with not a thought in his head but
where to purchase the best stockings!'

Catherine was sorely tempted to laugh aloud, but was
sobered by the thought that this complication might
have serious repercussions on herself if the truth were to
come out. She tried to concentrate on planning a way out
of the situation, but Jamie was distracting her by saying
tragically, 'You remember she told me she was not going
to the Assembly last week? Ah, but she did go—the
jade!—and made an exhibition of herself with this jack-
adandy the entire evening. Andy was there and saw
everything, and she denies nothing!'

'Oh, heavens!' Catherine moaned, wishing that Judith
were present that she might shake some sense into her.
'Surely she was able to offer some excuse?'

Jamie shrugged listlessly. 'Only that her brother
changed his mind about taking her at the last minute.'

'And about Mr . . . the Macaroni?'

'What could she say?' he snapped, glaring at her as
though it were all her fault—which, of course, it was.

'Everyone saw him fawning over her all night. Marbrae must have been mad—or blind!—to have permitted it.'

Catherine chewed thoughtfully at her lip. 'Listen to me, Jamie,' she said, coming to a decision. 'I am going to tell you something that may be new to you. Judith is a dear sweet girl, but she is not . . . not exactly . . . well, she's not very worldly wise. I am willing to wager that she had never met a Macaroni before, and I'm quite sure she would be quite overwhelmed by all the frippery and the airs and graces. Don't you think so? I know that I—who have been much more in society than Judith— frequently find it difficult to deal with an audacious beau, and I would not find it at all surprising if Judith proved unable to put a Macaroni in his place. The fact that he took advantage of her inexperience has nothing whatsoever to do with her feelings for you, as I'm sure she would have told you if you had not put her back up.'

Jamie afforded this aspect of the matter several minutes of intense thought, and then cleared his throat manfully. 'You really think so?'

'I do,' said Catherine earnestly. 'It seems to me that you have treated her a little harshly over this, Jamie, and she may find it hard to forgive you. You had better go and find her and offer her your apologies.' She turned him about and gave him a slight push, but he hesitated, looking grim.

'You see what comes of not speaking to her brother?' he said, looking at her pointedly and giving a decisive nod. 'She is not properly chaperoned, and is able to meet all sorts of fellows at the Assemblies—here tonight— everywhere her brother chooses to take her. If I am not to lose her to some other man, I must approach her brother without waste of time. I don't know why I've waited so long. Marbrae is here now. I shall go and make myself known to him, and tell him I wish to call on him to discuss a matter of importance.'

'No!' Catherine gasped, getting in his way as he turned to go. 'No, I don't think you ought to do that, Jamie. Not . . . not tonight. I . . . I happen to know he is in a very bad mood. Better to wait.'

'How do you know he is in a bad mood?' Jamie demanded suspiciously. 'You haven't even spoken to Judith this evening, so who told you?'

'Well,' Catherine said, playing for time while her mind worked overtime. 'To tell you the truth, I know he will not be in a *good* mood because . . . because Judith told me . . . oh, it must be a week ago . . . when we were discussing this masked ball . . . She told me that Lionel hates masquerades and almost never attends them, and . . . and becomes very irascible when forced to attend one.'

'Well, bad-tempered or not, I'm speaking to him immediately—or as soon as I can find him in this mob. I'll make him agree to seeing me tomorrow, and then I'll speak to him man to man.'

'At least speak to Judith first,' Catherine pleaded, in a last feeble effort to avert disaster. 'You must have upset her very badly, you know. I shouldn't be at all surprised if she does not wish to marry you now, since you trust her so little. Hadn't you better find out before you speak to Lionel?'

'You don't really believe she would refuse to forgive me, do you Kate?' Jamie fixed her with a horror-stricken stare. 'She's not like you, you know . . . she has the sweetest of natures. But I'd better go and look for her at once. But if she says that she will have me still, I must speak to Marbrae tonight!'

There was no stopping him this time. He pushed his way into the throng as though pursued by demons, and

Catherine could only mutter a prayer that Judith would prove equal to the task of dissuading him from button-holing Lionel forthwith. In the meantime, if she herself could not keep Jamie from looking for Lionel, she could at least make sure that Lionel was hard to find, even if it meant luring him out onto the terrace. To go outside with an eligible young man might be considered *fast*, but at least she could console herself that, in this company, she was virtually unknown.

There were possibly other ways of keeping Jamie and Lionel apart, but, for some reason, she was unable to think of any.

She went hotfoot in search of him, fearing that he might be impossible to find in the throng, but to her surprise, he was still sitting on the couch where she had left him, watching the dancers with a frown. A scatter of hopeful young ladies had appeared in his immediate vicinity, much as wild flowers will take root in a sunny spot, but he appeared quite unaware of their giggles and sly glances. He saw her when she was still some distance away, and her heart turned over as he sprang up and came striding towards her with evident impatience.

'You came back! I didn't think . . .' He caught himself, pressing his lips together as though unwilling to admit to caring whether she came back or not. Forcing a smile, he went on in a lighter tone, 'I thought you might have disappeared into thin air again, as you did last week. Every time I suggest calling on you, you rush off in a panic.'

Catherine stared at him in wonderment. Try as he might, he could not hide the tension that ridged his jaw muscles and etched a small frown between his brows, and she knew suddenly, beyond all doubt, that he cared for her. He really had thought that she had disappeared again, and it mattered to him intensely.

'I'm sorry . . .' she said softly, trying to absorb the shock of this amazing discovery. 'It has nothing to do with your calling on me, it just seems that way. Indeed, you would be very welcome to call on me if my parents were not abroad at present, and . . .' She broke off, glancing about her at the press of people. 'Shall we go out on to the terrace, where we can talk in peace?'

His frown deepened, and as she turned to walk away, he caught hold of a fold of her domino, holding her back. 'I'm sure there is somewhere in here where we can talk.'

'But it is so hot in here,' Catherine said, making great play with her fan. 'And the music gives me a headache. I had rather step out into the fresh air for a moment or two.'

'I really don't think your chaperon would approve, you know,' he murmured with a soft chuckle. 'Look . . . Let me carry these two chairs across to the windows, where there is a current of air. No one will think it at all exceptionable if we sit there.'

'Oh pooh!' Catherine laughed airily, and with a brisk resolve that was born of sheer desperation, she turned and walked quickly out through the french windows into the darkness.

Beyond the fan of candlelight that spilled across the stone-flagged terrace, the night was velvet black and heavy with the scent of honeysuckle. Catherine sought the deepest pool of shadow, moving aside from the windows till she was brought up short by a waist-high parapet of pale stone. Lionel had followed her, as she had known he must, but he was plainly nonplussed by her brazen disregard for convention.

'You are full of surprises, Miss Frazer,' he said, coming to lean against the parapet but keeping an irreproachable two yards between them. 'You will not allow me to call upon you at the Saracen's Head, where you have your maid for chaperon, yet you are willing to step apart with me here in a manner which must surely give rise to comment and speculation. No doubt,' he added drily, 'the reasons for this paradox will become apparent in the fullness of time.'

Catherine eyed him obliquely but could make out only the straight line of his cheek silhouetted against the candlelight. There was, in his voice, just the faintest note of patient amusement, but it was enough to make her heart miss a beat with apprehension. Did he suspect that there was more going on than he was privy to? Had he followed her out here in the full awareness that he was being manipulated?

Shrugging off these absurd fancies, she said, 'Dear me, Lord Marbrae, I had not thought you to be such a stickler for the conventions! What can it signify if we are seen together? In these masks and dominoes we are surely quite anonymous, and who would bother to gossip about two uninteresting strangers?'

There was a smile in his voice as he said gently, 'You do yourself less than justice, ma'am. Believe me, you are neither uninteresting nor a stranger to many of your fellow guests. Within minutes of your arrival tonight, at least three gentlemen asked me if I knew the name of the lovely lady in the green domino, and, although I declined to enlighten them, I think we can be reasonably sure that someone will, by now, have thought to wring the truth out of Lady Crawford.'

This disclosure gave Catherine considerable pause, since it implied that Lionel had not only witnessed her arrival but had recognised her immediately. Why, then, had he not invited her to dance or, indeed, spoken to her at all till Fate had thrown them together by causing her to trip over his foot? Had he recognised her escort as the deplorable Jamie Frazer and decided to cut her acquaintance? If so, it had not taken him long to change his mind.

'What do you think?' he prompted, misconstruing her silence for one of remorse. 'Shall we return to the ballroom while we still have a shred of character left to us?'

Nothing was further from Catherine's mind, but she was reluctant to appear too lost to propriety. 'Do *you* want to?' she said, playing for time.

He hesitated, seeming at a loss for words, and then shook his head. 'I would be lying if I said I did, Miss Frazer, but I don't see any point in getting ourselves talked about. When you finally give me permission to pay my respects to your parents, for instance, I don't want your father to have heard reports that I am the sort of fellow to trifle with a lady's reputation. And that, I promise you, is the version that will reach his ears—not the truth, which is that it was *you* who dragged *me* out here!'

'Oh dear!' Catherine said, smiling at his exaggeratedly plaintive tone. 'It was rather thoughtless of me, I suppose. But it's so pleasant out here . . . I dare say it won't make much difference one way or the other if we do not go in immediately.'

He regarded her thoughtfully for a moment or two and then said softly, moving a little closer to her, 'I think there is a stronger reason for your not wishing to go back in.'

Catherine shied like a startled horse. 'What? No, indeed! Whatever can you mean?'

'Forgive me, I don't wish to pry, but I can't help feeling that something is worrying you.' His voice gentled her as his hands had gentled her brown mare that day on the road to Monkwood, and she found herself relaxing in spite of herself. 'I may be imagining things—perhaps it is only someone you wish to avoid speaking to in the ballroom—yet I get the impression, each time we meet, that you are under some kind of strain.'

Catherine could only be touched by his insight and concern, but was too bemused by the new tenderness in his voice to bestir herself to reply.

'Can't you tell me what's wrong?' he coaxed her, ducking his head in an attempt to see her face. 'If you are in trouble of any kind I wish you would confide in me. I'll help you in any way I can. Don't you trust me?'

The warm tones of his voice washed over her like waves on some tropic beach, and the longing to make a clean breast of everything ran through her with a physical pain. But she was not sure enough of his reactions to risk telling him about Jamie's love for Judith—especially after his remarks about men who trifled with a lady's reputation. However, she could not bring herself to lie to him directly, and so she said wistfully, 'I only wish I might tell you everything, but for a few days at least you must be patient with me. It's not that I don't trust you—I do, but you see . . . Well, there are other people involved.'

'Who? Judith?' he demanded quickly but when she looked at him in alarm he lifted an apologetic hand. 'No . . . I know. I have no right to question you. But you must see how hard it is for me not to worry when I see you ill at ease over some problem which you can't share with me.'

He took a step towards her and halted abruptly as though reaching the limit of a chain. His voice was a low rumble in his chest as he said softly, 'I do want to help you.'

Her lips parted slightly, and without her being aware of it, her body swayed towards him till she could feel his breath stir a tendril of hair against her brow. 'In just a day or two I will be able to tell you everything.'

'When?' he persisted, refusing to be fobbed off with vague promises. 'Next week? Monday?'

'I don't know . . .' She turned her head away, but his hand closed round her wrist and the light pressure of his fingers lit a flame that seemed to course through her veins like molten lava.

'When am I to see you again?' he said stubbornly. 'I'm tired of playing cat and mouse with you.'

He bent over her and the aura of yearning that surrounded him like a glow from a fire seemed to reach out and envelop her, turning her knees to water. To steady herself, she stretched out a hand and laid it against his chest, saying in a whisper, 'Don't make me promise. I am as impatient as you are . . . I will come to you as soon as ever I am able to do so.'

Beneath her hand his heart began to beat like a hammer and she heard him catch his breath before he said in a gravelly voice, 'I'm taking you back inside now, Miss Frazer.'

Yet he made no move to go, and it seemed to Catherine that Time itself had stopped. The moment that had hung between them, growing, since they had stood here together was now ripe, and life could not go on till they had lived it in all its promise.

She lifted her face to him, and tenderly he took her lips, her heart and every vestige of her being, his hands cupping her head as though he would drink her to the dregs.

The night melted round her into a vortex of staggering beauty in which the stars, the scented breeze and the distant strains of music seemed to ebb and flow in time with her pounding pulse. All rational thought suspended, she knew only that she was home, that she had reached the haven her soul had, unconsciously, been seeking ever since she could remember.

But as her arms curled about his neck he caught her wrists and held her away from him, murmuring huskily, 'No! . . . No, not like this. Don't let us make things any more complicated than they already are.'

She frowned at him in bewilderment, her breath catching on a sob. 'What do you mean by "complicated"?'

'My dear . . .' He held her hands tightly, kissing them with tight-reined passion. 'While your parents are abroad, I don't want to do anything to incur their disapproval, that's all. If your chaperon has missed you and learns that we were out here together there will be a very great fuss. Come, we must go back in now. I have my duties to Judith, you know, and she has already been longer without my supervision than I can comfortably square with my conscience.'

Catherine allowed him to draw her inexorably towards the french windows, but she had a vague suspicion that he had been less than frank with her, and the word 'complicated' remained in her mind as though it were a clue to some fact that she had failed to grasp. A morose conviction that something was about to go terribly wrong took possession of her mind, and she hung back unwillingly, her fingers tight on his arm.

Again the hankering to tell him everything almost overpowered her common sense, but the thought of her own shameful part in the drama put a brake on her tongue. Before she could tell Lionel Jamie's side of the story, it would be necessary to see Judith and make certain that she would say nothing that might connect Catherine with Mr Mather. If Lionel were to confront his sister with half of the story, she might too easily take it into her silly head that he knew the whole—and *then* the fat would be in the fire. Besides, it would be utter foolishness to gamble on Lionel's good nature at this stage in the game, just when all their plans were working out. Better to delay a few days, and let matters take their course.

'Wait!' she said suddenly, as she remembered that it was to avoid Jamie that she had inveigled Lionel out of the ballroom. It was now almost midnight, and Jamie would already be looking for her so that they could make their departure before the customary unmasking. How disastrous it would be if she and Lionel were to step in out of the darkness and meet him face to face. 'Perhaps it would be better if we were not to go in together. Let me go in first, and you may follow at your leisure.'

He hesitated for a long moment before nodding in agreement and letting go her arm. 'Very well. But make sure that no one is looking towards you before you go in.'

Catherine looked at him in the half-light, hoping that he might kiss her again, but his face was uncompromisingly blank and there was a stillness about him that showed he was holding himself firmly in check.

'Good night . . .' she said lingeringly, postponing the moment when she must leave him, but he gave her no encouragement to stay and she could only turn away with a sigh.

She stepped blindly into the ballroom, dazzled by the brightness and submerged in the most profound melancholy, as though part of her very soul had been ripped off and left on the terrace while she bled, painfully, from the raw wound. The contrast between this depression and the unalloyed bliss she had experienced only minutes before was sharp enough to make her eyes smart with tears, and she could not help but glance back—fruitlessly—over her shoulder in the hope of seeing Lionel for just a few more seconds before being enveloped by the crowd.

For the first time the full enormity of her charade came home to her with a vengeance, and she felt truly as though she were walking on a tightrope. One false step now and the truth would come out, and with Lionel turning out to be so unexpectedly stiff-necked, who could tell how he might react? What if Judith lost her nerve and confessed everything? What if Captain Smart failed to turn up at Duffy's tomorrow night? What if Jamie insisted on . . .

'Kate! You are the most provoking jade!' Jamie appeared before her, clearly in no sweeter temper than when she had last seen him. 'How you manage to disappear like a snuffed candle-flame every time I turn my back on you for a second, I really don't know. I'm sick to death looking for you. Come on. It's almost midnight, and I don't want to take my mask off if I can help it.'

Deducing from this that he had abandoned his plan of speaking to Lionel immediately, Catherine drew a sigh of relief and followed meekly at his heels. At least she had managed to avert disaster for another few hours, she reflected, but even this small success could not ease the strange foreboding that was closed like a fist about her heart.

CHAPTER
EIGHT

ALL THE WAY home in the coach, Catherine vacillated between unalloyed rapture and blind panic. At one moment, sitting dreaming in her corner, her body felt so suffused with happiness she was sure it must glow in the dark. Then that feeling of impending doom would descend on her like a foul miasma and her hands would twine themselves together in a mute prayer for divine protection.

Just let me get through tomorrow night, she thought feverishly, and at the prospect her stomach shrank to the size and texture of a dried prune. It was a comfort to know that Lionel would be twenty-five miles away in Greenock well before she would have to sally forth to Duffy's, but she wished with all her heart that she could think of some other way of finding the money to pay off the mysterious extortioner. The very thought of donning Mr Mather's outlandish costume made her feel queasy, and she could not wait to have done with him once and for all. From being her beloved brain-child, the fruit of her intellect and imagination, the Macaroni had grown to be a monster that threatened to destroy her. She hated him now with an intensity that could not have been greater if he had been a real person, and she looked forward with relish to the moment when he would meet his end in the flames of the farrier's fire.

Across from her, Jamie stared morosely into the

darkness beyond the window, wrapped in silence and moving only to crack an occasional knuckle. Finally his immobility stirred Catherine's curiosity, and she said tentatively, 'You decided not to speak to Lionel, then?'

'What?' He started and looked at her with a frown as though he had forgotten she was there. 'Lionel? No . . . I didn't speak to him. Judith was so set against it, and she was already so upset—because of our foolish quarrel, poor lamb—that I had to agree to wait till Monday.' There were bluish shadows beneath his eyes, and the tension-lines about his mouth showed that the evening had been just as much a strain for him as it had been for Judith. 'She was quite right, in any case. This evening would have been quite the wrong time to approach her brother. He would scarcely have been pleased to be button-holed on such a matter in the middle of a masquerade. I might have set his back up and put paid to my chances once and for all—and all because I was thrown into a fury by this Macaroni fool who has been trying to ingratiate himself with Judith. By God, let me but set eyes on the fellow, and I'll give him a piece of my mind, I promise you!'

'Now, Jamie . . .' Catherine shifted uneasily on her bench. 'Please don't get into another scrape. Remember what happened with Lord Marbrae. For all you know, this Macaroni may be a perfectly nice person with the greatest respect for Judith.'

'Rubbish! The man's a despicable cur! If he had any respect for Judith, he would not have encouraged her to make an exhibition of herself in front of all the gossiping mamas in Glasgow. A gentleman does not behave like that.'

Catherine had already heard enough on this subject from Lionel, so she said pointedly, 'Nevertheless, you have no right to interfere, Jamie. I hope you will try to

remember that if you should happen to run across this
man. You must learn to bite your tongue, you know,
otherwise you are bound to end up in real trouble sooner
or later.'

The possibility of meeting Jamie face to face during
one of her Macaroni impersonations had always been at
the back of her mind, but hitherto the terror of being
exposed by Lionel had eclipsed it almost entirely. Now it
loomed large in her imagination, and she realised that it
behoved her to give some serious thought to the problem
of keeping Jamie away from Duffy's card-room on the
following evening.

Only now did she realise that the masked ball had
occupied too much of her attention during the past
week. She should have been mulling over her plan of
action for the card-game and making sure that everything that could go wrong had been considered and
countered. Instead, she had pushed all thoughts of the
meeting to the back of her mind, and was now quite
unprepared to deal with either Jamie's threats or the
equally worrying fact that Captain Smart had very nearly
recognised her in the ballroom.

Both of these eventualities might have been foreseen
and plans formulated for dealing with them as they
arose, but it had taken Jamie himself to give her warning
of the first and a fortuitous stumble to save her from the
second. There was, of course, still the possibility of
Captain Smart connecting Mr Mather with the lady in
the green domino, but now that she was prepared for it,
Catherine felt confident that she could convince the
Captain that the two were brother and sister. Jamie,
however, posed a much more serious problem.

Throughout the night, even as she slept—or so it
seemed—her mind worried at the difficulty like a dog at
a bone. Jamie would have to be got out of the way

somehow, either kept within doors or engaged in some activity which would prevent him deciding to visit Duffy's. But the sun rose on a morning of heavy skies and drizzling rain without bringing even the germ of a good idea.

The morning was well advanced before she saw anything of Jamie. Jessie had just come in with yet another letter from Grandmama Frazer, but when Catherine saw Jamie entering hard on her maid's heels, she thrust the envelope unopened into a drawer lest he should voice an interest in its no doubt vituperative contents.

'Oh God, what a dull city Glasgow is,' he growled, staring out of the window. With his hands in his pockets, his shoulders hunched and his head poked belligerently forward, he looked the very picture of disgust. 'If we were at home at Transk, or even in Edinburgh, there are a dozen things we might be about, but here one may as well stay in bed. On a day like this, there is nothing whatsoever to do.'

'You told me when I arrived that Glasgow was a most entertaining and interesting place,' Catherine pointed out, with perfect truth. 'What about Mr Fowlis's works of art, and . . . and the theatre and the wonderful shops?'

'Yes, but I've *seen* all those. The trouble is, everything costs money. Or at least, those things that don't cost money are no fun unless one has good company, and at this precise moment I have neither friends nor money.'

Catherine was too used to her brother's ways to be hurt by this implied criticism of her social skills. 'You must surely have made some acquaintances in Glasgow in the time you've been here,' she said. 'You know Lord and Lady Crawford, for instance.'

'Oh, I've known them for an age. I met them in London, and, to be honest, I only called to pay my respects after Judith told me she had received an invitation to their masked ball. If I hadn't wanted an invitation for myself, I doubt very much if I'd have bothered to renew our acquaintance.'

'You can't have spent all your time dangling after Judith, surely? Did you not make any friends at the cockpit?'

Jamie looked a little brighter. 'Oh, well . . . Yes, a few, I suppose. They are a cheery lot, you know, and remarkably stout fellows, but one never sees much of them till the evening.'

'Then why don't you bespeak an early dinner and meet them tonight? It will give you something to look forward to and help to pass the day.' She knew it was her sisterly duty to offer her own company as a sop to his depression, but she needed some solitude to think about her coming ordeal and the hours seemed to be slipping away at an alarming rate.

'I suppose I might do that,' Jamie muttered, not altogether enthusiastically. 'There were some lads from Inverness in the Black Bull the other night. I could go round there first and see if they want to come with me.'

He lounged around for a while longer, preventing Catherine from attending to her own problems and getting in Jessie's way till she took to muttering Gaelic maledictions under her breath; but finally, feeling painfully sorry for himself, he left them in peace.

Catherine could well understand the agony he was going through. If he felt for Judith a fraction of what she felt for Lionel, the delays that had been imposed on him over the past weeks must have driven him almost insane with worry, and now the added blow of finding that he had a rival for Judith's affections in the shape of Mr Mather was clearly preying heavily on his mind.

'Poor old Jamie,' she said to Jessie, 'I hope he enjoys his evening at the cockpit. He really needs a little light-hearted diversion.'

'Oh, he'll find plenty of diversion at the Black Bull,' Jessie nodded, and gave her mistress a knowing wink. 'The devil could cast his net there any night of the week and get a fine catch, or so I'm told. All the Highlanders stay there when they come to Glasgow to let off steam.'

'Well, I don't care what he does,' Catherine returned with conviction, 'so long as he stays away from Duffy's. Besides, he doesn't have enough money to get into trouble, and won't have, unless he is extremely lucky at the cockpit.'

With Jamie safely out of the way, she felt quietly confident as she set forth for the Gallowgate that evening. Each time she donned the Macaroni outfit it became easier to assume the character of Mr Mather. Her voice now dropped in pitch almost automatically, and the exaggerated gestures and manner of speaking seemed to come so readily that they felt quite natural.

Mindful of Captain Smart's sharp eyes, she had taken over an hour to paint her face, and felt now that only a very unlucky chance could give her away. She might, at worst, appear a little effeminate, but that was by no means unusual in a Macaroni and would excite no suspicion. As long as Captain Smart did not expose her to too large an audience, she was sure there was no need to worry.

Duffy's proved to be an unassuming two storeyed building, the exterior of which gave no hint of the tasteful comfort within. Instead of the dingy and smoke-filled room that Catherine, half unconsciously, had expected, there were a series of well-appointed salons where a number of games of chance were in progress. She had no need to go in search of Captain Smart; he was sitting reading a newspaper in the lobby with one eye on the door.

'Ah! Mr Mather!' He came hurrying forward, his guileless face wreathed in smiles. 'Delighted to see you, sir. Really delighted!'

He held out his hand, and Catherine was forced to give him her own to shake, although she was aware that the strength of her own grip left much to be desired. The Captain, however, seemed unaware of this and led the way upstairs, chatting with great *bonhomie*.

'And how was Edinburgh, dear boy? Cold, I'll wager. Can't abide Edinburgh at *any* time of year. That east wind goes for my wound—Oh, just a scratch I got in the Peninsula, but it still gives me twinges from time to time. Now then, what is it to be? Faro? Hazard? Just say what you prefer.'

'As I told you before, Captain, I am not really much of a gambler,' said Catherine, regarding the faro table through her quizzing-glass with an air of faint boredom. 'Yet I must admit to enjoying the quiet game of Chinese whist we played last week. But perhaps you prefer a more exciting game? If so . . .'

'Not at all, Christian—I may call you by your given name, I hope? And you shall call me "Peter", for "Captain" is a great deal too formal—No, Chinese whist has always been a particular favourite of mine. Not perhaps for hardened gamblers, but one of the best two-handed games that have come to my notice. Shall we sit here, or do you prefer the table in the corner?'

Catherine, not surprisingly, opted for the corner table and made sure that she was sitting with her back to the room. Although she had not recognised any of the faces she had seen on her way in, she had no doubt that some of the other gamblers must have been at the Assembly the previous week and would not have forgotten her.

There were a few raised eyebrows, here and there, and the occasional smile, but she forgot about these as she won the cut and dealt out the first hand.

From the outset it was quite clear that Captain Smart's concentration was no less erratic than it had been at their first meeting. Each time Catherine took a trick, he would frown in a puzzled manner and make a fresh effort to attend to his cards, but seconds later he would be distracted by exclamations of despair or triumph from a neighbouring table or find himself reminded of some anecdote which he could not resist repeating to his much diverted companion.

The pile of guineas at Catherine's elbow mounted steadily, but the good Captain's smile never wavered, and the depletion of his own funds seemed to be of no moment to him. Indeed, apart from an occasional laughing reference to Catherine's run of 'good luck', he showed very little interest in the game and appeared to take more pleasure in chatting about his years in the 16th Dragoons and his interest in terrier-breeding.

Thus encouraged, Catherine forgot to feel guilty about taking his money and settled down to enjoy herself. A few glasses of wine relaxed her still further, so that she barely raised her eyes from her cards when her opponent began to speak of the ball the evening before.

'An appalling crush!' he said, rolling his rather protruberant eyes with disapproval. 'And the rooms so ablaze with candles we were like to be roasted alive. But nicely conducted, as Lady Crawford's functions always are; the wine and refreshments of the finest quality and the orchestra quite passable. She has four daughters to be married off, you know, so it behoves her to entertain lavishly.'

Catherine smiled absently, trying to calculate how

much was in the pile of winnings beside her. She would have loved to count it, but did not wish to appear too interested.

'Quite a few Names there, too,' the Captain was saying. 'Although, to be sure, one can't always tell if one has guessed correctly till the masks come off. Viscount Basford was certainly there, and—I'm pretty sure— Lord Marbrae and his charming sister . . . Yes, and one quite amazingly beautiful lady in an emerald green domino who seemed to be a mystery to everyone.'

His eyes, as he spoke, were on his cards, otherwise he could not have failed to notice the change in Catherine's expression. However, she had resumed her bored exterior by the time he glanced up with a frustrated shake of his head.

'Tall . . . green-eyed . . . neck like a swan! We were all trying to find out who she was, and—do you know, Christian,—I'll swear I've seen her before! Can't for the life of me think *where*, but I know I've seen her.'

'Deuced irritating,' Catherine murmured, patting a yawn in the hope that he would take the hint and talk about something else.

'You're right, dear boy, it has been niggling me all day. I looked for her after the masks came off, but she was nowhere to be seen. I don't suppose you happen to have met James Frazer's sister, have you?'

The question took Catherine so completely by surprise that she felt the colour flooding into her cheeks. She could only keep her head down and take a careful breath before she replied, a little tardily, 'Ah . . . Sorry, I was not attending. Whose sister?'

'Jamie Frazer's.' His smile was one of hopeful enquiry. 'There was a rumour that the lady might be his sister Catherine. I wondered if you knew what she looks like.'

'No, I don't think so. As far as I am aware, we have never met.'

'Ah . . . too bad. They tell me she is an acknowledged Beauty.' He returned to sorting his hand, and added in a preoccupied manner, 'Quite a respectable dowry, too, or so I should imagine. A nice prize for some lucky man.'

Catherine looked at him in some amusement. 'Perhaps for you, Peter?'

'For me?' He looked surprised, and then gave an appreciative chuckle. 'You're hoaxing me, of course! No, no. Quite beyond my touch. Not that I'm hanging out for a rich wife, in any case. I have been too long a bachelor, and the idea of giving up my freedom no longer appeals to me.'

A slight disturbance by the door heralded the arrival of a group of noisy young men and he turned to glare at them, giving Catherine the opportunity to reckon up her winnings. Thirty-five pounds. Only another fifteen to win and it would be all over! Her fingers shook with tension as she shuffled and dealt the cards.

'Talk of the devil,' muttered Captain Smart, gathering up his hand, and at her vague look he jerked his head in the direction of the newcomers. 'James Frazer! Just when we were speaking of him. Looks a little under the weather to me.'

The spots on Catherine's cards swam momentarily before her eyes and she was forced to blink rapidly to bring them back into focus. She simply could not believe that Fate would deal her such a dastardly blow. Of all the places in Glasgow that Jamie might have chosen to end his evening's roistering in, why did he have to pick Duffy's? She took a moment to steady herself before she turned to look at him, and it was as well she did so, for what met her eyes was worse than she had expected.

Jamie was with half a dozen or more young bucks—his

friends from the cockpit or from the Black Bull, no
doubt—all of them noticeably the worse for drink, but
not quite obstreperous enough to be asked to leave.
They were commandeering a table at the door, dragging
chairs to it so that they could all sit together, and reaping
not a few pained glances from neighbouring tables. In
contrast to the jovial mein of his friends, Jamie's appearance was that of a sabre-toothed tiger with an abcessed
canine. His hair was dishevelled and his face unnaturally
flushed, and before Catherine could drag her eyes away
he suddenly glanced up and looked straight into her
face.

They were separated by the length of the room, but his
reaction was so violent that she was left in no doubt as to
his feelings. For a split second his jaw dropped in
surprise, then his face filled with an expression of such
loathing and malignity that she felt as though she had
been punched between the eyes.

Hurriedly she turned back to Captain Smart and
found him placidly sorting his hand, quite oblivious to
the fact that his opponent was speechless with shock.

'Well, now, Christian. It's me to lead, is it?'

It was well-nigh impossible to concentrate with
Jamie's eyes burning a hole in her back, but there was
nothing she could do except pray that he would go away.
If he had chosen to sit elsewhere she would have been
tempted to take her thirty-five pounds and run, but his
long legs were stretched right across the doorway and
she had no confidence in his willingness to draw them
back for her to pass. Clearly, she was trapped here in her
corner until he and his friends decided to move.

It was luck rather than brilliant play that won her the
next rubber, and as she took the final trick, Captain
Smart made a small irritated grimace. 'Christian, m'boy,
the gods are with you tonight, and no mistake. I confess I

had not expected to be so unlucky and have not come prepared. You will accept my marker, of course?'

It was a statement, not a question, and Catherine could only bow and smile. She would, in any case, not have dreamed of refusing since it ran at the back of her mind that one did not refuse a gentleman's IOU. As always, she was painfully conscious of the fact that the niceties of male etiquette were a closed book to her, and that this could so easily bring about her downfall. At the same time, it was a distinct setback to find herself playing for pieces of paper. She wanted her fifty pounds in cash, and she wanted it by six tomorrow night, but she could think of no way of putting this to Captain Smart without making him suspect that she was deliberately fleecing him. However, as long as Jamie lounged, brooding murderously, across the door, she might just as well continue playing as sit here doing nothing.

The evening dragged on interminably, and as game succeeded game, she discovered that she was collecting an incredible amount of Captain Smart's markers. She seemed quite incapable of losing to him, no matter how poorly she played, and though, conscience-smitten, she hinted that they cease playing, he would have none of it.

'Dear me, no! The night's young, m'boy! Haven't even scratched the surface yet! I have a feeling my luck is just about to turn.'

Catherine dealt again, helplessly. It was quite ridiculous. The whole thing was getting out of hand. At a rough estimate, Captain Smart now owed her a hundred and twenty-five pounds, which, added to the thirty-five he had already parted with, amounted to much too much. It was now well after midnight and she desperately wanted to go home, but Captain Smart kept dealing another hand and yet another, and Jamie still smouldered in the doorway like the embodiment of all the retribution she so richly deserved.

Gradually the tables began to empty as one group of patrons after another bethought themselves of home and bed. Soon it appeared that only Jamie's table and her own were still occupied, and she began to entertain the hope that, if Jamie had no intention of leaving before she did, he might at least—please God!—fall asleep. Turning round to check on the likelihood of this eventuality, she received another horrible shock.

Lionel—incredibly!—was sitting at a table in the chimney-corner, quietly dicing with an elderly gentleman and a cavalry officer.

It was several seconds before Catherine realised that she was clinging to the edge of the table as though to the mane of a bolting horse. Indeed, the frightening speed of events, the sensation of loss of control and the certainty of imminent disaster could not have been more acute if she had been hurtling, hell for leather, across a moor instead of sitting safely in this quiet room. All that was missing was the thunder of hooves, but the hammering of her heart rose in her ears and filled her with the impression of chaotic speed.

Her immediate reaction was to throw herself on the floor and drum her heels in a tantrum, but since this was clearly impractical, she set her teeth and tried heroically to control herself. There was every chance, she told herself firmly, that he had not yet noticed her. Thanks to the group round the faro table who had just left, she had hitherto been shielded from his line of vision, just as he had been from hers. It was quite obvious that Jamie was still unaware of his presence. Not only was his attention wholly on the person of his hated rival, but his back was towards Lionel and he was partially hidden from him by the jut of the chimney-breast. With any luck, Lionel had not spotted either of them.

She played a card at random and forced herself to take several deep, steadying breaths. If she could just get past Jamie . . . She could keep Captain Smart between herself and Lionel until they reached the door, and then dart out quickly. If Jamie tried to speak to her, she would simply ignore him and step out into the corridor. He might follow her and make a scene outside, but that was much the lesser of two evils. Let him do what he chose, as long as he did not attract Lionel's attention.

It took a supreme effort to smile as she played her last card and said casually, 'And there, my dear Captain, I must call a halt. Too many late nights play havoc with my constitution, you know. I shall have shadows beneath my eyes tomorrow as it is.'

The Captain shook his head at this with gentle scorn, but seeing that she was adamant, he capitulated courteously and cried with a grin, 'Then you shall come round to my lodgings for a nightcap. They are quite close by, and I have funds enough there to settle my markers.'

Catherine hesitated only momentarily as she swept the scraps of paper into her pocket. She would have given a good deal to have been able to exchange them for hard cash immediately, but although she was headstrong, she was not entirely foolish. Not for anything in the world would she risk visiting a gentleman's lodgings in the early hours of the morning. Not even when the gentleman in question was as harmless as Captain Smart. 'Oh no, you must excuse me, Peter. I am asleep on my feet.' She yawned convincingly, wondering if it would be permissible for her to suggest settling up tomorrow.

'Tomorrow, then,' he said, as though in answer to her thought. 'I am superstitious about owing money to a friend, and the sooner I can clear my markers, the better I'll be pleased. Where shall I find you?'

'The Saracen's Head.' She was so busy keeping an eye on Lionel that the words slipped out before she had time to reflect that she would have been wiser to have kept her address a secret. 'Er . . . That is . . . I have business there at the livery stable at noon. You might find it more convenient to meet me there.'

It sounded distinctly havey-cavey, as Jamie would have said, but Captain Smart was too much of a gentleman to look askance. 'By all means. Twelve noon it is, then. Perhaps we could call in at the Saracen's Head for our meridian. I'm told their salt herrings are the best in Glasgow.'

'Unfortunately I will be in something of a hurry.' Catherine drew a deep, shuddering breath, and began to sidle towards the door. All Lionel's attention seemed to be centred on the fall of the dice, but he had only to lift his eyes to see her skulking behind Captain Smart. She tried to keep talking as she passed Jamie, but as they neared him, it was all she could do to pretend to be unaware of his malicious stare and ominously clenched fists.

Perhaps the moment might have passed without incident—for Jamie did seem to be trying to keep his anger in check—but one of his cronies chose that moment to say in a stage whisper, 'Good God! If it's not Judith Cameron's new beau!'

Seeing the quick flush this brought to Jamie's cheeks, Catherine tried to spring past him, but suddenly her ankle was hooked from under her and only by grabbing frantically at the doorpost was she able to avoid measuring her length on the carpet. Biting off a cry of fright, she pulled herself upright and turned to find Jamie on his feet, his mouth curled in an evil grin.

It was at once apparent that he was very drunk indeed. He could scarcely stand upright without swaying, and she could see that he was having difficulty in focusing his eyes on her face. This circumstance seemed like a gift from the gods. If she could but keep her head, there was still a chance that he might not recognise her.

A quick glance told her that Lionel and his friends had noticed nothing of the incident, that Jamie's boon companions were looking on in shocked disapproval, and that Captain Smart had inexplicably disappeared. Unfortunately, her way out was still blocked, so she had no option but to try to talk her way out. Keeping her face as much in shadow as she could arrange, she said quietly,

'Your pardon, sir. I did not see your foot.'

Jamie gave an insulting laugh and said rudely, 'No, but I saw yours, you little runt!'

A sudden white-hot surge of temper shook Catherine to the heels, and her hand itched to slap his face. Here she was, risking her reputation—risking her future happiness, no less—to get him out of trouble, and she had to put up with his drunken insults! She was heartily sick of him, and her eyes blazed with fury as she turned on him like a wild-cat. 'Runt I may be,' she spat at him, clearly and with slow emphasis. 'But there is yet time for me to grow. You, sir, are not so lucky. Once a fool, always a fool.'

There was something odd about the silence that greeted this remark, and it was only when she saw the slow smile spreading over Jamie's face that she realised she had given him what he wanted. All along, he had been trying to needle her into insulting him so that he could call her out. He had succeeded very well.

One of his friends, a golden-haired lad who appeared much younger than the others, stepped forward from the gallery of watchers and laid a hand on his arm, but Jamie shook him off without a glance, snarling, 'You will give me satisfaction for that remark, sir! Name your seconds.'

Catherine was undecided whether to laugh or cry. The whole business was too ludicrous for words. But as she blinked at her fuddled brother, the young lad again laid hold on him, saying urgently, 'For God's sake, Frazer! What are you about? You can't go around picking fights for no better reason than that you dislike the cut of a fellow's coat! You're drunk, Jamie!'

'Keep out of this . . .' Jamie pushed him away roughly, but he was back again in an instant, buzzing at him like a hornet and arguing loudly.

'This is disgraceful! I tell you to your head, man, you'll regret this in the morning. Recant, for God's sake!'

He was a tall, slim youth, instantly recognisable as his mother's darling, and he was wholly enraged by Jamie's boorish treatment of an apparent stranger. He stepped resolutely between them and continued to argue, but Jamie merely leaned round him and snapped at his bemused sister, 'Name your seconds, damn you!'

'Certainly,' said Catherine, realising that only thus could she bring this farce to a speedy end. In another moment Lionel might become aware of the fracas, and besides, if this fair-haired boy continued to act like a gadfly, Jamie might lose his patience and swat him. She looked around for Captain Smart, but there was no sign of him, and seeing her predicament, the youth stepped forward and gave her a short bow. 'Edward Seton, sir. If I may be of service to you, I would be most honoured.'

'Thank you.' Catherine bowed gratefully, and deciding that it would do no harm to turn public opinion against Jamie, added rather plaintively, 'I am a stranger in Glasgow, and quite without a friend to call upon.'

Seton flushed with chagrin, and sending Jamie a scathing look he beckoned over another young man.

'Allow me to present my cousin, Francis Allardyce. He would be happy to act for you also, wouldn't you, Frank?'

This seemed to meet with everyone's approval, and upon Jamie naming, quite arbitrarily, two of his cronies, the party broke up. Catherine was in a hurry to disappear as she was fairly sure that she had managed to keep the group of onlookers between herself and Lionel, and she did not want to spoil things now. However, her seconds had other ideas.

She was expected, she discovered, to wait downstairs while Seton went back into the card-room to discuss the possibility of a reconciliation. This was, of course, nothing but a waste of time, since she had no intention of fighting Jamie in any case, and she would have loved to tell Seton not to bother, but she was afraid of making a gaffe. There seemed to be so much punctilio involved, so many niceties to be observed, that it seemed wiser simply to go where she was led and say nothing to arouse their suspicions.

She had to force herself to keep up her foppish mannerisms and foolish chatter. The excitement of the evening was beginning to take its toll, and her whole body ached with tiredness as she waited for Seton to return. When he finally did so, he was white-lipped with anger.

'I can only apologise for my friend, Mr Mather,' he said, looking bitterly ashamed. 'That you, a stranger to our city, should have been offered such an abysmal indignity . . . It is quite unforgivable! By God, I could call him out myself! Yet, to be honest, it's not like Frazer to be so churlish. I can't think what got into him. You couldn't . . . I know it's unlikely, but . . . I don't suppose you could have done something to annoy him? Perhaps on an earlier occasion?'

Catherine flicked open her snuff-box and applied a

thoughtful pinch to either nostril. 'Annoyed him? Not that I recollect. I may have commented unfavourably on his waistcoat, for I must confess that it offends me prodigously. Would he call me out for that, think you? Surely not, unless it were one of his favourites, which I am persuaded it cannot be. Not puce and gold, my dear fellow. *Surely* not?'

The two seconds, standing shoulder to shoulder, attempted to exchange glances without actually turning their heads, which was quite interesting to watch. Then Seton said,

'In any case, there is no getting him to back down. The only thing to be done is to meet him at dawn in Herries Wood, as he suggests. I will speak to him again at that time, and we shall hope that Frazer sober has more decency than Frazer drunk. I chose swords, provisionally. I hope that is acceptable to you?'

Catherine shrugged with convincing nonchalance. Swords, pistols, bare teeth or bowls of custard, it was all the same to her. At dawn tomorrow she would be fast asleep in her bed. She tried again to take her leave of them, but Seton was not easy to shake off. He was at such pains to make amends for the way Mr Mather had been treated that he offered to walk home with her, and in the end, she was forced to hail a chair on the pretext of extreme fatigue.

'Till tomorrow, then,' he said, taking Catherine's hand in a painful grip. 'Allardyce and I will call for you at your lodgings.'

'Er . . . No . . .' Catherine muttered hurriedly. When Mr Mather disappeared into thin air, as he was about to do, she did not want anyone sniffing round the Saracen's Head for him. 'I'm afraid . . . for various reasons . . . that will not be possible. I will meet you at Herries Wood.'

That this was decidedly irregular was immediately apparent from Seton's raised brows, but he merely shrugged and stepped back with a bow. 'As you wish. I give you good night, then, for what's left of it.'

It was such a relief to be finished with him—to be finished with all her dangerous play-acting—that she fell back against her cushions and let her fatigue sweep over her. What an evening! It was nothing short of a miracle that she had come through it unscathed when she had been within an ace of being recognised by both Jamie and Lionel, and—who knew?—perhaps by Captain Smart as well. Good God! If she had known what a knife-edge she would be living on when she dreamed up this escapade, she would never have given it a second thought.

Jessie was waiting for her with slightly befuddled anxiety, having been beguiling the passing hours with a large bottle of porter, and she was much relieved to see Catherine stride in and throw her wig on the bed.

'Certes! I was beginning to wonder what had happened to you! Are you all right?'

'Oh, all is well, but more by luck than good judgment.' She dropped wearily into a chair at the fireside and kicked off her shoes. 'Just about everything that *could* go wrong did so, but I think I've managed to scrape my way out of it without too much damage being done.'

She gave Jessie a brief résumé of the evening's events while she waited for the return of sufficient energy to make the effort of getting undressed, and, somehow, the act of translating the incidents into words made her narrow escape seem even more incredible.

'So what about the extortion money?' Jessie asked when she had heard the whole story. 'How are you going to find the remaining fifteen pounds?'

Catherine shrugged helplessly. She had been trying

not to think about the money, but now she put a hand in her pocket and drew out the crumpled promissory notes, staring at them with bitter amusement. 'There's one hundred and twenty-five pounds there, and all it will cost me is a short walk down to the stable-yard at noon tomorrow. Yet I tell you , Jessie, I'd sooner work a year for the money.'

'Ay, I wouldn't mind working a year for it myself,' said Jessie, to whom the sum represented more than ten years' income. 'So you won't want me to be burning those clothes tonight, after all?'

'No,' Catherine sighed. 'I suppose not. That cursed Macaroni has a charmed existence. As often as I plan his demise, circumstances arise which make it imperative to keep him alive. Will I ever be rid of him?'

'It won't take more than a few minutes to get the money from Captain Smart tomorrow,' Jessie said comfortingly, shaking the folds out of Catherine's nightdress and draping it over a chair by the fire to warm. 'Your brother will probably go back to his bed when he returns from Herries Loch, so you should be in no danger of running into him. It's just to be hoped he is not wounded in the duel, but I don't suppose that's likely. He's a good swordsman, isn't he?'

'What are you talking about?' Catherine frowned at her in bewilderment. 'You can't think I'm going to fight him, surely?'

'No, but if *you* don't turn up, your second has to defend your honour by accepting the challenge. Isn't that so?'

'What?' Surprise brought Catherine bolt upright, her hands flying up off the arms of the chair like startled seagulls. 'I didn't know that . . . Are you sure, Jessie? How do you know?'

Jessie set her hands on her hips and concentrated her

thoughts by staring at the fire. 'Well, I don't know *how* I know . . . I suppose someone must have told me. Anyway, what's the point of having seconds otherwise?'

It did seem only logical, when one thought about it. Logical, that is, if one regarded it from the point of view of the small imaginative boy who, Catherine suspected, had originally formulated the rules by which these affairs were conducted. As far as she could ascertain, the seconds had no other duties other than to make the arrangements and try to bring about a reconciliation. They might have other functions to perform tomorrow, but since it was impossible to find out whether Jessie's information was accurate or not, she had to assume that young Seton would have to face Jamie's blade at dawn.

There was, of course, no question of her allowing such a confrontation to take place. It was unforgivable of her to have involved that nice young lad in the affair in the first place. It was only due to Jamie's embryonic self-control that he had avoided being slapped down earlier in the proceedings, and the danger of him being hurt in any conflict with her brother was unthinkably high.

'That's that, then,' she said, finally accepting defeat. 'There's nothing else for it but to tell Jamie the truth. He will know what to do about calling off the duel. You'd better go and see if he has gone to bed yet. Whether he has or not, tell him I must see him immediately.'

'He'll kill you,' said Jessie in a hushed whisper. 'Can you not think of something else?'

'Can you?' Catherine muttered, in complete despair, and then made an impatient gesture. 'Oh, go and get him. We may as well get it over with.'

Jessie moved towards the door with leaden feet. 'I don't think I want to watch this,' she said cravenly. 'If you need me, I'll be round the bend in the passage.'

Catherine dropped her head in her hands and tried to

force her tired mind to suggest some way of breaking the news to Jamie. If she had had some good news to give him at the same time, it might have been so much easier. If she could have told him that she had the wherewithal to pay off the extortioner, for instance. But now he would probably forbid her to meet Captain Smart tomorrow, even if it meant acquiring the final fifteen pounds. But then, that was a part of the story she need not tell him. Hurriedly she crammed the markers into her pocket, and turned as the door opened behind her.

But it was only Jessie, alone and wearing an expression of indescribable relief. 'He hasn't come home yet. His door was unlocked, so I went in to make sure, and his bed hasn't been slept in.'

Catherine chewed at her lip with vexation. She would as lief have had it out with her brother immediately than sit worrying about it till he arrived home. 'Oh, the devil fly away with him!' she said impatiently. 'It's clear he has decided that it's hardly worth while going to bed now, and is still roistering with his scapegrace pot-companions. Still, he will have to come home to change his clothes before going to Herries Wood, so I shall leave him a note telling him I must see him before he goes. Beshrew me if I'll sit up waiting for him all night.'

Her eyes were smarting with lack of sleep, but she forced them to stay open while she penned a few hasty but imperative lines warning Jamie of dire consequences if he proceeded to the duel without first having speech with her. This done, she made direct for her bed, where, undisturbed by considerations of conscience or of imminent retribution, she fell asleep at once.

Yet, drugged with exhaustion as she was, there remained at the edge of her consciousness the knowledge that the night was passing and still Jamie had not come.

CHAPTER
NINE

SOME SIXTH sense awoke her before the dawn, her mind
reeling with tiredness but warning her that something,
somewhere, had gone decidedly wrong. Only after
several minutes thought did she realise that Jamie
should have read her note by now, and yet he had made
no move to contact her.

Could he already have come and gone without seeing
the note? Or had he decided—on sober reflection—not
to pursue his quarrel with Mr Mather, after all? Rejecting an impulse to turn over and go back to sleep, she
threw a shawl round her shoulders and pattered down
the passage to Jamie's door.

There was no response to her knock, so she stepped
inside and saw at once that the room was empty. The
bedcovers were unruffled, and the note that Jessie had
slipped under the door still lay, untouched, on the mat.

'Oh no!' she said aloud, stamping her foot with vexation. 'What on earth is going to go wrong next?'

It did seem a piece of unbelievably bad luck that Jamie
had decided to go straight to Herries Wood without even
bothering to change his evening dress for something
more suited to the occasion. The implication, she very
much feared, was that Jamie had continued drinking and
was now too obfuscated to care about appearances. All
the more reason to prevent the duel before somebody
got hurt. But how?

She returned to her own room and drew back the curtains to estimate the time. There was just the faintest shimmer of light on the eastern horizon. She had, perhaps, fifteen or twenty minutes before Jamie and Seton would assume that Mr Mather had defaulted, and if Jessie's information was correct, proceed to the next step in their infamous ritual. She had to think of something—quick! quick!—before it was too late to stop them crossing swords.

She spun round and was feeling her way to her bedside table to light a candle, when Jessie's voice made her jump.

'What's the matter? Why are you creeping about?'

'Oh, Jessie! What a fright you gave me! I thought you were asleep!'

Jessie gave a laugh that was almost a groan. 'I haven't shut an eye for worrying what would happen when Mr Jamie learned what's been going on.'

Catherine got the candle alight and turned, holding it high to see her maid's face. 'Well, we have more than that to worry us now. Jamie hasn't come home. He must have ridden straight to Herries Wood, and he is probably, even now, preparing to fight poor Mr Seton. I can't think of any way of stopping him other than by going after him myself.'

'Oh no!' Jessie wailed, in real alarm. 'Couldn't you break it to him gently? If you spring it on him like that—and in public—he will fly into a temper, and that will be the end of me! At the very least, he'll turn me off!'

'Don't be silly, Jessie.' Realising, belatedly, that she was afraid, not just for her mistress's sake, but for her own livelihood, Catherine laid a hand on her shoulder and gave her a gentle shake. 'Why should he turn you off? All of this was my fault. You had nothing at all to do with it.'

'You couldn't have done it if I hadn't helped you,' said Jessie, with calm fatalism. 'He'll say I should have told him what you were about, and your grandmother will jump at the chance to be rid of me. She never did like me.'

'Well, I don't give a hoot whether she likes you or not!' Catherine retorted hotly, waving the candle about dangerously. 'It's what *I* think that matters! It would be scandalous to turn you off because you were faithful to me! I won't let them.'

But Jessie's look was anything but confident, and Catherine had to admit to herself that if the truth came out about how she had been occupying her time in Glasgow, she would be hard put to it save her own hide, far less Jessie's.

'What can I do?' she asked helplessly. 'I can't take the chance of either Jamie or Mr Seton being killed—or even wounded! I have to go and stop them fighting, and the only way of halting the duel is to tell them that I was Mr Mather.'

Jessie sat down on the end of the bed and began to cry. 'Oh . . . I don't know why you agreed to go through with the duel!' she sniffed miserably. 'When he called you out, you might easily have apologised and saved all this worry and upset.'

'Well, I wasn't sure if that was allowed in the rules. And I had no intention of going to Herries Wood, so it didn't seem to matter much . . .' Catherine paused suddenly, struck by a new idea. 'Could I apologise now, do you think?'

'What? . . . How?'

It was a mad idea, and the chances of its succeeding were very slim indeed, but it offered one last opportunity to avert retribution altogether. 'Hurry, Jessie! Get out Mr Mather's clothes. He is going to beg Jamie's forgiveness! I'll go on my bended knees to him if I have to, but I'll make him withdraw his challenge! Quick, there isn't much time.'

'But how can you?' Jessie cried, as her mistress began lavishly painting her face. 'No amount of paint will prevent his recognising you in broad daylight!'

'He didn't recognise me last night, and if my suspicions are correct, he will now prove to be a good deal less sober than he was then. Besides, if he does recognise me, he will surely have more sense than to blurt it out in front of everyone, so we shall be in no worse case than if we had not tried. Where are my boots?'

The Mr Mather who presently galloped away from the Saracen's Head was not the impeccable fop of his previous appearances, but if his costume bore signs of having been donned in a hurry, his face was as thickly painted as ever and his wig was firmly set low on his brow.

Herries Wood was only a few minutes' brisk ride away, but the sky was almost light by the time Catherine reached the edge of the trees. Mr Seton and his cousin met her there with open relief, and guided her through the bramble thickets to a small clearing well hidden from chance observers. Jamie and his seconds were standing beside a town carriage and some saddle-horses at the far side of the glade, and at a little distance, stood a tall dark man whom Seton identified as the doctor.

As she had surmised, Jamie was still dressed as he had been at Duffy's the previous evening. His face was pale now, and very blue about the jaw, and she saw him stagger a little as his friends helped him off with his coat. He looked so ill and miserable that she was suddenly stricken with remorse. She had been furious with him the night before not only because he had insulted her but because his undignified behaviour made her ashamed of him. But, this morning, she could see his pain and unhappiness, and she knew that, for at least part of it, she was to blame. No wonder he had tried to drown his sorrows in brandy last night, and no wonder also that he hated the very sight of Mr Mather.

'I have approached Mr Frazer in the hope of effecting a reconciliation,' Seton was saying as she dismounted. 'But I'm afraid he is in no way willing to retract.'

Catherine offered no reply to this, as she was sure she was in a dangerous situation. Everyone was behaving with such grave formality that it was clear that one ill-considered action would immediately be noticed. All of Jamie's party were behaving as though Mr Mather's group were not there, and *vice versa*. Both Seton and Allardyce were strutting about like marionettes, making preparations with exaggerated gestures, and speaking in clipped tones.

'I must just have a word with Mr Frazer,' she said to Seton, and glancing at him as she spoke, saw his jaw drop with astonishment.

'You . . . ?' He seemed to collect himself. 'Oh, I'm sorry. I thought for a moment that you meant *now* . . . before the contest.'

It didn't take a genius to discern that she had made a *faux pas*. Quickly she turned away to hide her blush, and managed to drawl, 'Good God, no. Later. I shall give him the name of my tailor in Edinburgh. That waistcoat is depressing, even by Glasgow standards.'

To play for time, she allowed Allardyce to help her off with her coat and boots, but retained her waistcoat since its stiff braided front covered her chest like a breastplate and formed a necessary part of her disguise. All the time her mind was racing, searching for a way of presenting an apology to Jamie without giving away her total ignorance of the rules. His party were now showing signs of moving out into the middle of the clearing, and Seton had produced two identical swords which he laid, parallel, across his arm. Snatching at a last straw, Catherine remarked, with spurious innocence,

'Duelling is a fool's game, y'know, Seton. I tell you frankly, I had rather apologise to the fellow than get blood on these buckskins.'

Seton gave a small lop-sided smile in reply. 'I fear that would avail you nothing, sir. I made sure to ascertain last night—and again this morning—whether an apology, if tendered, would be accepted. Unfortunately, Frazer will be satisfied with nothing but your blood.'

Catherine's face fell. She could not help it. Her despair and dejection were so complete that she cared not if Seton noticed it. Now the fat was truly in the fire, and the only thing left for her to do was to walk out into the clearing with him and to whisper to him, there in front of everyone, out of earshot—she hoped—that she was his sister Catherine.

It was risky. Jamie would be utterly staggered by the revelation and might easily cry out something incriminating, but that chance would have to be taken. If she were to attempt to speak to him now, he would most likely refuse to step apart with her and she would be forced to blurt out the truth for all to hear.

'He has the advantage of you in reach,' Allardyce muttered as they walked across the greensward shoulder to shoulder. 'And he will probably try for a quick finish, so you would do well to keep well out of range, if you can, and concentrate on wearing him down gradually. He is in an evil temper, which is to your advantage since it will affect his concentration and may well give you an opening.'

Catherine nodded, pretending an interest she did not feel. She had fought Jamie so frequently that she was confident she could hold him off long enough to make him aware that he was engaging his own sister. In fact, her only serious worry was that her wig might come off and give her away.

At close quarters, Jamie's face looked as threatening as a clenched fist. He, apparently, could not bring himself to look his rival directly in the face, but fixed his eyes, coldly, at a point some inches above Catherine's head. At another time she might have thought this quite fortuitous, since it prevented him recognising her, but now she tried desperately, with much throat-clearing and head-jerking, to make him catch her eye. But it was to no avail, and in a matter of moments it was too late.

That was when the whole shaky edifice of her machinations began to tumble like a house of cards and did not stop until all her hopes and dreams lay trampled into the mud of Herries Wood.

The instant the seconds sprang back, Jamie opened hostilities with such a furious rain of blows that Catherine was completely taken aback. This was not at all the same activity as they had engaged in in the stable-yard at Transk! She had never suspected at the time that Jamie had been cosseting her to such a degree, but now the strength and rapidity of his unexpected attack had her running backwards, retaining her grip on her sword only by sheer will-power. There was never a moment when she had the least chance of uttering his name, far less identifying herself, and she knew beyond a doubt that she was about to be seriously wounded, if not killed.

Then, suddenly, their swords were struck upwards by a blow that sent hers flying from her grasp, and a voice seemed to crack like a whip over their heads.

'Enough of this folly!'

As Catherine staggered backwards, her arm numb to the shoulder, Jamie whirled like a daemon on her saviour, and shouting, 'By God, I'll kill you for this, Seton!' drove the hilt of his sword full in the other man's face. The other moved like lightning but yet not fast enough, for, although the full force of the blow failed to connect, the edge of the hilt caught him on the temple, knocking him to the ground.

Catherine found a tree at her shoulder and clung to it, sickened by the violence, and then it seemed to her that the very ground beneath her feet heaved like an earthquake as the man on the ground sprang up, and she saw that it was not Seton, but Lionel!

She was not immediately thrown into a panic for the simple reason that her mind refused point blank to accept that this could be happening to *her*. It was almost as though she were watching a theatrical performance, and not with any great interest. She saw the seconds begin to run over from the edge of the clearing. She watched Lionel step towards Jamie, white-faced with anger, his cheek streaked with blood. She heard him mutter something unintelligible, and she watched with total detachment as Jamie turned to stare at her with incredulity and horror.

Now the seconds were upon them, and everyone appeared to be shouting at everyone else. Jamie's seconds were shouting at Lionel; Seton and Allardyce were shouting at Jamie, and the doctor was trying to justify his existence by examining Lionel's wound and getting no co-operation from anyone. No one had a thought to spare for Mr Mather, and since Catherine's only remaining instinct was to remove herself from the scene of contention, she simply wandered away. Without having any clear idea of where she was going, she moved like a sleep-walker across the glade to where she had left her coat, but just as she picked it up, hurried footfalls behind her made her stop and turn.

'Where are you off to?' Jamie caught at her arm with a grip that hurt.

She shook him off, but the fury in him was so frightening that the words of defiance died on her lips, and she could only shrug and shake her head.

'Get in the carriage and wait for me.' He looked at her with hooded eyes, and his voice shook with passion. 'And, Kate . . . If you play any more tricks on me, I won't answer for the consequences, do you understand?'

He strode back to the knot of arguing figures, and as he joined them, Lionel left the group and walked to the edge of the trees. She saw then that his bay hunter was tethered there behind a bramble brake, and as he untied the reins she waited, hoping in spite of everything that he would turn and look at her. As he turned his horse's head towards the path, she must have been almost in the corner of his vision, but his eyes looked straight ahead and his pale face looked as though it were carved out of marble.

She watched him until he disappeared among the trees, and her gaze moved over him hungrily, so that if she should not see him again she would remember for ever the long line of his back and the way his body moved as one with the tall brown horse.

It was inconceivable that, after managing to maintain her pretences for so long, she should be overtaken by such sudden and total disaster. She felt like a juggler who had been keeping twenty plates whirling above him, only to find them crashing down, one after the other, on his head. But a few minutes ago, everything had been possible: Jamie's extortioner silenced, his offer for Judith accepted, her own love for Lionel returned, and Mr Mather reduced to ashes. Now only the last eventuality seemed likely to occur.

She drew a deep, painful breath and got into the

carriage, leaning back against the cushions and closing her eyes. All at once she was overwhelmed with tiredness. She wanted to climb back into bed and sleep for a week. This had always been her method of dealing with emotional upsets, and she knew that by hiding away from her problems, by shutting the world out with her bed-curtains, she would wake stronger and better able to face facts. But there was to be no rest for her yet awhile.

Jamie's voice sounded outside the window, barking an order to the coachman, but she resisted the impulse to open her eyes as he climbed into the carriage and sat down facing her. His audible breathing and the air of tension he brought with him told her plainly enough that he was still in a towering rage, and she found herself extremely reluctant to meet his eyes.

He waited till the carriage had lurched across the greensward to the path before speaking, and when he did so, it was evident from his tone that he would far rather have been communicating with blows.

'I could choke the life out of you!' he opened, with a frankness Catherine could not regard as disarming. 'I hope you realise what your meddling has led to, you insufferable jade! You've just ruined my life, that's all!'

He paused, breathing heavily, but she said nothing, and after a moment he went on, with a break in his voice, 'I'll never see Judith again. He'll kill me if I ever cross his path again!'

Catherine opened her eyes. 'Did he say so?'

'Not in front of the others, of course not.' He had a hand across his eyes, and his mouth was twisted with pain. 'We had to pass it all off as a misunderstanding. With Judith involved as well as you, we couldn't take the chance of the truth getting out. Ye gods! Did you stop to think for one second before you involved *her* in your foolish pranks?'

'I *did* it for Judith . . . and for you!' Catherine returned with some heat, knowing that nothing would be gained by quarrelling about it, but unable to resist defending herself.

'Then you must be mad! What, in all the world, did you hope to achieve?'

'What I very nearly *did* achieve,' Catherine retorted, now thoroughly incensed, 'what, in fact, I would have achieved, if it hadn't been for your infantile jealousy and . . . and your foul temper, was Lionel's consent to your marrying Judith! Can't you see? If he thought Judith were about to run away with a Macaroni, he would have been delighted to receive *your* proposal—the lesser of two evils!'

'You *are* mad!' stated Jamie with conviction. 'You really think Marbrae is the sort of man to settle for the lesser of two evils? He's simply not subject to that kind of pressure. Certes, he would send Mather—*and* me—packing in ten seconds. In any case, he knew from the first that Mather was you.'

'*No!*' she cried out, refusing to admit that horrific possibility for a second. 'You can't know that! I don't believe it.'

'Well, what the devil made him turn up at the duel, then? And why was he at Duffy's last night, when he gave it out that he was going to Greenock?'

'You *saw* him at Duffy's?'

'Only when he followed you out. I suppose he was following you to see what you were up to. God, he must think insanity runs in our family!'

Catherine fell back in her corner and chewed dismally at her lip. She couldn't bear the thought that Lionel had known all along that the grotesque caricature that was Mr Mather was Catherine Frazer making a fool of herself. 'I think you are wrong,' she said stubbornly.

'Probably he told Judith that you had challenged Mr Mather to a duel, and she—thinking we might really come to blows—told him the truth so that he would put an end to the duel.'

'What does it matter when he found out?' Jamie grunted, turning to stare blindly out of the window. 'He'll never forgive me for knocking him down in front of everyone. That's out of the question. He'll make sure I don't even see Judith to say goodbye. If you had planned to bring about my total destruction, my dear interfering sister, I doubt me if you could have made a more thorough job of it!'

'You brought about your own destruction!' responded his dear interfering sister with considerable feeling. 'I may have shown myself to be lacking in good behaviour, but it was you and you alone who dealt your hopes the *coup de grâce*!' She slid forward until she was perched on the edge of her seat, and all but shook her fist in his face. She might be partly to blame for this débâcle, but she wasn't going to accept all the blame. He might not know it—perhaps he never would—but it was his temper that had delivered the final blow to her own dreams of a future with Lionel. It was just possible that Lionel might have overlooked her hoydénish behaviour, but he would never forgive the insult of being knocked down in public.

'I'm sick of listening to you blowing up like a volcano every time something displeases you,' she shouted at him, her chest heaving with tribulation. 'It's time you grew up, Jamie Frazer, and stopped behaving like a spoiled brat! Maybe this will teach you a lesson you should have learned years ago!'

If the carriage had not, at that moment, pulled into the inn-yard, a battle royal would have broken loose, but under the interested stares of the ostlers Jamie could only simmer speechlessly and hustle her up the stairs at a speed which made her dread being alone with him.

Thrusting her into her room with a roughness that appeared to turn the anxiously waiting Jessie to stone, he stuck his head in after her, to snap, 'Jessie! Get packed up. We leave for Ayr first thing tomorrow morning.' The head was withdrawn, but before the girls could even exchange glances, it appeared again and a narrowed stare was directed at Jessie, together with the words, 'Yes, and I will have a word with you later, my girl!'

Jessie barely waited for him to slam the door before bursting into tears and sinking into a huddled heap at the fireside. 'Oh mercy! I knew this would happen! What am I to do? Oh lord, what am I to do?'

Catherine was in two minds whether to join her. A good cry would go a long way towards relieving her feelings, but it was a luxury she could not at present afford. There was Judith to write to, and Jessie to comfort, and then, after a little rest and perhaps a bite to eat, she would sit down and contemplate the ruins of her life and see what could be salvaged.

'Jessie,' she said firmly, laying a hand on her maid's heaving shoulder. 'I give you my solemn promise that I won't let you suffer for my folly. If I can't prevent your being turned off—and, yes, I will admit that I'm not sure I can—I swear I'll see you don't starve. I'll find you a new position soon, and in the meantime I'll make sure you have enough money to live on . . . somehow.'

Somehow. That was the operative word. Still, she could think about that later. She dried Jessie's eyes and drew her to her feet, smiling confidently. 'You'll see, Jessie. Everything will be all right. You'll feel better once you've had something to eat. See what you can procure for us downstairs before I starve to death.'

Left alone, she sat down at the writing table and tried

to compose a letter to Judith, who, she knew, would be just as unhappy this morning as she herself, and who might otherwise never know exactly what had happened at the duel.

It was far from the easiest letter she had ever been called upon to write, and she was sharply aware that Judith might now be heartily wishing she had never had a friend named Catherine Frazer. She took a long time about mending her goose-quill and then sat staring at the blank sheet of paper till her eyes grew heavy, and finally she fell fast asleep with her head on her folded arms.

When she woke, she was shivery and stiff-necked, and the waistband of her buckskin breeches was cutting into her stomach. Jessie was fast asleep in the chair at the fireside, her eyes red from weeping, and there was a platter of assorted provender and a bottle of wine on the table beside her unwritten letter. She no longer felt hungry, but a glass of the wine sharpened her appetite and presently she found herself busily making up for the fact that she had eaten nothing since the previous evening.

As she ate, her eyes were drawn repeatedly to the sleeping Jessie, noting the lingering signs of weeping around her eyes and the way she still sobbed in her sleep, and her conscience stung her like a nettle. Life was so unfair. What had Jessie done but keep faith with her mistress and obey her orders without question? Why should she be made to suffer for doing her job?

It was quite unthinkable that Catherine should permit this. Clearly, she could not live with it on her already overburdened conscience. There must be some way of preventing Jamie from sending her packing, but it was extremely unlikely that he would listen to argument, and pleading with him was even less likely to bear fruit. Her credit with him was not at all high even now, and he had yet to learn that, in the process of ruining his life, his erstwhile beloved sister had incurred a considerable burden of debt for which she expected him to be responsible. The bills had already started to arrive, and although Catherine had barely glanced at them before throwing them into a drawer beside her grandmother's unopened letters, they had begun adding themselves up, willy nilly, in her head, and it was only with great difficulty that she was able to ban the total sum from her consciousness. The landlord's claims would also have to be satisfied before their departure in the morning, so Armageddon could not be long delayed.

Propping an elbow on the table, she leaned a cheek on her fist and stared bleakly out of the window. There were too many sore hearts, this morning, which could be attributed directly to Mr Mather—all right, to Catherine Frazer! Before she could begin to lick her own wounds she had to think of some way at least to *begin* to make amends, particularly to Jessie, who, less than anyone, deserved to suffer.

She could hear, beyond the window, the musical chimes in the Tolbooth steeple ringing out the hour, and with a start she realised that it was already twelve o'clock. Inevitably she thought of Captain Smart who would, no doubt, be waiting in the stable-yard for his contemptible and predatory friend. Someone else whom Mr Mather had wronged, not only by taking advantage of his friendship, but by taking his money, and, now, by making him waste his time waiting about in the cold. The money could be returned, of course, and would be, sooner or later, but it was a shameful way to treat a friend.

A hundred and sixty pounds! She could not resist a tiny smile of self-satisfaction. What a pity she had no one to whom she could brag of her achievement. To have won so much in just a few hours was really something to brag about, particularly if one considered the strain she had been under at the time. If only it had all been in cash. All her money problems would be over and she could even pay off the extortioner, for although Lionel already knew all that could be told, Jamie would surely not wish it known that he had exposed Judith's reputation to such a scandal. She could give the tradesmen something on account until her next allowance was due, and there would still be plenty to take care of Jessie while she was arranging employment for her.

There could be no argument about what she had to do. It would take only a few minutes, and if she was quiet about it, even Jessie need never know that she had been out of the room. It was a heaven-sent opportunity, and she could not refuse it.

Her hands trembled a little as she tucked her hair, yet again, into the loathed wig and perched the ridiculous little cocked hat on top, but it was haste, not nervousness, that made them unsteady. She had no longer any need to be nervous, since Lionel was lost beyond recall and Jamie, even if he found out, could get no more angry than he already was.

She met no one on the back stairs except a laundry-maid with a basket of wet linen, and there was no one about the yard when she emerged. Nor was there any sign of Captain Smart. After lurking in the doorway for a minute or two, she took a few steps towards the entry and then she spotted him. He was leaning from the window of a town carriage which was stopped in the street beyond, and he was beckoning her imperiously. She had no choice but to go to him.

'My dear Christian!' he cried as she approached, opening the door and stretching out a hand to shake hers. 'A very good morning to you, my boy! Forgive me for not getting down. My wound. I am quite crippled with it this morning, and would not have come but that I would not otherwise have known where to find you. Come up . . . Come up! Don't stand there in the road!'

Catherine hesitated, but he had retained a grip of her hand and was now tugging at it inexorably. 'I myself am in something of a hurry . . .' she began, but Captain Smart waved a peremptory hand.

'Come up, my friend, and let us conclude our business in private!'

Catherine flushed a little, realising that, naturally, it would not be the done thing for two gentlemen to stand exchanging money in the street. Quickly she ran up the steps, but before she could seat herself the door slammed to behind her and the carriage gave a sudden leap forward, throwing her to the floor. For several seconds, as the driver whipped up his horses, she was flung about like a cork on a fountain, skinning her knees and elbows and fetching the back of her head a crack that made her see stars. Finally she got a grip on a seat, but as she began to pull herself up, Captain Smart extended a shiny boot and pushed her back to the floor.

'A thousand pardons, my dear Miss Frazer,' he said with an oily mock-servility that was quite different from his usual *bonhomie*. 'But, for the time being, it would better suit my purpose if you remain where you are.'

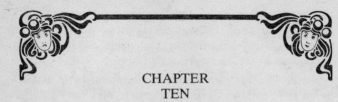

CHAPTER
TEN

THE CHANGE in the Captain was so startling that she felt she might have walked past him in the street without recognising him. Yet he had changed only in his expression, which was no longer genially open, and in his attitude, which now eloquently demonstrated his amusement and self-satisfaction. She could scarcely believe that she had thought him a benevolent and harmless old fogey and had felt thoroughly unhappy at the necessity of taking advantage of him. If she had seen him as she was seeing him now, his mouth twisted in a leer and his protuberant blue eyes like chips of ice, she would have had no hesitation in assessing him as the evil brute he really was.

She glared at him, fighting down a wave of such cowardly panic that she would have died rather than let him see it. 'How dare you! What do you mean by this, you cheat-gibbet?'

'Manners! Manners, dear lady!' he sniggered unpleasantly, but in a curiously high pitch, which told her that he was nervous and excited. 'You need not be alarmed! No harm will come to you, provided you do exactly as I say.'

Pushing aside his boot, she raised herself on one elbow, but the coach was careering along at such a speed that she had to be content to stay on the floor. 'What do you want with me, Captain Smart—if that is indeed your name? Where are you taking me?'

'You will see soon enough, my dear. I don't want to spoil the surprise!' He was dividing his attention between watching his prisoner and peering out of the window as though he were afraid of pursuit. If he had known, as Catherine most poignantly did, that none of her friends even knew she was out of the inn, he might have rested easy.

Suddenly the carriage made a sharp turn, lurched over some uneven ground and drew to an abrupt halt, throwing Catherine painfully against the door.

'Up!' barked Captain Smart, grasping her by an elbow and jerking her to her feet. 'And please . . . don't let's have any unpleasantness, Miss Frazer. It will avail you nothing to start screaming and struggling, for there is no one by, as you will see, and I would prefer not to use violence if it can be avoided.'

He threw a heavy black cloak about her shoulders, and pulling the hood well over her face, threw open the door and leaned out, saying, 'All clear, McPhee?'

The apparition that manifested itself beyond him was huge and hairy and grotesquely fat, with a head like an Ayrshire bull and expression of such terrifying imbecility that Catherine stepped involuntarily backwards. One massive fist gripped a coachman's whip and the other was clumsily letting down the steps, while a pair of bright blue eyes probed past the Captain to fasten on Catherine with a greedy intensity.

The Captain ignored him, and after a hasty glance to left and right, dragged Catherine behind him down the steps. They were on the bank of the river, no great distance from the dock area which, although out of sight, was still close enough for her to hear the shouts of the sailors and carters and the rumble of heavy wheels. A straggle of low willow trees grew close on either side and paddled out into the water, screening them from anyone to whom she might have cried out for help.

There was no place to run to, even if her shaking legs had been capable of the effort, and had she summoned up the courage to scream, the puny noise she might have made would pass unnoticed among the babble of noises surrounding the dock.

'Get moving, McPhee!' the Captain snarled, aiming a kick at his monstrous servant, who seemed unable to remove his gloating gaze from Catherine. 'Get the boat in the water, and don't take all day about it!'

Closely followed by the Captain and, perforce, by Catherine, the half-wit shambled down to the water's edge and uncovered a flat-bottomed dory which had been hidden among the roots of the willows. He handed the painter to the Captain, and pushing the boat out into the shallows, he turned with the obvious intention of lifting Catherine into it.

She could barely smother the cry of revulsion which rose to her lips, and with a shudder she struck his hand away and hurriedly waded through the calf-high current to scramble unaided into the stern.

Captain Smart gave a short laugh. 'Is McPhee not to your taste, my fine lady? Well, see you don't give me any trouble, and you'll have no need to worry about him dirtying your fancy coat.'

Catherine summoned up all her resolution to stare him straight in the eye as he followed her into the boat. 'You may think you have a defenceless woman in your power, sir, but you will soon find that you have landed yourself in trouble up to your scrofulous neck. My father will have you on the gibbet for this!'

'Hold your tongue!' he snarled, betraying his lack of nerve by a violent over-reaction. He was sweating profusely, and his eyes were showing a good deal of white around the iris as he scanned the river-bank for onlookers. 'I have not brought you here for the pleasure of your company, miss, so you may keep your opinions to yourself—otherwise you can have McPhee for company. You'd like that, wouldn't you, McPhee?'

McPhee grinned horribly, exposing a set of brown tooth-stubs and a wet red tongue that seemed to have outgrown his mouth. His reply, although unintelligible to Catherine, was quite unmistakably lewd, and although she knew that by betraying her revulsion she had given the Captain a stick to beat her with, she could not repress a shudder.

If the Captain had held a pistol to her temple he could not have ensured a more craven submission to his wishes, but while both her captors were engaged in edging the dory furtively out of the screen of willows, her eyes were busy searching for something that might, if necessary, be used as a weapon. There were scraps of fishing-nets and some old floats beneath her seat, and as she dragged these out a fraction with her foot, her eye fell on a long sliver of curved green glass caught in the meshes. It was only three or four inches long, part of a smashed float, but it came to a sharp point and could do considerable damage if wielded with determination.

In seconds it was snatched under her cloak, and no mother ever clasped her first-born to her bosom with more heartfelt affection.

Keeping close to the wooded bank, the dory turned down river, McPhee's powerful arms making it fairly skip over the water. In seconds a small lugger, the *Pallas*, came into view, anchored well out in mid-stream, and McPhee made a sharp turn and headed straight towards it.

Catherine's faint hopes of effecting an escape flickered and went out. From an ordinary place of confinement, she might have had at least a small chance of winning free. Almost all rooms have windows, even cellars have doors, and few places are devoid of passers-by who might hear a cry for help. But . . . a ship! Even if she could evade her two jailers, how could she hope to reach the shore? She had never in her life swum more than a few strokes in the river at Transk, and she would have to be very hard pressed indeed to risk leaping into this fast-flowing current.

They came alongside with much cursing from the Captain and a good deal of obscure rumbling from McPhee, whose accent was so thick and whose vocabulary so foul that much of his conversation was, mercifully, lost on Catherine.

'Where are you taking me?' she asked sharply, not, in truth, because she had any expectation of being told, but because her pride demanded that she show a brave front—the more so because her teeth were chattering audibly and she was afraid that the Captain, at her side, could feel her trembling.

No one took the slightest notice of the question, and she was pushed roughly towards a rope ladder that hung down the ship's side.

'Up you go, my lady,' the Captain snapped, laying a steadying foot on the bottom rung. 'And move sharply, unless you want McPhee to give you a hand.'

Spurred on by this threat and unhampered by trailing skirts, she was on the deck in seconds, but before she had time to do more than glance about her, Captain Smart was at her elbow, pushing her impatiently towards the bows where a small area of deck had been roofed in to form a tiny cabin.

'In here,' he said curtly, opening the door and thrusting her inside so hurriedly that she struck her head on the low lintel. She stumbled forward, blinded by the abrupt transition from sunlight to semi-darkness, and crashed into a low bunk that half-filled the compartment. The door slammed to behind her, a bolt was thrown, and without wasting another word on his prisoner, Captain Smart was gone.

For a long time she stood quite still, *not* sobbing, she told herself stubbornly and with almost complete truth, but merely bringing her breathing under control. She was shuddering with cold and terror, water squelched in her shoes and dripped from her clothes, and her body hurt in a dozen different places, but her eyes were dry and her chief emotion was one of rage and chagrin.

Gradually the room began to take shape about her, and she found herself in a low-roofed, triangular cuddy that smelled pungently of tar and fish and of a number of other odours which she tried hard not to identify. What little light there was came from two tiny portholes, one on each of the two longer walls. Neither of them was anywhere near big enough to escape through, but they gave her a view of both banks and admitted faint reflections of the sun on the water outside, which flickered across the ceiling like silver ripples. Apart from the bunk, which was topped by a straw-filled mattress and a filthy blanket, the only other feature that caught her eye was a narrow shelf along the bulkhead on which stood a bottle of water and half a loaf of bread.

There were footsteps on the deck and she could hear the rise and fall of voices, but she could distinguish no sound to indicate that her captors were preparing to set sail. Luckily, the door was ill fitting enough for her to be able to hear a little of what passed between the two, and, although McPhee's remarks were largely undecipherable, she was able to guess at much of the conversation.

'. . . I'll be back on board by half past six . . . with this wind . . . plenty of time to clear Dumbuck ford . . . still enough light to see the channel markers . . .'

The Captain seemed to Catherine to be trying to convince himself, more than McPhee, that he could delay sailing until the evening without finding himself grounded at low water in the shallows at Dumbuck. She listened avidly to McPhee's reply in the hope of discovering why they were not making off with their prize while they still had plenty of water beneath their keel, but she could make out only the words, '. . . my three pounds . . .'

Her lip curled at this. If McPhee thought he could trust the Captain to reimburse him for his assistance in the abduction, he was even stupider than he looked.

'You'll get your money!' swore the broken reed, with an energy that carried clearly to Catherine's ears. 'As soon as I get my hands on her brother's two hundred pounds.'

'*What?*' Catherine said aloud, so stunned by the discovery that her body sagged weakly against the door. Captain Smart—Jamie's extortioner? But of course he was! It was so obvious that she would have known it at once had she not, since discovering him to be a rogue, been so taken up with worrying about her own predicament. Indeed it was she herself, she now realised, who had given the Captain all the information he needed to put the bite on Jamie, boasting of his expectations and making clear that he was no impoverished younger son.

She sat down on the bunk and gave herself up to contemplation of this man who now held her in his power. That his intentions towards her had always been purely evil was now beyond question. Even when he had befriended her at the Assembly, he must have seen her as a young buck, fresh upon the town, and with a good deal more money than sense. No doubt his intention, then, had been merely to let his victim win enough so that he would be ripe for the plucking at their second meeting but by the following week he had discovered that 'Mr Mather' was, in fact, the daughter of Frazer of Transk, and a bigger prize than he could have hoped for.

That night at the masked ball . . . if he had not recognised her there and then he must have realised the truth almost immediately afterwards. Certainly, he knew when he met her at Duffy's that she was Catherine Frazer, and . . . surely! . . . he had allowed her to keep on winning only in order to keep her there until most of the others had left and he could expect the streets outside to be deserted. His intention had been either to snatch her away as soon as they emerged or to inveigle her up to his lodgings and to imprison her there. No doubt Jamie's unexpected interference must have seemed like a serious set-back, if not a disaster, and she could imagine his jubilation when she had, miraculously—and so stupidly!—kept her appointment with him at noon today.

Her attention was alerted by sounds of increased activity beyond the door, and, standing up, she pressed her ear to the wood in time to hear the Captain say, '. . . and if she tries to attract your attention while I'm gone, ignore her, do you understand?'

McPhee replied in tones that she had no difficulty in recognising as salacious, but Captain Smart shouted viciously, 'No, you won't, you great doddering bedlamite! That door will be padlocked while I'm gone, and you'll sit there and keep your eyes open, or I'll flay your hide!'

She heard him approaching the door and skipped hastily back to the bunk, but he was so confident that she could get up to no mischief that he did not even look in on her as he fixed the padlock to the bolt. Minutes later she heard him clattering into the dory, and, from the porthole, caught a partial glimpse of him as he pulled away, still glaring at McPhee.

As the sounds of his departure diminished, there fell an uneasy silence. Catherine was very sharply aware of McPhee's presence only a few yards from the door, and as she strained her ears, her eyes unseeing on a strip of sunlight that shone through a gap in the door-jamb to etch a short silver line on the floorboards, she could hear him muttering softly to himself.

Then, abruptly, that silver line was blotted out and she knew that he was standing at the door, his eye pressed to the crack, and, in spite of herself, a low moan of anguish escaped her as she shrank back into the shadows. There was a scrabbling sound which lasted perhaps two or three seconds, and then there was silence again while the patch of sunlight came and went on the floor like a distress signal.

A few seconds later, she heard a sound on the roof of the cabin and whirled round just in time to see his grotesque head appear, hanging upside down, outside one of the portholes. With a choked scream she ran at it, snatching off her cloak as she moved and hooking it feverishly over the screws that held it closed. Instantly he wriggled over to the other porthole, but she was there before him with the blanket, blotting out the sight of his insane leer.

In seconds he was back at the door, gabbling to her in his queer *patois*, his face pressed to the gap in the jamb. There was nothing she could do but try to plug the gap with anything that came to hand, but before she had completed this, she heard his footsteps retreating and laid her own eye to the crack to see what he was doing.

Her view of the sunlit deck was better than his view of her shadowy prison. She could see his broad back stooped over a locker, from which he was removing sundry boathooks and marlinspikes and testing them for strength.

Catherine's nails scraped on the door as she clutched at it for support. He was looking for an instrument with which to force the padlock! At that moment she discovered, for the first time, what it was to be afraid, and indeed she was never sure, afterwards, whether or not she actually fainted for a few seconds. It may have been only the strength in her legs which suddenly ebbed, depositing her like a sack of potatoes on the floor behind the door. Sure it was, however, that it was that inadvertent descent that reminded her that she had a weapon.

Feeling something prick her in the leg, she put her hand in her pocket and drew forth the sliver of glass, grasping it with a fervour that drew blood from her own finger. Quickly, for she could hear his footsteps once more approaching the door, she ripped off her neckcloth and wrapped it thickly about one end of her blade, her hands shaking with such agitation that she could scarcely grip the cloth to draw it tight.

Fear was a searing pain in her chest as she bent to peer through the gap again, and in that very second she saw his bright blue gaze appear on the other side, his cheek pressed close to the wood and his loose lips mouthing some sentiments which she could only be glad were unintelligible to her. Without stopping to think what she was doing, she took lightning aim and jabbed the glass blade through the gap with every ounce of her remaining energy.

His scream of rage and agony exploded through the door with a bellow that drew a cry of horror from her own lips. Dropping her makeshift dagger to the floor, she sank on to the bunk and covered her eyes with her hands, rocking back and forwards in distress. Only the necessity of listening for sounds of retaliation prevented her from bursting into sobs, and only the need to see clearly kept her eyes dry. Her whole body revolted against the thought of what she had just done, and she knew that, even if he were to break down the door and attempt to lay hands on her, she could not bring herself to use the blade on him again.

But there was no need to repeat her attack. McPhee withdrew, like a sick animal, to the far end of the deck, from where she could hear him weeping like a child and comforting himself with a long querulous monologue. After a while, she forced herself to peep out at him, and saw to her relief that her lunge had missed his eye but had left a deep gash on his cheek, which was bleeding sluggishly but would heal soon enough. She watched him for some time, but when she was sure that he had put aside all thought of breaking into her prison, she returned to the bunk and tried to think constructively about how she could possibly break free.

She could not allow herself the luxury of hoping that anyone had even noticed her absence yet. Jessie had clearly been tired out by her sleepless night and could continue to doze for hours unless she were disturbed. It was just possible that Jamie would decide to resume berating his sister later in the afternoon, but by then the trail would have grown cold and it would be almost impossible for him to trace her to her cell in the middle of the Clyde. He might even—and who could blame him?—conclude that she had run away rather than return to Ayr.

No. If she were to escape the clutches of the despicable Captain, it would not be by sitting snivelling on this bunk and praying for help to arrive. She would have to fend for herself. Yet she had never in her life felt less capable of doing anything practical. Already, she knew, she had let slip the best opportunity she might have for winning free. She should have allowed McPhee to force the door, and, once he was inside, knocked him out with the bottle and concealed herself on deck ready to leap into the dory once Captain Smart left it unattended.

Admittedly, it would have been a dangerous plan, abounding in pitfalls, but anything was better than sitting worrying in the half dark. It would still, of course, be possible to attract McPhee's attention, and, perhaps, prevail upon him to make another attempt on the padlock, but now he knew that she was armed and would be on his guard.

But if she had lost her chance of overpowering McPhee, at least she had the seeds from which another plan was already beginning to sprout. She had in her possession one fact which might prove her salvation: when the *Pallas* finally sailed, sometime after half-past six, she would be racing the tide to Dumbuck ford. Therefore, if Catherine could but delay their progress sufficiently, they would find very little water under their keel when they got there. It might be shallow enough for her to swim or even wade ashore—always assuming, of course, that she could devise some way of escaping from the cabin. They might even run aground, which would be better still, since the resultant confusion would afford better possibilities for breaking loose.

She took stock of the tiny cabin, noting everything that might come in useful, which was little enough. The blanket, if dragged from the porthole, might slow the *Pallas* considerably but it would certainly be discovered within seconds, and Catherine rather dreaded to think what retribution Captain Smart might consider appropriate.

Using the glass splinter as a tool, she tried to dig a hole in the ship's side, below the waterline, but the wood was like iron and the shard was too short to grip firmly. Finally she gave up, and was tugging hopefully at the boards of the bench when she heard the creak and splash of oars, followed by a volley of abusive oaths as Captain Smart climbed the rope ladder.

She had her eye to the crack in time to see his head appear over the side, and his expression would not have encouraged even McPhee to assume that his visit ashore had been one of undiluted glee. His pale blue eyes fairly bulged with resentment, and he lashed out at McPhee as the idiot hindered him over the side with such lack of dexterity that the Captain's sword got between his legs and almost tripped him up.

'Mind what you're doing, damn your eyes! You near broke my neck with your stupid blunderings!'

McPhee cringed back like a dog, his finer feelings grossly offended, but the Captain had seen the blood on his cheek and caught him by the collar the better to see the wound.

'What's this, then? Where did you come by that cut, eh?'

McPhee shook his great head and mumbled cryptically, his face grotesquely twisted in an expression of alarm.

'I'll have none of your lies, McPhee!' roared the Captain, and Catherine almost smiled to see him threaten his servant with a fist. McPhee could have strangled him between thumb and forefinger, but the thought did not appear to have occurred to him. 'You don't get a gash like that without knowing how you came by it. What have you been up to?'

Catherine saw him jump, as the suspicion struck him. His head swung round, and for an instant his eyes seemed to be glaring into hers. Then he darted across the deck towards her and she heard the padlock rattle as he checked it. The discovery that it had not been tampered with seemed to have an immediately calming effect on him, however, for after listening at the door for a moment—till, in fact, Catherine obliged by shuffling her feet—he began issuing orders as though McPhee's wound was of no further interest to him.

'Make fast the dory and get the sails hoisted, then. I want to get under way before the light starts to go, otherwise it will be pitch dark before we make Dumbuck.'

McPhee fixed him with a slightly less vacant stare than usual, his loose wet mouth working with the effort of abstract thought, then he stretched out a hand and said clearly, 'Three pound.'

Captain Smart rushed at him and fetched him a blow on the head with the first instrument that came to hand, which happened to be a belaying-pin, and which would have killed him had the idiot not taken part of the force on his arm.

'Three pound, is it, you misbegotten pile of garbage! You'll get your money when you've worked for it, and not before! Now get moving before I try knocking some sense into that turnip head of yours!'

For the space of perhaps a second Catherine wondered if McPhee would retaliate, but when he lumbered aft to make fast the tender she was uncertain whether to be disappointed or not. If the Captain's henchman should turn against his master and put him, either temporarily or permanently, out of action, she might find herself in an even worse situation, alone with the imbecile. On the other hand, with only one captor to evade—and a simple one, at that—her chances of escape could be marginally improved.

Her mind played with this consideration as she watched the two scoundrels making ready to sail. Already the sun was a ruby red fireball low on the western hills, and the river was dark with the coming of dusk.

The sky was beginning to cloud over with a thick, billowing layer of dark grey, promising early darkness and a moonless night. If only she could manage to add as little as fifteen or twenty minutes to their time, it might make all the difference between clearing the shallows and going aground.

She felt the *Pallas* lurch as the anchor cleared bottom and was stowed, with a terrifying and prolonged rattle of chain, on the cabin roof. Then the banks began to slip by on either side and the cabin tilted to starboard as the little ship leaned into the wind and headed downstream. For a minute or two the Captain and McPhee were kept busy trimming the sails to make the most of the light breeze, but Catherine, standing at the starboard port-hole, had the leisure to notice that the anchor chain had not been stowed properly. Every time the *Pallas* leaned over, a short loop of chain, dangling down from the cabin roof, swung across the margin of the window.

Realising she might have only seconds to act before the Captain noticed this, Catherine attacked the screws that held the porthole closed. There were three of them, and each one was twisted down to the last thread, but at last the little round pane of glass swung on its stiff hinge, and she thrust an arm through the aperture to grasp the loop of chain. There was no point in trying to be stealthy. As soon as she gave the loop a tug, it rattled fit to wake the dead, so she took a firm grasp and wrenched with all her strength, running the chain through her bruised hands with a speed born of sheer desperation. For once, luck was on her side, and she found that the loop had been within a few feet of the anchor, which, almost immediately, was hauled overboard and plunged into the water, dragging the remainder of the chain behind it.

The little ship halted as though she had hit a brick wall, throwing Catherine onto the bunk, but she scrambled up in haste to fasten the screws again before Captain Smart should think to blame her for the sudden halt. It soon became apparent, however, that he had no suspicion that anyone other than the luckless McPhee might be responsible, and he could be heard cursing and beating his servant unremittingly for the several minutes it took to haul up the anchor and get, once more, under way.

The success of this operation filled Catherine with optimism, and she set to knotting the blanket to her cloak, just in case she met with an opportunity to attempt a similar manoeuvre. Weighted at one end with the water-bottle and a piece of loose board she had found under the mattress, the material would certainly slow the ship and might even catch on some underwater obstruction and stop it altogether.

As she worked at this invention, she kept a constant watch on her two jailers as well as on the stretch of river visible from the portholes. The sun had dipped below the hills, now, and long grape-purple shadows lay across the water and made the figures on deck colourless and indistinct. Their voices, too, were hushed: McPhee's a low rumble; the Captain's still bitter with dissatisfaction.

Small wonder he was dissatisfied, Catherine thought with a wry smile. The non-appearance of his two hundred pounds must have come as a severe disappointment to him and might well interfere with his plans for disposing of his prisoner. It was amusing to reflect that, had he paid his gambling debts like a gentleman, the money would have been waiting for him at six o'clock as demanded. 'Captain Smart,' she would have liked to say to him. 'Let this be a lesson to you. The more you put *into* life, the more you get out of it.'

She could hear McPhee's bare feet on the roof above her head. He had moved for'ard as the light faded and was shouting sporadic instructions to the Captain, who was at the tiller. As her ear became attuned to his accent she could interpret an occasional phrase, and was aware of his relief when he commented to his master that they could not be so very close to low tide since another craft was following them downstream.

'Rubbish! What fool would set sail at this hour—my God!' The Captain's voice went suddenly shrill with alarm, and the *Pallas* zig-zagged erratically for several seconds as though in sympathy. 'We're being followed, you fool!'

Catherine sank on to the pile of blanket, her hands clasped over her thudding heart, her mind stunned into inertia by this unexpected ray of hope. Above her head, heavy feet raced up and down as ropes were tightened, sails set more efficiently, and the dory cut loose to lessen the drag.

'Get for'ard with the lead,' the Captain interrupted a stream of monotonous and creative cursing to snap. 'I want to know how much water I have under the keel.'

She ran to the door, pressing her ear to the crack in an effort to hear McPhee's voice as he called the soundings. The words were incomprehensible but he seemed re-assured, and this suspicion was confirmed a moment later by Captain Smart, who said with a shaky laugh,

'Ay, fine! Couldn't be better. We'll just make it by the skin of our teeth, and if this fool behind us draws as much as an inch or two more than we do, he'll be stuck high and dry!'

'No! Oh no!' Catherine whispered, rearing back from the door in alarm. If the following craft was indeed coming to rescue her, the time had come to put her invention to the test. Even a few seconds, at this juncture, could narrow the gap between the two ships sufficiently to bring them within hailing distance—or perhaps within pistol-shot.

Her fingers were like toes as she tried to fasten one end of her cloak to the hinge of the porthole, and her efforts were further hindered by the fact that she could not quite stand erect due to the lowness of the roof. By the time she had effected a bulky but reasonably secure knot, her head was well-nigh twisted from her neck and she could feel a nervous sweat dampen her brow and throat. She was just about to start launching her contrivance when she detected a note of excitement in the voices on deck, and reached the door just in time to hear the captain say, '. . . not a great depth of water, but we'll make it all right. There's one marker, and . . . look . . . there's the other! The channel is narrow, but we're right on course. Steady, now!'

Without waiting to hear any more, she darted back to the porthole and peered out into the dusk. Yes! She could see the channel markers for herself, one through each porthole, and only yards ahead. There was no time to feed the blanket out lengthwise. She had to snatch it up and force it through the window in a lump, and this, she realised at once, was the wrong way to go about it.

The bottle wedged sideways in the aperture, surrounded by a knot of material which caught on the screws, resisting her pushing and pulling while precious seconds ticked away. Sobbing with frustration, she at last managed to drag the entanglement back into the cabin, tearing it loose from the screws with maniacal strength, and was just gathering it up for another attempt when she was suddenly hurtled forward against the wall and came to rest in a heap on the floor.

Although it was not a violent jolt, and cushioned by the wadded blanket in her arms, she was not at all hurt, she was quite dazed with surprise and it took her a moment to realise that—quite miraculously and without apparent reason—they had gone aground.

CHAPTER
ELEVEN

PANDEMONIUM REIGNED on deck for several minutes. Neither of the two mariners could understand, any more than could Catherine, how their navigation could be so much at fault, and much time was lost in pointless recrimination before Captain Smart collected his senses and took time to think what must be done.

Since they were now without a tender, they had to choose between wading ashore or attempting to free the *Pallas* while there was still time to find a deeper channel and escape down river. Catherine had no way of knowing how far behind them the pursuing craft now was, but she guessed that it must still be reasonably distant because the Captain chose the second course and sent McPhee overboard with instructions to try and rock the keel off the sandbank.

Presently the *Pallas* began to lurch furiously from stem to stern as the half-wit brought his strength to bear on the problem, his master shouting insults and encouragements impartially from the port rail.

'That's it . . . a bit more . . . it's coming. There's only an inch or two in it. Try this rope . . . Keep pulling, and I'll get all the weight to the stern.'

She watched him hurriedly dragging all the heavy gear away from the bows and piling it against the stern rail, and she realised that by lightening the forefoot of the ship where it was jammed into the sand, he might permit it to float free. She could think of no way of counteracting this see-saw effect except by cramming every movable object she could find into the apex of her triangular prison and sitting atop the pile like a cock on a midden. Seconds later, however, Captain Smart decided to add his prisoner's weight to the other end of the see-saw. Catherine heard him hurriedly unfastening the padlock and jumped to her feet as he stuck his head under the lintel.

'Out of it!' He caught her by the wrist and dragged her forth—quite unnecessarily, since she was as eager to emerge as he was to have her do so—and propelling her the length of the deck with a hand between her shoulder-blades, he produced a piece of rope and secured her by both wrists, twisted behind her, to the stern rail. During this entire process Catherine was on the *qui vive* for an opportunity to escape, but with the Captain's fingers clamped about her wrist and MacPhee splashing about like a leviathan somewhere over the side, it would have availed her nothing to struggle.

By straining her head round over her shoulder she could just see the following ship, not as close as she had hoped but closing fast, her white sails spread to the wind like the wings of a gull in flight. The light was now too poor to allow her to guess at the identity of the figure at the helm, but she could have sworn that an arm was lifted in salute and her name called out with a whoop of triumph.

The *Pallas* had now ceased rocking and appeared to be settling even deeper into the silt, and the significance of this was not lost on Captain Smart. 'MacPhee?' he roared, completing Catherine's immobilisation with a sharp tug. 'What are you up to, you great witless slug! Get back on that rope!'

He went striding round the deck, peering over the rail

into the mist that was beginning to mask the surface of the water. They were in a part of the river that was wide and marshy, dotted with flat reed-covered islands that would be submerged at high tide. The end of McPhee's rope was floating out sideways in the current, but there was no sign of the man himself, and neither Catherine nor, apparently, the Captain could conceive of any near-by feature that could be concealing him from their view.

'Devil take you, McPhee! What are you playing at?'

The Captain stepped up on to the cuddy roof to peer over the bows, and at that moment a quick movement among the reeds of a little island caught Catherine's attention and she swung round in time to see a shadowy figure leap up out of the mist, and with barely a touch to the rope ladder, land sure-footed on the deck.

His back was towards her, and in the half-dark, even that was not at all distinct, but she knew only one person who could move with that characteristic loose-jointed strength, and all at once the fear and tension ebbed from her body like a receding wave.

'*Lionel!* Oh, thank God!'

He turned his head to look at her, his face hidden in shadow. '*Catherine!* Are you all right?'

'Yes . . . *Look out!*'

The Captain, with a cry that rang with terror rather than challenge, had launched himself from the cabin roof, his sword slashing viciously at Lionel's exposed throat. But Lionel was ready for him, his own sword naked in his hand, and parried the blow easily, swaying backwards out of reach, and following up with a flurry of blows that forced his opponent back against the cabin door.

There was no question about who was the better swordsman. Lionel, as always, was incomparably dextrous, but, more than that, there was a new cold resolution in his style that had not been apparent when he was fighting his friend Enoch, and which made him appear quite deadly. There was no laughter, now, in his narrowed eyes, and not the least suspicion of enjoyment or even satisfaction in the way he laid about the unfortunate Captain, and it came to Catherine, quite suddenly, that she was about to witness a murder.

That Captain Smart shared this suspicion was immediately apparent. He was so panic-stricken that she could scarcely bear to look at him. There was something almost indecent in such explicit horror, and she felt ashamed to witness his degradation, but she could not avoid watching the conflict.

His eyes, which were prominent at the best of times, were stretched to their fullest extent and seemed about to burst from their sockets. His mouth, too, was alarmingly dilated into a rictus that distorted his whole face, turning it into a mask that was barely human. At every exertion, a whimpering gasp of despair was forced out of him, and each time Lionel lunged at him he yelped like a puppy, too demoralised even to hide his fear.

Yet he fought like a madman, slipping and scrambling on the wooden deck, crashing into obstacles, tripping over ropes, yet always managing, by painful and desperate effort, to stay upright and to defend himself against such unequal odds that it seemed to Catherine a miracle that he should survive, even for a matter of seconds.

Then she saw, to her horror, that Lionel was playing with him. Over and over again the opportunity to make an end of the matter presented itself, but each time, Lionel let the moment pass, giving the Captain time to recover, or aiming a blow that had clearly no chance of connecting. It was quite appalling to watch the effect of this on the Captain. In moments, his intermittent gasps had given way to a sustained gibbering, and his strength seemed to ebb visibly till he could no longer keep his blade from wavering.

Then, suddenly, he was down, flat on his back, his sword spinning slowly away across the deck, his eyes, terrified, on the man who stood over him with the point of his steel pressed uncompromisingly against his throat.

The silence, for a moment, was broken only by the lap of water against the hull and the dry sobs escaping from the Captain's stretched lips. Then Lionel said steadily, without removing his gaze from the wretch at his feet,

'Tell me the truth, Catherine. Has this man harmed you . . . in any way?'

'No!' cried Catherine quickly, seeing how the sword-point dimpled the skin over the Captain's Adam's apple and how his eyes rolled beseechingly towards her. Much as she hated him, she could not enjoy seeing another human being brought so low, and the thought of what Lionel might do if she were to answer 'Yes!' made her feel faint. 'No! Really!'

Tardily, and with every evidence of extreme reluctance, Lionel removed his point from the captain's throat, and bending down, caught him by the neckcloth and hauled him brutally to his feet. 'Very well, my lion-hearted adventurer! You live to fight another day. But take my advice and eschew a life of crime. You have neither the brains nor the mettle for it.'

His voice was level and matter of fact, but there was very little gentleness in the hands that threw the limp body against the cabin door and whipped a length of rope about his arms and legs. This done, he was thrust into Catherine's erstwhile prison and the door bolted behind him.

'Well, now . . .' Lionel murmured thoughtfully, turning to regard Catherine with a speculative frown. 'What are we to do with you, I wonder?'

She was taken momentarily aback, and then saw the expression in his eyes. 'I hope, sir,' she said, smiling, 'that you will set me free.'

'You think you deserve that?' He began to move towards her, but slowly, his eyes devouring her. 'After all the trouble you've caused, driving your brother and me nearly demented?'

Catherine took a step towards him, forgetting in her urgency that she was still bound by the wrists to the stern rail. 'But I shall make amends, Lionel . . .'

'Indeed?' he said softly, slipping his hands about her waist. 'Then you had better begin . . .'

All the privation and harassment of the afternoon were wiped from her mind in the first instant his lips came down on hers. His arms closed about her, cradling her with such tender strength that she abandoned all reticence and gave herself up totally to his embrace, straining against her bonds, moving her mouth hungrily against his.

Later—how much later she would have found it impossible to estimate—there were lights in the darkness and the sound of sails flapping, and suddenly a tall-masted vessel appeared, broached to, on their port bow.

'Ahoy, *Kelpie*!' Lionel ran over to the rail, making a megaphone of his hands. 'Don't come any further to starboard. I've moved the channel markers and there's virtually no water at all over here.'

'Ahoy, *Pallas*!' came Jamie's voice out of the darkness. 'All's well?'

'All's well.' Lionel turned to Catherine as though inviting her to corroborate this, so she called, a little weakly but with spirit,

'What took you so long, Jamie?' and was answered with a ragged cheer from more than one throat as Jamie and his crew celebrated the success of the mission.

'Listen!' Lionel shouted. 'I'm going to leave the rest of the work to you, Jamie. Catherine is exhausted, and I don't want her staying out in the cold, so I'll take her across to the inn at once. There were only two of them. Smart is in the cabin, and the other one is on an islet on our port bow. All right?'

'Ay, ay, sir!' Jamie replied in accents of purest enjoyment, and leaving his sister in not the slightest doubt but that his afternoon's activity had done much to lighten his gloom. 'I'll meet you at the inn as soon as I can.'

'You seem to be on surprisingly good terms with my disreputable brother,' she mentioned, as Lionel set to work on the knots that held her fast. 'I confess I had expected you two to be at each other's throats after what happened this morning.'

'Not at all.' He smiled a little grimly. 'My sympathies were entirely with Jamie this morning. You drove him to breaking-point—and he broke! What did you expect?' He flicked the tip of her nose chastisingly with one finger, and followed it up with a kiss. 'No. Jamie is all right. He knows how to keep his head in an emergency, and he can stop to think when everyone is screaming at him to *do* something. He had already done all the right things before I met him this afternoon.'

'Where *did* you meet him? And how?' Catherine asked, as the last knot came free and the rope dropped to the deck, but Lionel shook his head and set an arm about her shoulders, leading her towards the ladder.

'Later, my love. When you are warm and dry and have a good hot meal inside you, I will tell you everything. Come, now.'

The tide was at its lowest ebb, and there was scarcely enough water to reach the cuff of his top-boots as he carried her ashore. Behind them they could hear the creak of oars as Jamie and his crew prepared to board the *Pallas*, and before them on the bank of the river a lamp shone out fitfully, silhouetting the figures of a man and woman.

'The innkeeper and his wife,' Lionel murmured. 'I told them to watch out for us so that they can take you in by the back way. The fewer people who see you dressed as you are at present, the better I'll be pleased.'

'Oh dear!' Catherine rubbed a hand hastily across her face in the hope that much of her paint and powder had already disappeared. 'What will they think? I'll have to make up a story!'

'Darling!' Lionel gave her a tiny shake, smothering a chuckle. 'No more stories, *please*! You don't have to tell them anything. I've already paid them enough to still their curiosity and they understand the need for discretion. Let them suspect what they will. It's of no moment, and I am sure they will keep their own council.'

Stepping out, presently, on to the grass-covered bank, he set her on her feet, and she was instantly borne off by the goodwife to the accompaniment of whispered commiseration and promises of immediate succour. They entered the inn by the back door, hurrying down a stone-flagged passage that led them past still-rooms and pantry and afforded one fleeting glimpse into a bright kitchen hung with hams and redolent of roasting meat and fresh baked bread. Unobserved, they climbed a narrow staircase, and found at the top the landlady's own bedroom, where Catherine could see that preparations had been made to receive her.

There were dry clothes to change into, hot water to wash in, and a cup of fresh-brewed Bohea to put warmth into her chilled body. The landlady treated her guest like an invalid, drawing her to the fire and chafing her hands, and later, when she had washed and changed, making her sit with her feet in a bowl of hot water while she pinned up her hair with her own hands.

Throughout these ministrations, Catherine could not hide her impatience to return to Lionel, and on learning that he had ordered a meal to be served in the private parlour downstairs, she wasted no time in joining him.

Here, too, everything was in readiness, a small table spread with a white cloth and set for three, and a low sofa and footstool pulled close to the fire. When she was comfortably installed like—as she protested—some decrepit old crone, and the landlady had departed kitchenwards, Lionel sat down beside her and took her firmly into his arms.

'I don't quite know how I'm going to manage it,' he said, looking thoughtful and a little worried. 'But I can see that it will be necessary for me to readjust my entire lifestyle so that I can operate satisfactorily with only one hand. It appears to be indispensable to my contentment and peace of mind that I should have at least one arm about you at all times, and one can see that this might give rise to problems.'

'We do have four arms between us,' she said reasonably, wriggling closer to him. 'I dare say, if we put our minds to it, that something could be arranged.'

This remark being rewarded with a kiss, and one kiss leading to another, there was very little conversation until a tap at the door heralded the arrival of the innkeeper and his wife laden with steaming dishes.

'You don't feel we should wait for Jamie, then?' Catherine said, investigating the covered platters and finding a leg of mutton, a crab pie, a haggis and a tureen of good hen broth.

'Certainly not.' He drew her to the seat nearest the fire, and made her sit. 'Jamie will not be here for at least an hour. I've warned the landlord to expect him later, and there will be something hot ready for him when he gets here.'

'You do like to have everything planned ahead and under control, don't you?' she laughed, and indicated the room with a wide gesture. 'All this . . . the hot meal . . . the change of clothes . . . You must have been very confident that we would go aground at Dumbuck shallows!'

'It was certainly my intention that you should do so,' he said matter-of-factly, filling her glass and motioning her to drink.

'*Your* intention?'

He looked at her in surprise, as though he had expected her to know without being told. 'At that stage of the tide there is only one channel deep enough to take the *Pallas*. It's marked by two buoys, one on either side. My only problem was to get here well ahead of the *Pallas* so that I had time to move them to a shallower part of the river where they would guide Smart on to a sandbank.'

'Oh, Lionel . . . !' she breathed, bending on him a look of such hero-worship that he dropped his knife.

When he had recovered himself and kissed her several times, he said, 'It was the longest half-hour of my whole life—sitting out there in the reeds watching the *Pallas* tacking towards me and praying that nothing would go wrong. I'd already made so many mistakes: in not forcing Judith to tell me the truth earlier, in allowing you to proceed with your masquerade for so long . . .'

Catherine choked on her soup. She could feel the blush sweeping hotly up from the base of her throat, and had to force herself to say, still looking at her plate, 'You . . . You knew about that . . . all along, I suppose?'

'I realised that first night at the Assembly, but . . .' He became aware that she was dying a thousand deaths, and added, apologetically, 'Not immediately, of course. You had me fooled for quite a few minutes—and at close quarters, too. Really, you were amazingly convincing.'

'Don't!' She covered her burning face with both hands. 'Oh certes! You must have thought me such a fool! Why did you let me go on making a fool of myself?'

She felt his hand on her head, tenderly smoothing back her hair, and he sighed as he said, 'Because it was the only hope I had of finding out what you and Judith were up to.'

She could make neither head nor tale of this cryptic remark, and so was forced to drop her hands and say, 'What do you mean?'

He propped his chin on one hand and stared at her thoughtfully, drawing a finger down her nose and touching it lightly to her lips. 'I don't know a lot about women, my love. I've never had much room for them in my life, and Judith's the only one I'd claim to begin to understand. But it seems to me that, if they don't want to tell you something, it will do you no good to ask. Right?'

Catherine regarded him blankly, so he answered himself.

'Right. Now, I knew—had known for some time— that Judith was seriously worried about something. She was off her food, jittery, ready to burst into tears at the drop of a hat, yet she would not confide in either my mother or myself. That night at the Assembly I could see she was in a fine taking, and I'll admit, I did think, when I saw her new beau, that I had discovered the reason for her megrims. But, of course, the Macaroni turned out to be you.'

He sat back in his chair, sipping reminiscently at his wine and chuckling deeply. 'Catherine, you really floored me! I had no idea what I was expected to do, but I knew that if I were to say, "Try pulling the other leg!", I might never discover what was driving Judith to such desperate measures. My only hope of finding out the truth was to play along with you.'

Catherine helped him to a second serving of crab pie. 'Well, if you knew at the Assembly that I was Mr Mather, you were certainly exceedingly uncivil to me when you waylaid me in the wood the next morning. In fact, I was so quelled I couldn't wait to get home and burn everything that could connect me with the Macaroni.'

'That's exactly what I had hoped to achieve. Or at least I hoped to prevent you from making any more public appearances and keep you out of the clutches of Smart, whom I had seen setting you up for fleecing at the Assembly.' He spread his hands and shook his head helplessly. 'I couldn't bring myself to believe that you would be so foolhardy as to keep the appointment I heard you make with him—to play cards with him at Duffy's. But, at the last moment, I decided to cancel my arrangement to go to Greenock and go instead to Duffy's to make sure you were not there.'

'But, of course, I *was* there,' Catherine muttered, not without embarrassment. 'How else could I have raised the cash to buy off Jamie's extortioner? You must have realised that?'

'I? Certainly not. Until this afternoon, I knew nothing about Jamie being threatened. Indeed, I don't scruple to tell you, my love, I had not the slightest idea *what* you were up to till I forced the truth out of Judith last night, after hearing you accept Jamie's challenge.'

Catherine pushed her plate away and folded her arms on the table. 'So it was Judith who told you the whole story?'

'By no means. Judith didn't know the whole story. Nobody did. Each of us knew only our own little segment, and it wasn't until we pieced them all together that we realised who had abducted you and how we could trace him.'

'Wait a minute.' Catherine frowned. 'You are too fast for me, Lionel. How did you and Jamie come to be pooling information? The last I saw of both of you together, you seemed to be on decidedly less than friendly terms.'

Lionel's hand went to the purplish bruise on his temple where the hilt of Jamie's sword had left its mark. 'The least said about that incident, the better,' he said sourly. 'If I hadn't been so terrified that you'd been hurt, I would have been alert enough to deflect the blow entirely. As it was, I only caught the edge of the hilt.'

'But . . . you rode off without a word to me . . .'

'Darling, we were trying to draw attention *away* from you . . . fobbing the others off with some hazy story about a misunderstanding . . . If I had shown myself to be upon friendly terms with you, the others might have drawn you into the discussion at that point and discovered that you were not a man. It wasn't easy to leave you standing there so white and dazed, but I knew—or *thought* I knew, that I would be able to speak with you at the Saracen's Head later in the morning. However, I was delayed, talking to Judith, and it was almost one o'clock when I got there.'

'And that, I suppose, was when Jamie discovered I was not in my room.' Catherine grimaced. 'I'll bet he was as wild as fire!'

'No, he had discovered your absence some time earlier when your maid came to his room in search of you. I must say, I thought he handled the matter quite creditably. Instead of leaping to conclusions, he had sent to discover if either you or Mr Mather had hired a horse from the livery stable and, finding that you hadn't, he then began to make enquiries in case anyone had seen you leave. Luckily, a laundry-maid had passed the Macaroni on the back stairs only ten or fifteen minutes previously, and your maid, hearing this, confessed that you had probably gone to meet someone who had lost a good deal of money to you at Duffy's.' He seemed to wince a little, and his lips curled in a rather wry smile. 'It was at this point in the proceedings that I turned up.'

'Yes . . .' She could imagine her brother's embarrassment at seeing Lionel walk in on such a scene of family drama. 'I take it that Jamie was less than welcoming?'

'Well, I admit I thought him a trifle stiff at first, and I could see that he was not at all himself . . . pacing about . . . hardly attending to what I was saying . . .'

'Cracking his knuckles?'

'Precisely. Then he suddenly decided to confide in me and enlist my help, and from then on we worked very well together. I was able to identify your gambling partner, so we found out where Smart lived and went to his lodgings, only to find them empty. We rode to several posting houses in the hope that you or he had been seen, all to no avail. Then it occurred to Jamie to mention that he had received an extortion demand that he was due to pay tonight at six. That was the final clue that completed the answer to the puzzle. We realised that the extortioner was Smart, and we knew where Smart would be at six this evening. We had only to wait for him to go for the money, and then follow him to you.'

Seeing that she had finished eating, he rose to draw back her chair and lead her to the couch, setting a cushion behind her and the footstool beneath her feet.

'I wish you might have saved me before the *Pallas* sailed,' she said, submitting happily to his cosseting and arranging herself comfortably in the crook of his arm. 'There were some very nasty moments during our passage downstream.'

'Ah, but you see, my love, we had no means of knowing what they might do to you if we attacked them openly. While they held you hostage, we had to be careful. Happily, instead of going to Greenock yesterday to pick up my new yacht, I'd had two of my crew sail it up to the Broomielaw, so we decided that Jamie would follow you in it while I rode like the wind for Dumbuck shallows to lay my little trap. We had planned to board the *Pallas* in force—together with my two crewmen—but I was lucky enough to surprise the half-wit while he was concentrating on knotting a rope, and so decided to deal with Sharp while the opportunity presented itself. I dare say Jamie will not be pleased to have missed all the fun, but I suspect he enjoyed his sail on the *Kelpie*.'

'He certainly appeared to be quite elated when he caught up with us,' Catherine agreed, and added tentatively, 'It made me wonder if perhaps you and he had found time to discuss his relationship with Judith?'

'We did touch on the matter, yes . . .' He paused tantalisingly, teasing her.

'And . . . ?'

'And I was unable to find any cogent reason for forbidding the match. However, I insisted they wait a year before the wedding. I have no objection to them announcing their engagement immediately, but one wedding in the family is enough to be going on with, and I refuse to share mine with anyone, even Jamie. I do like your brother, Catherine, and I'm sure he's just the man for Judith. If you'd seen him taking charge this afternoon, sending out messengers, collating information, and managing, the while, to keep your two grandmothers totally in the dark as to what was really happening . . .'

'*My what?*' Catherine squealed in such close proximity to his ear that his face contorted momentarily with shock. 'When did my grandmothers arrive?'

'I assume, since they seemed well settled in by the time I arrived, that they must have reached the Saracen's Head within minutes of your leaving it. They had spent last night at the White Horse, at Eaglesham, and the little one—Mrs Frazer?—seemed to think you should be expecting her as she had warned you, by letter, that she would be arriving today. Didn't you receive her letter?'

'Oh . . . I don't know.' Catherine muttered, considerably put out. 'I suppose I did. Every other day there was another letter from her, insisting I return to Ayr, complaining, threatening, cajoling. I stopped reading them after a while. Who would have thought she would pop up like Orpheus from the Underworld? And Grandmama MacIntosh, too. What on earth am I to tell them?'

'Oh, I wouldn't worry about them.' He seemed quite uninterested in the predicament, being engrossed in pushing his nose into her hair and inhaling deeply. 'I think Jamie had them believing you had gone to visit Judith.'

'Yes, but it's now too late to persist in that story!' Catherine pointed out, and would have objected further had not the sound of heavy footfalls approaching the door impelled them to leap hastily apart just as Jamie strode jubilantly into the room.

'Well, that's a job well done!' he announced, speaking directly to Lionel, his face alive with satisfaction.

Lionel jumped to his feet with an equal enthusiasm. 'Successfully?'

'Entirely. Our two friends are already embarked and sail for Barbados on the morning tide.' Receiving a congratulatory grin and a slap on the shoulder from Lionel, he went to crouch on the footstool at his sister's feet and took her hands in his. 'You really are all right, then, Kate? One hundred per cent?'

'A *thousand* per cent!' Catherine laughed, happier than ever to see the glow back in his eyes. 'I'm sorry I caused you such a dreadful afternoon.'

'If I could have got my hands on you ... .' he began balefully, and then broke off to round on Lionel with a suddenly lightened tone. 'But I'll tell you something, Lionel. That little craft of yours is as sprightly as a dragonfly! Did you see the way she gained on the *Pallas*? I'll swear we cut her lead by something like two-thirds! I'm determined to have one just like her, Kate, and as soon as possible. We shall have to think of a name . . . *Kelpie* was a strange one to choose, Lionel. It means some sort of water-nymph, doesn't it?'

'That's right.' Lionel sent Catherine a smiling look out of the corner of his eyes. 'I met one recently, in the forest at Monkwood.'

'You *met* one?' Jamie reiterated, but Lionel had turned away to part the curtains and look down into the yard, his attention caught by the rattle of wheels on the cobbles.

'Oh, no!' he groaned, stiffening in dismay. 'There can't possibly be *two* coaches like that!'

Neither Catherine not Jamie needed to ask 'Like what?' They both cried out in horrified unison, and Catherine ran to the mirror to tidy her hair.

'Oh, heavens! I look as though I'd been dragged through a hedge backwards! Go quickly, Jamie, and see if you can delay them while I tidy myself. Run!'

Lionel went with him, ostensibly to lend moral support, but in effect, Catherine suspected, because it might appear rather too cosy if the old ladies found him *tête à tête* with Catherine. She had done what she could to remedy her appearance and was sitting demurely by the fire before the door was thrown open and the two granddams swept into the room, side by side and looking ready for anything.

Mrs Frazer halted two steps over the threshold, casting suspicious eyes about the room as though she expected evidence of licentiousness and unspeakable debauchery to be hidden behind every cushion. She was wearing a wig at least twice as large as her head, and pinned atop it was a minuscule mob cap which reminded Catherine of a sprig of holly on a Christmas pudding. 'In all the world, Catherine . . .' she began, but was over-whelmed by Mrs MacIntosh, who overtook her like a rotund whirlwind strewing her cloak, gloves and black silk calash in all directions and enveloping Catherine in a hug.

'*There* you are, child! I *told* your Grandmama Frazer that she was worrying about nothing. But you *are* looking peaked, dear. You should be in bed. All this racketing about isn't good for you, as I told Jamie this afternoon. You should both learn to relax.' She spread herself on the sofa and beckoned Mrs Frazer to join her. 'Look at this lovely fire, Elspeth. Come and get warm, dear, or you'll have trouble with your sciatica. And then, since we are here, I dare say we may as well have something to eat. I had scarce started my dinner when you insisted upon following Lord Marbrae and I am faint with hunger.'

'You *cannot* be hungry again, Margaret,' stated Mrs Frazer, perching on the armless chair that Lionel had drawn to the fire for her. 'You have taken refreshments at every posting house between here and the Broomielaw. And, forbye, there are some questions that need answering before I shall feel free in my mind to think of other things. What game, for instance, have these young people been playing this afternoon, and who are these friends whom Jamie tells me he was seeing off on a journey to Barbados?'

'Grandmama . . . it's such a long story!' Catherine said earnestly. 'And, really, it's nothing at all for you to worry about. Shall we not leave the telling of it till tomorrow when you are less tired?'

Mrs Frazer drew a deep breath and allowed her critical stare to dwell, for a moment, on Lionel as though she were wondering if Catherine's story were known to him, and, if not, if it were fit for his ears. 'Very well,' she said firmly. 'But I make no secret of the fact, Catherine, that I am extremely dissatisfied with your behaviour and I shall require a full explanation tomorrow. Whatever your excuses, I fear your father will have to be told that you wilfully absented yourself from my care for an extended period, and refused even to reply to my demands that you return to Ayr.' Tucking in her chin in a scandalised manner, she reared back her amazing wig and fixed Catherine with what she clearly intended to be a piercing look. 'What steps he will decide to take, I shall not presume to predict.'

Catherine tried very hard to look crestfallen, but it would have been easier if she had not been able to see Lionel grinning at her from behind Mrs Frazer's chair.

'There was really no need for you both to come posting down here tonight, in any case,' Jamie said, resuming his seat on the footstool. 'Lord Marbrae has hired a carriage, and we would have been home by bedtime. But you—in that coach . . .'

'There is nothing wrong with that coach,' asserted Mrs Frazer, thoroughly incensed.

'. . . well, I think you would do better to stay here tonight. You've done enough travelling for one day, and this seems a tolerably comfortable house.'

'Yes, yes, you are quite right, Jamie dear.' Mrs MacIntosh beamed, leaning over to pat the top of his head as though he were still six years old. 'Go and bespeak chambers for us all, my love, and while you're about it, see if the landlord has something in his larder that he could offer us—a lobster or two, some game pies and a leg of pork with apples, would be nice. And perhaps, a morsel of venison and one or two fruit tarts. You young people will have eaten already, I suppose?'

Jamie denied this, and Lionel, not wishing to admit that he and Catherine had been indiscreet enough to have dined together in a private parlour, implied that he, too, would be glad of sustenance, so in the end they all sat down together.

It was, to Catherine, a dreamlike experience. Surfeited with happiness, mentally exhausted, every one of her emotions drained and re-drained by the events of the day, she went through the motions of eating and drinking as though she were acting a part in a play. Lionel sat beside her, as close as he dared, and presently he shifted his soup-spoon to his left hand so that his right could steal beneath the table to clasp Catherine's.

She kept her eyes on her plate, but gradually the strong pressure of his fingers began to fill her consciousness until she was aware of nothing else. A warmth seemed to spread, tingling, from the contact of his skin with hers as if something of his inner being were passing into her. He moved a thumb caressingly on the back of her hand, and her whole body thrilled. She twined her fingers in his, pressing their palms together, and her brain reeled with bliss.

The voices of the others ebbed and flowed, like the sound of a placid sea, and figures moved, shadowy, around the table, but they were in another, and distant, world. Sight and sound had retreated to the far edges of her consciousness. She had found that two people in love can be alone together in any company.

Slowly, she turned her head to look at Lionel, and seeing his parted lips and the wonder in his dark eyes, she knew that he had found it, too.

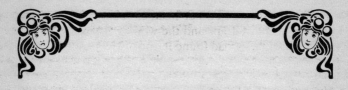

EPILOGUE

'WELL, MARGARET,' remarked Mrs Frazer, catching Mrs MacIntosh with a momentarily empty plate. 'If you are as tired as I am, you will be ready for your bed. Shall we leave these young men to their punch bowl? Catherine . . .'

There was definitely something strange about the girl this evening. She hardly had a word to say for herself and had eaten virtually nothing.

'Catherine, dear . . . I said, are you ready to retire?'

'What . . . ? Yes, I suppose I must,' Catherine sighed, looking about her in a dazed manner. Her eyes were huge and shining, and her cheeks tinged with what her grandmama instantly suspected to be an unhealthy colour.

'Bed,' she pronounced firmly. 'I shouldn't be at all surprised if you are feverish. Come along, Margaret.'

But Mrs MacIntosh had left her cloak on one chair and her fan on another and had misplaced her gloves altogether. Jamie helped her to look for them, but Mrs Frazer tapped her foot impatiently. Catherine and Lord Marbrae, she was quick to notice, had moved to the doorway and were conversing in low, and altogether too intimate, whispers. Admittedly, Jamie had hinted earlier, while they were at the Saracen's Head, that Marbrae was on the point of offering for the girl, but it was abundantly clear that the relationship had already progressed to a stage that was quite unseemly.

There was, in any case, no guarantee that Catherine's father would accept such an offer. One knew the family, naturally, and there could be no doubt of their being of the first respectability, but the boy himself . . . well, really!—one had only to look at him! Those riding-boots hadn't seen a lick of polish in days, and his breeches looked as though they had been soaked and dried out again! She turned to frown at him, and discovered that both he and Catherine had passed through the doorway out of her line of vision.

'Margaret, for goodness' sake stop fussing!' she snapped, moving into the doorway to counteract this infringement. 'Surely you can look for your gloves in the morning?'

Lord Marbrae had halted at the foot of the stairs, and Catherine was standing on the bottom step with her eyes on a level with his. A second earlier, Mrs Frazer was absolutely certain, his hand had covered hers as it lay on the banister, but it was impossible to comment other than with a strongly disapproving cough.

'I shall go up without you,' she told Mrs MacIntosh, trying quite unsuccessfully to look both ways at once, 'if you do not stop wasting time on so trivial a matter. Jamie can find your gloves for you if you are so worried about them.'

'Oh, Elspeth!' Mrs MacIntosh murmured, joining her in the doorway with a smile. 'Have you forgotten what it is to be young and in love? Surely we can allow them a few moments together to say good night.'

Mrs Frazer stared at her round-eyed, as though she could not believe her ears. 'They have already *said* good night. *Twice!* Once here at the door and once at the foot of the stairs. They are about to say it once again at the top of the stairs, and if we do not join them immediately they will be saying it again at the door of her bedchamber!'

Mrs MacIntosh smiled a particularly youthful smile. 'I am persuaded, dear, that no great harm will come of it if they do. Lionel is such a charming young man, and so well bred. We need have no doubts about his sense of propriety. Do you know, Elspeth, there is something about him that reminds me so forcibly of James when we were first married. His smile, I think, or the way he holds his head.'

'Moonshine! He's nothing like James,' replies Mrs Frazer, turning again towards the hall. '*There!* You see, Margaret?' she cried, as the two miscreants disappeared round the bend at the top of the stairs. '*You* must go after them, for I simply cannot take stairs at a rush any more.'

'No more can I!' Mrs MacIntosh laughed. 'I fear they have stolen a march on us. Most reprehensible, of course, and we must really speak severely to Catherine. But really, Elspeth, don't you feel we are fighting a losing battle? It takes a strong man to keep Catherine in check, and the sooner Marbrae takes over, the happier I'll be.'

Mrs Frazer halted with one tiny foot on the stair and an arrested expression on her face. Then she turned slowly to Mrs MacIntosh, and in her eyes was all the wonder and delight of a child on Christmas morning. 'I can't believe it's true, Margaret! Who would have thought that someone would *offer* to look after Catherine?'

Masquerade Historical Romances

New romances from bygone days

Masquerade Historical Romances, published by Mills & Boon, vividly recreate the romance of our past. These are the two superb new stories to look out for next month.

THE GRETNA BRIDE
Olga Daniels

THE HUNGARIAN ADVENTURESS
Ann Hulme

Buy them from your usual paperback stockist, or write to: Mills & Boon Reader Service, P.O. Box 236, Thornton Rd, Croydon, Surrey CR9 3RU, England. Readers in South Africa-write to: Mills & Boon Reader Service of Southern Africa, Private Bag X3010, Randburg, 2125.

Mills & Boon
the rose of romance